BODY

and

BREAD

BODY *and* BREAD

A NOVEL

NAN CUBA

Engine Books
PO Box 44167
Indianapolis, IN 46244
enginebooks.org

Epigraph used gratefully with the permission of Ian Johnston, who translated the story for a 2009 collection titled *The Metamorphosis, A Hunger Artist, In the Penal Colony, and Other Stories.*

Also available in hardcover special edition and eBook formats from Engine Books.

Printed in the United States of America

10   9   8   7   6   5   4   3   2   1

ISBN: 978-1-938126-06-2

Library of Congress Control Number: 2012945051

For Paul Barton Brindley, 1944–1970

"No one pushes his way through here, certainly not someone with a message from a dead man. But you sit at your window and dream of that message when evening comes."

—Franz Kafka, "Imperial Message"

PROLOGUE

ZEUS OR YAHWEH, some metaphysical trickster, flipped a switch, and I stepped into *Yopico*, the fifteenth century *Tenochtitlan* temple. While I stood at its cave-like entrance to earth, agave cloth scraped my shoulder; the air reeked of copal, roasted corn. My feet, cloddish, reluctant, stepped around the sunken receptacle where supplicants left offerings to the soil. Inside the building's packed dirt patio, I molded crushed amaranth (*huāuhtli*) and maize seeds, tepary beans, jicama, and blood into a figure bigger than any man: *Xīpe Totec* peering from beneath a flayed captive's skin. The victim's hands hung at the god's wrists; the skin reached to *Xīpe's* ankles. He wore a *quecholli* feather wig, golden ear plugs, and a skirt of *tzapotle* leaves. I tied a red bow at his forehead, a gold trinket in its center. The outer layer I painted yellow, the body underneath, red. The gummy dough smelled nutty, malt-like. I tasted that sweetness, heard fertility rattles at the end of a long staff, saw a shield with red and yellow feather spirals. His body was made to be broken apart: communion, transubstantiation.

The face was startled, as if privy to sudden insight at the moment of death: the inner force of *teōtl's* ceaseless self-generation.

I waited.

CHAPTER 1
1958

PLEASE HELP ME SAY THE UNSAYABLE: My first life ended when my brother Sam committed suicide.

Before that, when he was thirteen and I was nine, he taught me his version of truth. We attended church services that May Sunday, ate lunch at my grandparents' house, took a nap. Around three o'clock, we drove in two cars through the farm gate, past the tenants' clapboard house, past the barn and slatted animal pens and patch-bald corral, toward our shaded table by the creek. Low-lying limestone cliffs bordered with cattle trails banked the water's edge. Farther out, seasonal rains brought out bluebonnet clusters radiant as lakes, alongside prickly pear and bull nettle, whose thorns left stinging wounds.

Freight trains, their whistles catastrophic, sad, slid like snaky sun gods across our property. Nugent had once been Texas' central connection for the Gulf, Colorado & Santa Fe Railway. The ornate station house stood three blocks from the municipal auditorium. Each Sunday afternoon I checked for evidence of stowaway campers near our picnic table, hoping an engine would barrel past, freight cars slinking behind.

My father parked the station wagon parallel to the tracks. They ran along a mesa that wound across our fields. I found a torn cotton shirt and a tiny pyramid of white pebbles. My legs stretched at awkward angles, beggar's lice already dotting my socks, my tennis shoes pressed into ashes and dirt. Kneeling, I imagined a bare-chest man juggling the stones, then balancing them, one by one.

My mother, whose name was Norine, moved close. "Look, Mama." I pointed, then chewed a fingernail. "What is it, you think?"

"Here, give me that," she said, reaching for the bundled shirt, "and take your fingers out of your mouth." Her brow pinched. "Look at this." She tapped her loafer at burned branches, snatched a Snickers wrapper. She glared, bit her pouty lip.

"But, Mama—" I pointed at the pyramid again. Still she didn't see. I wouldn't learn about hobos marking camping spots until years later.

"These people are tramps. Don't touch anything." I nodded, and she talked on, more to herself than to me. "I'd call the police if it would do any good." Her elegant, hook-nosed profile belonged on a nickel. "I hope Gran doesn't notice," she said, turning. "That's *all* we need."

I flinched whenever she spoke. Her Nile green eyes contrasted with my beady polka dots, and while I chose my shorts or skirts according to their buttons and snaps—the fewer the better—she stayed ahead of trends. Wearing her trademark silks, she applied face creams and liners in sponged and penciled stages, the whole job softened with a cosmetic brush. I'd never meet her standards for cultivated beauty. I hoped I wouldn't be a disappointment.

My brothers—Kurt, who was fourteen, Hugh, who was five, and Sam—checked for iron pyrite around the murky creek. When our mother wandered from the campsite toward the picnic table a few yards away, I didn't follow. I cupped one of the pyramid's stones. Chalky, I thought, like those rocks by the creek. I counted twenty-four, mostly round, one thinner, heavier, maybe an arrowhead. Indians, I marveled, may have once touched it. I tried to imagine walking in buckskin moccasins through burrs and wild rye in search of cottontails for dinner.

I pitched up a small pebble then caught it with both hands. Some man maybe sat here waiting for a train, I thought, and he held this, probably rolling it in this way. I'd seen open boxcars passing through intersections, the bells clanging, a candy-striped arm blocking the street. Now I imagined bouncing on a smudged wooden floor, darkness split by threads of flashing light, wheel clicks, honking blasts. I pictured the stranger lounged on a cardboard cushion, his back pressing the corrugated metal wall, his sunburned ankles crossed. If I could sit beside him, he'd tell how he'd been to places beyond Nugent, how nobody could stop him even though he was illegally hopping trains; then he'd hand me a shelled pecan. Oh, I thought. His pyramid of stones had been a thank-you to my family, a gift he'd made. I balanced the pebble back on top.

My grandfather rode his horse down the road from the barn. The animal, a thoroughbred grandson of Man o' War, pranced, angling sideways, the reins so taut the stallion sometimes bobbed its long head and snorted, its nostrils ruffling, its agitated lips showing yellowed teeth. My grandfather, not looking his seventy-four years, rode as if floating, directing the animal with his knees. His legs squeezed, pressing, and the horse whinnied, pumped its head. My grandfather kicked, yanking the reins to his chest. The horse lurched then reared, waving its front hooves, working its tongue at the metal bit.

I stepped back. My mother ambled toward the creek.

My grandfather jerked the reins harder, gave another kick. The horse bowed then quivered, stumbling, sullenly righting itself. Its eyes bulged; blood drooled from the split corners of its mouth. A moment later, it padded forward, ears pricked. As they approached the table, my grandfather waved his fedora, a one-man parade, his pedigreed mount subdued. All of us except my mother pointed, calling out as we hurried toward him.

He dismounted, and my father slapped the stallion's neck. "You've been taking a few lessons?" he teased my grandfather. "Like a nice ride in the park," he added, holding the reins, his grin a false note. I checked the tension around his eyes, thinking maybe I'd mistaken his irritation for teasing or that he'd somehow decided hurting a horse was okay. After all, his slap had been hard, even if it hadn't drawn blood like my grandfather's jerks at the reins did.

"Fine animal," my grandfather said. He rubbed its rangy forehead then smacked its flank; the horse flinched, shifted its footing. "He's spirited but manageable."

"Yes, sir," my father said, one hand behind his back, the other still holding the reins. His posture gave no indication of his feelings. Relaxed, his was the straightest back I'd seen. His flat expression and stiff back, though, made me sad.

"I expect you to show him a thing or two, boy."

"Yes, sir," my father answered, nodding in regimental rhythm, his gaze on the empty horizon.

That look reminded me of the times he'd playfully hung me or one of my brothers over our second-floor banister, or once, when he pretended to shut Sam in the car trunk. I thought my brother would suffocate and begged, "Daddy, don't." My father wasn't being mean. In fact, we all laughed when Sam tumbled out, our father tickling us both. But we were never to show that we were frightened. There were rules. I was sure they were meant to teach some lesson, since, at other times, he would pull me close and explain one of his "points of philosophy":

#1. Happiness is primarily an attitude.

#2. Even Moses was punished when he made his one mistake.

#3. Problems can be corrected through a systematic identification of facts.

Although I couldn't give a reason for not saying *sometimes you scare me*, I always kept silent.

Sam approached, pulling back the horse's lip. "Is his mouth cut?"

"No, boy," our father said, pushing Sam's hands. "Go see if Gran needs help unloading the car."

"Where's Norine?" my grandfather asked, waving in her direction. "Hey, girl, I'd like to see you ride," he shouted.

Sam frowned then turned toward the creek.

My mother squatted at the bank. She wore a frayed straw hat and looked through cat's-eye sunglasses over her shoulder, swatted the air twice then turned back.

She'd bragged that her name appeared by itself on the farm deed. While my father was overseas tending wounded soldiers during the war, she'd moved in with my grandparents and scrimped each month to pay the token fifteen-dollar mortgage before buying necessities for herself, Kurt, who was a baby then, and Sam, who arrived a few months after our father left. "Investment," my grandfather had reminded her.

"Consider it my thanks to a son's faithful wife."

Now, as he watched her, the horse nudged him off balance. He shoved back, and the animal thumped its rear hooves, yanked its head.

"Ho," my father said, holding out his hand. I wondered if he always believed Granddaddy was right. Would he do *anything* his father asked? I hoped not.

"You go then," my grandfather said, his face red, puckered. "Get Hugh, there, and convince me I wasn't wrong to pay good money for that sorry piece of horse flesh."

"Yes, sir," my father said, calling Hugh.

"I'm checking the peach trees," my grandfather said to no one in particular as he waded through broomgrass toward a small orchard my father had planted on the other side of the road.

Once he'd plopped Hugh behind the saddle horn, my father swung up, their bodies snug in the leather seat. "That way," Hugh said, signaling toward the barn. "Cows. Daddy, hurry." He waved as they swayed with each of the horse's steps, their hips ticking right, then left.

My mother strolled toward a mass of vines below the train trestle, then disappeared, collecting mustang grapes in a coffee can. My grandmother headed for evening primroses clustered next to a crepe myrtle.

"We don't like lemonade, I hope you didn't bring lemonade," Sam said as my grandmother snapped flower stems, discarding all but perfect blooms.

"Whoever perished, being innocent?" she said, pity shaping a smile, a typical condescension whose source was mysterious. Then she sang, her reedy voice garbling lyrics, except in the occasional clear note, the words "blessing" and "thou."

"Last one to the water—" Kurt yelled; then he, Sam, and I raced each other to the creek. My brothers had worn bathing suits under their jeans, so they peeled off their pants, left them on the bank. Stripped to my panties, I stepped into the cool water, and Sam dove past me into the shadowed depths. Kurt soaked me with a cannonball dive. Fine silt blackened our bottoms as we slid from algae-slick rocks to mud soft as feathers. If I stood flat-footed in the small swimming hole, the top just covered my head. We slapped water at each other, and I barely escaped their pinches and efforts to push me under.

We forgot we were two boys and one girl with rules we'd learned about how one should behave with the other. Just three children in the water and mud, our tanned arms and legs gleaming, sharp stones pricking our toughened feet. Every so often, one of us called another's name, and these shouts, mixed with giggling and thwaps of splashed water, echoed back toward our mother, father, grandparents.

By the time my grandfather had returned to the table with a basket of peaches, we'd put on our jeans again, and we raced toward him. My grandmother joined us, strands of gray hair stuck to her damp face. Kurt and Sam threw their pits at each other as our father and Hugh came riding up.

"*I* want one," Hugh cried, reaching toward the basket, slipping, tumbling to the ground. He whimpered, clutching his arm; my father stepped down.

"Guess we could amputate, just about *here*," he teased, the side of his hand slicing above Hugh's elbow.

"No," Hugh whined, rubbing. "It's okay, honest."

We laughed and shoved him, but our father's message was clear.

My grandfather took the horse's reins in one hand and used his other to motion again in wide arcs. "Now, Norine, I'd like to see what *you* can do."

She'd gathered stalks of purple horsemint and wispy old man's beard in a peanut butter jar and was leaning over the table, but she stopped, her arm a warning flag. "No. Thank you," she said, her words heavy as the heat, and set down the flowers.

My grandfather dropped his hand and watched her poking her arrangement. "Now, Miss Norine, come on, girl." He stroked the horse's neck. "No reason to be afraid. He's a thoroughbred, but a baby could handle him."

My mother stiffened. Only her head turned. "It's not that I *can't* ride him," she said. "I just don't care to right now." She rubbed the table with a cloth.

My grandfather stood, a corner of his shirttail hanging, and removed his fedora, then wiped his forehead with his sleeve. We all grew still. "You want everybody to think you can't ride a little ol' horse, I guess that's your business." He replaced his hat, pushing it back, not looking at her.

She faced us—her straw hat's brim a halo, her sunglasses white horns. She marched over, reached toward my grandfather, snatched the reins, and swung onto the saddle.

My hands went to my mouth. I winced, ready to cover my eyes.

Leaning right, she flicked her heels. The horse twirled, cantered, then galloped toward the trestle at a high speed. At the edge of the field she turned, hunched into the wind, and aimed at us, her finish line. As the horse gathered speed, its rocking gait smoothed into a streak. When they stopped, dust and dirt kicked our feet. Dismounting, my mother tossed the reins back at my grandfather. "I *told* you I could ride him," she said through clenched teeth. "What I said was that I didn't want to."

"Yeah, she told *you*," Sam whooped.

But to me, a child whose world was still family, my mother's defiance was like cursing God in the middle of a sermon. I'd never seen anyone, particularly a woman, talk to my grandfather like she had. Even Gran called him Dr. Pelton, and she never questioned anything he said or talked back. Neither did my father. The church taught about resurrected saints, betrayals in the garden, so I knew that committing a sin was scary; Dad's switch had proved it. But this time, I knew my grandfather was wrong, and, sin or no sin, I wanted to tell him that, but couldn't.

My grandfather slapped his leg with his hat then repositioned it. He led the horse toward the creek for a drink. My mother rolled up the cuffs of Hugh's jeans then gave a hugging laugh while patting his bottom. Why wasn't my grandfather mad? Had my mother known she could talk to him like that? Maybe there were times when rules could be broken. But which ones, and how? At least, now, I knew to ask.

"Sam, I need my number one helper. Over here, please," my grandmother called. "Will you carry some things from the car?" She brushed a damp curl from her forehead.

"Only if I can hold your hand," Sam said, clutching hers. My father, my mother, and Hugh followed them to the Cadillac.

I escaped with Kurt upstream, our cane fishing poles in tow. We guided our rods between trees, past clumps of scrub and brushwood, leaving behind the adults and my questions. Insects dotted the stream's surface, bringing perch and bass up from the bottoms, but Kurt, as usual, lost patience. A typical firstborn, he conjured images of snappy salutes, troops marching in coordinated steps. He'd forgotten his glasses again, so his face wrinkled from habit into an ornery squint. "These fish are either stone dead or geniuses," he said, frowning, flipping his line back and forth.

When Sam appeared, he slid my hook through the back of a cricket he'd found under a rock, then swung his own line next to the far bank. "Over there, Sar," he said, pointing at a quiet water hole to the left. I aimed, then consulted his broad, full-lipped face. He nodded.

Unlike Kurt's tight-cornered ways, Sam had an impish quality, like a pet parrot that flirts while maneuvering to snatch someone's food. His laugh was a high-pitched giggle that wrenched from his body like a spasm, his face all creases and teeth, his arms flailing until he hugged his stomach. He loved to talk, though his conversation was never easy. At any moment, he might do something that I had to think about.

"I swear they got a bead on my hook," Kurt said, plopping his worm farther right.

Sam and I watched for movement in our lines, while Kurt wiped his forehead, fidgeted. Sam signaled for me to look past our brother. A turtle, head wagging, floated on the murky surface then went under, small waves spreading, fading.

"Hey, Kurt," Sam called, "your fishing's so bad, you got an audience," and he jerked his head toward the turtle. Even though they occasionally wrestled, sometimes punching each other, today Sam's smile was an arm around Kurt's shoulder.

"Man!" Kurt said, dropping his pole, scrambling toward the floating creature. He reached into the dirt near his feet, then tossed and skipped rocks one after another, plunking them near the bobbing target.

The turtle had greenish skin and a shell covered in algae. It paddled its webbed feet and sometimes flipped a tail that bore scales like a crest.

"Stupid!" Sam stifled a shout. "You're scaring the fish."

"They're spooked anyhow," Kurt said, biting his lip, reaching a stick toward the turtle as it passed in front of him.

He poked, and the creature gazed, stunned, then dipped its wobbly head. "Kurt, stop. I'll call Mama," I whined, running toward him. I shoved him and tried to grab the stick.

Kurt raised his elbow, blocking my waving arm, a buzzing he barely noticed. He squinted, jabbed again. This time, the turtle yanked its head and snapped its jaws onto the stick, cracking it. Sam stood next to me, clasping his sides, laughing.

"You're hurting him. Leave him alone," I shouted, almost crying.

Kurt skipped a pebble off the animal's shell, and Sam frowned, staring, his gaze like a cranky conscience.

I turned to run, but a terrible thud made me stop. My grandfather had yanked the horse's reins then made my father's face go blank, and later he'd forced my mother to ride when she'd said she didn't want to. Now Kurt and Sam were throwing rocks at a turtle. I pictured them cackling, leaning toward the water, the turtle belly-up, its legs flopping. Sam disappointed me most; I'd thought of him as a person who couldn't hurt anything without a good reason.

Somebody called my name, and when I turned, Sam stood by the cattle trail, motioning me over. As mad as I was, I couldn't resist his singling me out; we left our poles on the bank and wandered upstream, hidden from the others by juniper, Arkansas cane, the creek's curve. Stepping in time with him, his breaths whispery, even, I trusted that he'd explain his meanness.

"Stay here," he said and waded into the creek. He stopped and stared into the darkness. This time, his breathing hardly raised his chest. Only his eyes moved, following some creature below as it passed. Another turtle? The two middle fingers on his left hand twitched. Cicadas rattled like tambourines, the stream pattered across rocks, mosquitoes whirled.

Sam's hands pierced the surface and fell deep, the water above his elbows. I ran to the edge; the toes of my tennis shoes sank into silt. He lurched backward, then tossed the creature and a tunnel of water forward; drops fanned around his head, thumping as they splashed.

Almost a foot long, the fish flopped, slithering in the muddy shallow. When I reached him, Sam held the fish while its mouth yawned then closed, and the tail curled like a tongue, the body all muscle as it jerked, flipping in my brother's hands.

I imagined the bass, with its green back, black side-stripes, and orange circles around popping eyes, flopping between my own fingers, wanting its cool home.

"Daddy and Granddaddy cut open bodies so they can see the stuff inside," Sam said. He crouched on the bank, reached into his pocket.

I bent next to him but pressed my fists to my chest. The fish's gills fluttered.

"I saw you watching all them." He motioned with his head back toward the others as he withdrew a knife, pulled out its blade with his teeth. "Don't let it get to you. We're not like that." His eyes peered into mine. "I want you to see this. Can you take it?" When I nodded, he knelt as he slid the steel into the anus, then sliced forward through white belly, splintering ribs. The wafer-like flaps still puffed as he cut through them on either side. He laid the knife next to his knee and pulled back on the head, cracking bones, then yanked it off. He set the head next to his knife; one orange-haloed eye stared at sky.

"Why'd you do that?" I asked, not letting myself turn away. My brother had killed it, killed it just so he could show me something. I had to watch.

"Sometimes you got to do ugly things," he said, but he didn't look at me. Even though he was mangling the fish, I trusted him because he always took care of me.

Sam stuck his hand inside the body, tugged at the gullet casing. He ripped the intestinal sac loose with a snap. He dropped the bass, holding its insides in the air, the torn end that had once connected to the head pointing at the ground. About the size of our father's index finger, the sac was pear-shaped and gray with threads of red membrane, muscle. It tapered into something like a tail.

Pinching what had been the bottom of the gullet, Sam squeezed, raking the casing in jerks. A larval insect with a crowd of legs popped out, landed on the ground, and thrashed its whip-shaped body back and forth, its head sprouting pincers that searched for a target. Then the sac spit out pill bugs and algae, snails, tiny clam-like animals, all dead. Alive, they'd been cramped inside what must've seemed like a cavernous pouch.

Sam pressed again, and shells and plants oozed free until something larger neared the opening. It was brown and had a tiny curled paw. He punched at the casing, and the dark mass fell next to the wiggling grub. This new creature had a face and white eyelids, delicate in their tiny perfection. Hair covered its limp body, and the feet touched one another, while the head curved toward the tail as if to rest there. I rubbed the fuzz around the mouse's ears. What had it been doing in the water, and why hadn't it chewed its way out of the fish? When a green liquid squirted from the sac onto the pile of creatures and plants, Sam tossed the limp casing to the side.

"Know what this is?" he asked as he picked up the writhing insect, allowing it to creep across his palm, fingers, back of his hand.

I giggled nervously, imagining how it would feel to swallow something alive, hoping he wouldn't expect me to hold the thing like he'd once dared me to touch a jumping crawdad. "Uh-uh, what?" I said.

"Hellgrammite. Turns into a fly with a giant claw and only flies at night," he whispered. "Looks a little like Granddaddy, don't you think?"

He rested the flat of his hand on the dirt, and the insect scuttled into the grass. He flipped open one of the clam-like shells; inside laid a soft animal, cupped.

"Can you eat those?" I asked.

"I don't know," he said, "let's see," and he scraped one loose, rubbed it onto his tongue. He chewed twice, shrugged.

"What'd it taste like?" I imagined salty flesh, slipperiness as I swallowed.

"Too little," he said, poking at the pile of small animals and debris. His hands were child-sized but muscled, meticulous as a surgeon's.

"Those could be you and me, Kurt and Hugh, right?"

He smiled.

"And the mouse has to be Mama," I said.

"Nope, *that's* you," he said. "And these," he pointed at the shells, "are all your babies."

They were fluted, smaller than thumbtacks.

"I was hoping to find a young bass. They're cannibals, you know."

His eyes commanded an answer, so I shook my head, no. Did animals realize they were eating their own kind or did they gobble out of instinct? "Fish don't feel stuff. I mean, they don't hurt like us, right?"

"No, not possible," he said. "Their brains," he made a tiny circle with his index finger and thumb, "are no bigger'n your fingernail." The circle's ratio to fish body was disturbing when compared to my brain/body proportions.

He wiped his knife on his thigh, popped it closed, slid it into his pocket. "Help me pick this stuff up. We'd better get back." He gathered bass parts in his hands.

I scooped up the fish's head and reached for the mouse—the orange-circled eye glared from one palm, the sleeping baby curled in the other. The fuzzy hair and scales, the delicate paw and loose gills were now familiar as my own skin. From then on, I decided, I'd be as devouring as a bass, a truth scavenger.

Sam led me along the creek's bank to a cluster of agarita bushes, and we left the animal pieces for raccoons. During our return walk, he tried to carry me at first, my body sliding down his back, my legs dangling. Near the picnic table, he tickled me and shouted for Kurt, who was climbing off the horse.

My grandfather held the reins, calling, "Okay, Sarah." He waved. "You think you can handle this animal as good as your mama?"

"I'll try," I croaked. Determined to practice my new resolve, I joined him. But while I stood waiting as he bent to shorten a stirrup, yanking the strap's buckles, an object glimmered in the grass. Leaning closer, I recognized his gold money clip, bills folded inside like handkerchiefs.

"That ought to be about right," he said, gauging my match-up with the readjusted stirrup. I muttered, "Yes, sir," so he moved to the other side of the horse. Casually, I edged closer. While he raised the second stirrup, I crouched, sliding the clip into my pocket. Jittery but smug, I popped my knuckles. Maybe I *was* like my mother.

Once in the saddle, my tongue-clicks and tug at the reins sent the horse trotting forward. Leaning, I loosened the reins, and the stallion cantered, his lumpy hooves whacking ground in a rhythm I controlled. A crisscross of branches and sagebrush expanded when I looked behind, so I stared ahead at patches of brown and blue. The wind pressed and whirled, while the horse, panting, waited for my command. Was Mother watching? I steered him under the train trestle, then back up the other side. His feet slid in gravel as he strained, heaving with jerking steps.

Standing, wobbly, on the ground, I scooped a handful of those stones, and in a flat area close to the tracks, I stacked them in another pyramid, twenty-four rocks in all, with my grandfather's clipped bills in the center. The stranger could come back and find my gift, his dirty fingers smudging the gold. Maybe I'd end up riding with him to New York or Mexico, nothing but rumbles and scattered light surrounding us.

I turned toward the clearing below, looking for Sam, not finding him. Only flicks of color and constant stirring, the rest didn't notice me:

#1. not my grandfather as his white shirt reflected the sun;

#2. not my father reaching into the basket of peaches;

#3. not Kurt fishing at the creek;

#4. not my grandmother;

#5. not my mother bending close to the ground.

I blocked the glare then shifted my arm, concealing my view of them with my open hand.

CHAPTER 2

SINCE I MISSED TEREZIE last month at my father's funeral, I wouldn't have recognized her but for having seen her eight years ago at my mother's service. When she was a girl, her nonchalance had been key to seducing Sam. Now, standing on my porch in Austin, her housecoat hugging a sausage waist, this woman only hints at the sister-in-law I knew. Seeing her brings me one-step-removed from Sam.

"I wouldn't be here unless I had a good reason," she says. "Sam would've wanted me to come. I've never asked you for anything before, but now I need to."

I let her in, of course, but mumble an apology that I'm meeting someone for lunch. It's an obvious lie, rude, cruel even, but I can't stop myself.

"As you know, I have a daughter, Cornelia."

I don't need to see the photo. Terezie introduced her while we stood together after my mother's funeral. If the daughter had knocked on my door instead, I'd have known her immediately. She's the Terezie I remember.

"She's a good girl, uncomplicated, hard working. Ma says she's 'old country.'" Terezie chuckles, thinking she's made a joke. "Thing is, she needs a kidney transplant."

I hold up my hands. "I'm sorry, Terezie. Don't you think you should talk to Kurt or Hugh about this?"

She licks her lips, taking back her photo. "We don't need your kidney, if that's what you're thinking. Cornelia's father's the donor, God bless him." She zips her bag. "But her condition's scary. She's got polycystic kidney disease and blood pressure so high it's really gotten her in trouble. On top of that, she's had a delayed autoimmune reaction. She's on dialysis and steroids to stabilize everything, but she's got to have the transplant at Mayo."

"Oh, this is way out of my league." I move toward the door, ready to usher her out. "Please, phone Kurt," I say, tugging Terezie's arm. "I'm sure he'll want to help."

"I've already talked to him." She shakes me loose. "Listen, since I teach part-time and my husband has his own business, we don't have insurance. I know how stupid that is, but who thinks something like this will happen?

"I've already told Hugh and Kurt everything, but they won't give me an answer." She winces; her jaw clamps. "Cornelia's got to be operated on in the next six months, Sarah, or she'll be in real trouble. If Sam were here, you know what he'd do."

After Terezie is gone, I reach for the phone, dial Hugh's number.

Hugh is driving over from Nugent, so I wake feeling pissy. I don't want to talk about the farm. I love my memories of little boy Hugh, but our past is all we've got in common. I've agreed to meet with Hugh today in part because my hallucinations are coming more often. The *Mixe* shamans in southern Mexico see dreaming and waking states as the same, and although I understand this, it scares the hell out of me. I never know what will trigger one of my *episodes*, so I'm trying to hang onto whatever's real.

At four-thirty, I dress then grade student essays, an intentional distraction. At noon, I treat myself to the gastronomic beau ideal, cinnamon toast. I fix two slices of a bran loaf I baked, as usual, on Sunday. As lunch browns, bubbling under the broiler, I put the butter away. The door closes with a suctioned click, and I think, *here*, this appliance is *now*.

The Frigidaire's nearly empty shelves (my usual diet: bran loaf,

Winesaps, camembert) are a relief, the porcelain and steel requiring no tending, the shell sturdy as a punching bag. Sometimes, deprivation can bring comfort, sanctification like the celebration of *Xīpe Totec* by the Aztec Triple Alliance. An effigy's flayed-skin costume commemorated the body's deterioration in a vegetable cycle of transformations. If the effigy was human, the worshipper emerged from the rotting skin after twenty days, signifying rebirth. A ghoulish ritual, to be sure, but so are enactments of Jesus' crucifixion. In both cases, the sacrifice brings solace. This morning, of course, my little ritual is free of gruesome drama.

When the first whiff of cinnamon, East Indian yet familiar as *Pelton*, turns to the stench of scorched sugar, it seems an omen. My brother, the farm sale papers tucked under his arm, might make fun of my unconventional life. But Terezie's poor child needs emergency surgery. I stack my charred toast on a fluted Royal Dalton and carry it with a matching cup of hazelnut espresso to my captain's chair, but the third mouthful gets me. I've bitten my tongue, and like most mature women at such moments, I have a tantrum. After that, I work on my book.

I write for an hour about the metaphysics and social hierarchies of the *Mexihca*. For another hour, I write about *ixīptla*: richly dressed and accoutered stone images, elaborately constructed seed-dough figures, ecstatic priests in divine costumes, captives prepared for sacrifice. Rituals transformed these into vehicles for *teōtl*, the self-generating, transmuting energy. Each was carefully constructed, named for an aspect of the sacred, adorned with characteristic regalia, and destroyed.

Īxīptla were part of *Mexihcayōtl* protocol designed to pacify the inscrutable, uncontrolled power called *teōl*. Rituals bombarded the senses. Drumming, jangling of shells, copper bells, cries from sacrificed victims, conch trumpets, flutes, and antiphonal chants merged with the smells of flowers, incense, and blood as dancers twirled, their feathers brushing.

Class divisions continued beyond the grave. Those who drowned went to the Southern Paradise. As I describe *Tlāloc*—his fangs, absent lower jaw, goggled eyes, elaborate headdress, with a lightning bolt in his hand, controlling rivers, thunderstorms, and crop-devastating hail—I think again: What kind of life is this, sitting alone, dissecting a pre-Columbian culture? I know the answer but have no idea how to change it.

A spatula on the kitchen counter, its tip blackened with crumbs; student papers in ordained stacks next to my chair across the room; sunlight in amoeboid patches in the fanlight of my front door. *Here. Now.* Hugh is late.

Hugh's six-year-old daughter, Norine, Mother's namesake, whines on the other side of my door: "She doesn't even have a TV."

"I know," Hugh's wife Debbie says.

Norine is first inside, and when she steps forward with her arm raised, I brace myself for a hug. Instead, she pokes my pant leg. "Aunt Sarah…Aunt Sarah…"

"Hello, Hugh, Debbie," I say. My rabbit-toothed little brother with hand-me-down t-shirt and exposed belly: now muscle, whiskers, sinew. His eyes: our father's eyes: my eyes.

"How come—" Norine continues, oblivious, "how come you're here all by yourself?" Mother's eyes, the same green. The same question.

Debbie and Hugh believe in immediate response to their daughter no matter whom or what is interrupted. Throughout years of infertility treatments, Debbie had two miscarriages before producing, at thirty-eight, a premature Norine so small that she wore doll clothes. After that, Debbie's sanctification of motherhood manifested in strange ways. Half porno-queen, half Virgin Mary, she wore tight, low-cut clothes while preaching La Leche philosophy and the carnal influence of Saturday morning cartoons and comic books.

Hugh's newfound religion emphasizes thou shalt *not*, a reincarnation of our father's blank expression and stiff back. Our grandfather's Bible probably sits like the Ark of the Covenant in his Nugent living room.

"Aunt Sarah's not married," Debbie explains, holding her daughter's hand and leaning, her thigh taut and tan. Was mine ever sexy? Maybe. And now? Veins, fat pockets, my body a traitor. The upside is I don't have to shave much anymore.

Hugh faces his family; he hasn't said anything yet.

"Look, you have the same chin," Debbie says, cupping Norine's face but looking up at me.

"Uh…well…" I say, waving, casually I believe, until my hand lurches sideways, tapping Hugh.

He watches Debbie hovering over Norine.

"Who's going to be the daddy?"

Enough, I think. "Norine, dear, would you come over here? I have something to show you." I've given up trying to connect with children. W. C. Fields said, "Anyone who hates children can't be all bad." I tend to agree. But I don't want to upset Norine, so I coax her toward my table. When I hand her my plastic model of the *Mexihcayōtl* Great Temple, complete with removable tops, her expression indicates the distraction quotient of a video game. "Pretend you're a goddess. Sit here," I say, "while your folks and I talk. Good girl," I add as she climbs onto a floor pillow. Then I pull chairs from various places, and Debbie, Hugh, and I sit in the kitchen next to the counter.

"Here, honey," Hugh says, holding a ladder-back for Debbie, "this'll be more comfortable." My youngest brother is approaching fifty, still my height (we tie as the family's tallest), his hair coiffed as a Baptist preacher's. During the work week, he wears his white coat. Along with Kurt, a cardiologist, Hugh, a gynecologist, works at the hospital that mushroomed from the practice shared by our grandfather and his two partners. "Is it a political thing or what?" he says. "I mean, why no furniture?"

Where's the farm contract? I want to ask. I've agreed to the sale, so can't we just get on with it?

"We're all sitting, aren't we?" I say, shrugging, wondering if he'll next mention the stench of burned toast. Oddly, none of them seems to notice, while smoke swirls directly above their heads. I blurt a quote reminiscent of our father's proverbs: "'Rough treatment gives souls as well as stones their luster.'" My eyes attempt a lighthearted signal. "Good to see you, Hugh."

"Yeah?" he says, running his palms down his chinos. "You, too." He teasingly arches an eyebrow.

He spots the five-headed Ganesh next to my laptop. "You never change."

"Everything changes, especially people." I'm thinking of us, but we're remembering Sam. "Except the farm, maybe that's the same."

"You haven't seen the house, have you? The tenant didn't keep up his end of the repairs. We're talking wiring, plumbing, roof."

"I guess he's not the buyer, then?" I picture children sitting cross-legged in weeds alongside the highway. "He doesn't have a family, does he?"

"Kurt's been dealing with that, but the guy's already eight months behind in his rent."

"Where will they go?" Am I being rude? I'm making him sound like Scrooge, when I've never offered to help. Or thanked him. I've clearly lost the ability to talk to my brother.

"I don't know, Sarah, but I'm sure they'll be fine. They can't stay at the farm, though. It's not safe."

I block more images. Cornelia is enough to worry about, and besides, the farm won't be ours much longer. "Remember swimming in the creek?" I say before I can stop myself. "I miss Mother and Dad, Sam, everything." Our parents lie under a single tombstone in the Nugent cemetery, Sam in the same lot shaded by a mimosa. Now, the farm is my only link to family. But if it isn't sold, what happens to Cornelia? Keep talking, I say to myself; you'll find a way. You have to.

"Can't look back," Hugh says.

"Remember that?" I say, pointing to an imitation jaguar mask hanging over my bed in the next room. The *Mexihca* believed the cosmos was a *xāyacatl*, or mask, of *teōl*. What we perceive as objects during our dreamlike earthly life—insects, cornstalks, comets, even humans—were *teōtl's* transmutation in disguise. Dualities—order/disorder, illusion/reality, life/death—were misunderstood as opposites. Since you could only know *teōtl* through a mystical union without language or categories, ritual masks had dualities on their surface, the effect intentionally ambiguous. Now, my jaguar's painted rosettes and leather tongue greet me each morning.

Hugh tilts back. "No, should I?"

"You were just a kid. Sam brought it from Laredo." I picture our brother, his puckish expression, his hazel-green eyes. As a graduate student at the Institute of Anthropologic Research in Mexico City, I learned *Nahuatl* and held a tenth century mother-of-pearl *ixīptla*. *Xipe Totec's* jeweled head peered from inside the open jaws of a flayed jaguar.

"Had to be somebody else," he says, pulling his ear lobe. "Look, Debbie." He leans, angling his finger toward the bedroom. She shudders; they laugh. "My big sister," he says with a smile, "the loco professor."

This from the boy who made a Pinocchio puppet out of socks, who majored in journalism and wrote an editorial about Camus' theory of the absurd proving the Viet Nam War's pointlessness. Where did that brother go? "Okay," I say, "I assume you brought the papers?" Cornelia. Six months.

"I was only teasing. Come on, can't you take a joke?" He massages the base of my neck. For years, no one has done that.

"I have an idea," I say, reaching toward a cabinet. I set a candle on the drain board then light it. I bring my Conway Stewart from the tea table. "Here," I say, handing him the pen, "you first. We'll make this a celebration."

"Sit down," he says. "There's something I have to tell you." His top lip folds under, disappearing, so different from Sam's.

"What now?" I moan.

"No big deal," he shrugs, "just, the sale's temporarily on hold." He balances his right calf perpendicular to his left knee, then grabs his leg, as though leaning across a desk. "To tell the truth, you didn't seem that fired up about selling anyway."

"I don't understand. What's the problem?" We didn't discuss Terezie, so he doesn't know she's been to see me. "Who's the buyer?"

"Our lawyer has to work out a few minor details. Like I said, it's no big deal."

"But we don't have time for that."

"Sure we do, a little breathing room. This kind of deal can't be rushed; you know that."

"But Cornelia, Hugh. She only has six months."

He flinches.

"Actually," Debbie interrupts, "she has longer than that." Norine slides off the cushion and lies prostrate in front of the pyramid. "In the meantime, we're trying to figure out how we can help her."

Hugh slumps; his head and shoulders fold over his lap.

"At least Debbie's being honest," I say. "Now, will you please explain what's going on?"

"I swear she'll get the operation," Hugh says, "even if I have to pay for it." He slaps his shoe, uncrosses his legs. "But our lawyer says Sam's letter could be a problem." I picture Sam's scribbled instructions to transfer all his possessions to his wife. "If we give her Sam's part of the sale now, then later, she could ask for a percentage of Granddaddy's estate."

Why should that bother me anymore than the idea of sharing our inheritance with my other sisters-in-law? The only difference is that she needs the money. "But if it's legally hers, what right do we have to argue?"

"Wills are contested all the time."

"But Hugh, a child's life weighs in the balance."

"What do you think I am?" Hugh says, rising. He fills a glass at the faucet. "I told you Cornelia would have her operation."

"So you're definitely going to pay for it?"

"I don't think that'll be necessary," Debbie interrupts.

Norine walks over, whispers into her mother's ear.

Debbie nodds. "All Terezie has to do is sign an agreement promising not to ask for anything else."

"Have you explained this to her?"

"Not yet," Hugh says. "But that's our next step."

"So you're going to ask her give away what our brother told us to make sure she got?"

"She's not part of this family anymore, Sarah. Nobody's talked to her in thirty years. You'd feel a lot different if you had children."

"Maybe." Now I stand but turn my back, press the bridge of my nose and inhale. "But I expect to be included in the meeting with Terezie."

"All right," he says, holding up his palms. "Whatever you want. We should know something in the next couple of weeks. I'll call you."

"Should I talk to Kurt?"

"No, I'll tell him." He gives a Boy Scout salute. "Promise."

"Sarah," Debbie says, "Norine would like a Coke if you have it." She sits with her arm around her daughter; they glance at each other, look back, smile, their movements synchronized.

Debbie's question is a command. I'm expected to accommodate the child who's assumed my mother's name, while another child and her mother are being manipulated. "No. Sorry," I say then blow out the candle. "As a matter of fact, just before you got here, I promised a student I'd meet her at my office in half an hour. Having trouble with her thesis. You understand."

"You mean you want us to leave?" Hugh asks, his head cocked. "But we drove all the way here."

I gather the scattered pyramid pieces from the floor. "Professors have emergencies, too." Hugh's specialty, gynecology, was chosen for its un-Pelton-like qualities, but he, like Kurt, heads his department at Latimore Memorial.

"Why do you do this?"

"Excuse me?"

Holding hands, Debbie and Norine walk toward the front door.

"You're my sister." He and Kurt have maintained the Pelton tradition of gathering for holiday lunches and periodic Sundays after church. My absence must worry them.

"Yes, and I appreciate you coming." Mother and daughter move into the front yard. "And bringing your family with you." *Liar! Liar!* Miraculously, he doesn't notice.

"At least call sometime."

"Sure." I walk him outside, tap his back, the bones pliant yet sturdy.

"I pray for you every night," Hugh whispers with such tenderness, I can't bring myself to point out his implied insult.

"When did you get so pious?"

His fingers furrow his hair, exposing strips of scalp. "When Sam died, I got mad," he says, his eyes suddenly wet. "There didn't seem to be a point to anything. Church was nothing but morons preaching a hyped-up myth." He shifts his stance, shoves his fists into his pockets. "Then I found the Lord." He nods, as though I'll understand. I don't. Sam would've known what to say. Hugh's grief would've prompted Sam to give comfort. Now this Christian brother is hesitating to help Terezie's daughter, and I am silent.

While Norine stands at the curb, Debbie crouches, her denim skirt barely covering her crotch. Hugh joins his family; when he squats, he cups his daughter's chin with one hand, grips his wife's thigh with the other.

Odd, I think, the variations in dress and behavior female animal species use to attract males. Then, *cheer-lee churr* sings from the pecan tree across the street. "Western bluebird, *Sialia mexicana*," I mumble, "Sooty gray feathers that camouflage during nesting. Unlike grouse in estrus, who shove their swollen parts in the air."

While Norine runs to the side of the house, out of view, Hugh helps Debbie stand. He whispers something, rubs her back.

The white bass squirts orange eggs, roe, as she flutters her silver sides in the shallow water.

When Norine returns, she holds something I can't see.

"Beautiful," Hugh says, stroking her arm.

Still, human females outdo them all, I think while I reach for the door knob: from painting their nipples and elongating their necks, to the Dayak girls in Borneo wearing corselets of rattan hoops covered with brass rings, silver and shells. Or American women who squeeze into denim.

When I turn from the doorway, Norine hands Debbie a fistful of wild rain-lily stalks. As I whisper, "*Cooperia pedunculata*, diminutive amaryllids," I notice the child's and mother's same sorrel-colored hair and Norine's stance, tilted forward, like her father's.

My eyes close. Burning sage. Drumming? Shells jangle.

On my bed two hours later, I stir, groggy.

CHAPTER 3

A WEEK LATER, I drive to Nugent, where I get lost trying to find Kurt's house. Circling through the subdivision, I spot a familiar screened porch, a three-car garage with a basketball hoop, the street with a seventy-five-degree drop that neighborhood children coasted down on skateboards and bicycles. Bewildered (How does a person lose her brother's house?), noticing the same orange front door for a third time, I skid to the curb midway through the next block.

I'd like to go through the front door, but my sister-in-law, Randy, would think that odd, so I head toward the back. As I latch the gate, two Doberman pinschers appear, their hatchet heads jerking with each chopped bark. Kurt has always owned big dogs, so I stroll toward the door, acting unfazed, convinced that he, Randy, or one of his two children is watching, that my ability to arrive unruffled might be a test, one I hope to pass.

Stooping, her thin leg a barricade, Randy wrestles the Dobermans away from the door. In the kitchen, cilantro, garlic, almond waft from a pot on the commercial range. Oriental lilies half fill a cut-glass vase; more lay on waxed paper, their perfume mixing with herbal steam. Silverware gleams in stacks on the granite counter. "Did I come at a bad time?" Maybe I have the appointment wrong. I thought Kurt said Saturday at 9:00.

"No, why?" Randy says, clipping a lily, sliding it into the arrangement. "It's Supper Club, no biggie. Can I get you anything?"

Her cell phone rings; she swivels as though stepping into a dance routine.

"Mom, you said…" Kurt Jr. whines while rounding the corner. He looks thirteen or fourteen, gangly, with droopy, obliging eyes.

"And I'll say it again," she interrupts. "You need a haircut." She checks the oven. "Now tell your Aunt Sarah hello." She tips her auburn head in my direction, finally answering her phone.

"Huh?" he says, scowling, his Adam's apple bobbing.

"You don't remember me, but I'm your dad's sister. The last time I saw you, you were a baby."

"No way. I'd forgotten Dad had a sister. That's totally weird," he says, snickering, his insult meant as a compliment. I almost hug him.

"Hey!" Randy says, holding the receiver with one hand, snapping her fingers with the other. She checks her watch; the stove timer buzzes.

"What-ev-er…"

"Don't be rude, mister." Turning, Randy mumbles into the mouthpiece while walking to the pot; she stirs, adjusts the flame.

"Can we bail then, Mom?" he says, huffy. "Dad'll kill me if I'm late." He leans on one hip, his legs like stilts, his hands catcher's mitts.

"Get your gear then," she says, hanging up. "I'll meet you at the car."

I don't say how familiar this scene feels. Spooky. "Is Kurt home? Was he expecting me?"

"Oh," she says, checking her watch again. "He's in his lair," she sighs, stepping toward the doorway. "But we'll have to hurry."

Randy talks on her cell, reading from a folded piece of paper she's pulled from her slacks pocket as we pass through labyrinthine halls. "Horseradish," she says, "yes, two." She points to a door. "I told you I saw them together last week," she says, wheeling, disappearing back down the carpeted passageway.

Kurt sits cross-legged on the floor, next to his ten-year-old daughter, Emma, and behind a small transformer. A model train, its steam engine whistling, puffing smoke, whips over a track that winds under two bridges, through a tunnel, past houses, a diner, a loader that dumps miniature logs into one of the cars, and a gateman in blue overalls who comes out of his shanty waving a red lantern. Each time the train veers toward Emma, she kicks her feet, shuts her eyes, holds her ears. Kurt rests his hand on her back; she flinches, flapping her hands. "Here she comes," he sings, "woo, woo."

"Train," Emma says, blinking. She rises, shrieking, and steps toward the swerving caboose. Was the layout for him or for her? Whichever, Kurt's tenderness is the issue. Fate, with its inexorable aim, has pierced his seemingly invulnerable heart. Even his international connections can't give his developmentally challenged daughter a normal life.

"Oh," he says finally. "It's you." His face has lost its pudginess, but without glasses, he's got his usual squint.

When the train stops, Emma flops to the floor, swaying, biting her hands. "Em," Kurt says kneeling, "go work on your puzzle." He waits, glancing down. "Your puzzle," he says, leaning into her plank-like face. She walks to a small table next to the wall, fingers jigsaw pieces in a cardboard box.

Kurt sits at our father's oak desk, checking inside one drawer after another. I take an armchair across from him. He wears jeans and a plaid cotton shirt whose faded red blocks and tight shoulders are familiar. Was it Sam's?

"So let's get this over with," Kurt says, setting a box of shotgun shells and a bird whistle next to a kettle of bones Dad kept in the same spot. "I'm meeting Nyank at the farm in twenty minutes."

"Nyank?" Kurt's frankness is typical but never mean-spirited. "Do I know him?" The name sounds familiar.

"Wade," he says. "Wade Nyank?" I frown, and he adds, "Sam's friend. Remember him telling how Nyank almost lost his ear at 32 Bluffs?"

"Oh, yeah, how is he?" I guiltily resent Kurt knowing what seemed a confidence Sam had shared only with me.

"Okay, I guess." Before I can ask how Kurt and Wade became buddies, he reminds me of why I've driven here. "You can't come to the meeting with Terezie." He shoves the whistle in his shirt pocket.

"What do you mean I *can't* come?"

"Cut the crap, Sarah. You can't join the game at halftime and expect to know which play to run."

A football analogy. Sometimes I forget this is Texas. "*You* cut the crap, Kurt. A priest doesn't deny counsel to a dying woman simply because she reminds him of his sins."

He stands and walks to his gun cabinet. "I'm sure that was your version of an insult," he says, taking out a 12-gauge, cracking open the stock. "You honestly think you're the expert." The gun snaps shut. "Here," he says. "Catch."

"No," I call, but the weapon is already airborne, so I grab the handle with one hand, the pump with the other, clutching the contraption to my chest. "This better not be loaded," I say. I lay it on top of the desk and sit back, rubbing my eyes.

"Like I said, you're no expert."

"Expert on what?"

"On Sam."

"That's absurd. You don't know what you're talking about."

"No, it's important. It's the reason you shouldn't come to the meeting."

"That won't work, Kurt. Nothing's going to keep me from being in that room."

"You think Sam told you everything, don't you? Well, he didn't. You act like you're the smart one, battling us poor morons." He leans close. "Trust me. There are some things you *don't* know."

I want to say, *and some things you don't know either.* "I don't get it. Could you be a bit more specific?"

Kurt taps my shoulder. "You're *not* the only person he was close to."

"Look," I say standing, "if you know something that affects Cornelia's situation, you're morally obligated to reveal it."

He squints, picks up the gun and walks to Emma. "Let's see if Mom's home," he says, and Emma rises. He follows her to the doorway, so I shoulder my purse. "As far as Cornelia's concerned, you don't need to get your panties in a wad. She'll have her transplant; you can bet on it. 'Cause Terezie's going to sign our agreement, guaranteed. Then we'll all shake hands and trot politely back to our corners."

CHAPTER 4
1961

WHEN MY GRANDFATHER leased his new farm in 1910 to tenants—
Antonín Cervenka, his wife and four children—the family hired
Otis Settle to help them grow corn and cotton and tend turkeys,
Durac hogs, White-faced Herefords. My grandfather admired Otis'
agricultural knowledge and his stamina, even at fifty-seven, while
bundling cornstalks or swabbing the cattle's occasional lesions. But
Otis' childhood years as a slave to Sam Houston, captor of Santa Anna
at the Battle of San Jacinto, first president of the Republic of Texas,
so impressed my grandfather that he hired Otis to be the janitor of
his medical partnership's new hospital. Since Otis' wage was almost
double the one he'd received from the Cervenkas, they wished him
well, never acknowledging the hardship his leaving must have caused.
My grandfather moved Otis behind his house into a cottage that before
the Civil War had housed field slaves. Ten years later, Otis' seventeen-
year-old bride, Ruby, moved in and worked as my grandparents' maid.

During the early 1950s, my grandfather would coax Otis, who
was then in his nineties, to describe his years as Houston's servant.
"Oh, no, Doctor, shame on you," he'd say. The older Otis got, the
more he spoke to my grandfather in exaggerated dialect. He'd shake
his white head, his mouth disappearing behind a white mustache, his
black eyebrows balancing his light-toned face. People guessed his age
at around seventy. "Don't you know," he'd add, "these poor people gots
to be tired of an old man's gibberish?" Then he'd disappear. Unfazed,

my grandfather would point toward the empty hallway. "Abigail and I," he'd say, "are now blessed to have this good and faithful servant taking care of our family." He actually said it: *servant*.

That Otis was not the person I knew. He taught my brothers and me to make whistles from blades of grass, the vibrations tickling, and to fertilize plants with eggshells and limp banana peels splayed like starfish under the surface soil. He showed Sam how to feed a baby pigeon with an eyedropper, and how to fold an origami dove with wings that flapped when he pulled the tail. He also told me his Master Sam stories, memories no one else mentioned and I kept to myself. Now, I hope they weren't revisions, given condescendingly, like he would have to my grandfather to accommodate an expected version of his life. After all, my fascination with his slave experience was, to say the least, imprudent. I longed for a connection to a historical figure. And I wanted to know why Otis could be devoted to his slave owner but contemptuous of my grandfather, a man I'd been taught to revere.

Two of Otis' stories were favorites, and I'd often beg for them. "Not now, child," he'd always begin. "Don't bother an old man." But that was his signal for me to plead. I'd pull him a chair, usually at the backyard wrought iron table, and he'd sit, then poke at one of his hearing aids, his tongue clicking as loud as a mockingbird. Sometimes, he'd tell me to get Sam, but Sam was always off somewhere with Kurt.

In his first story, the chief of a Texas branch of the Coushatta tribe complained about the Confederate government's mandatory draft, which forced Native Americans to travel to Virginia to fight in a war they didn't understand. "Chief Billie Blount brung along twenty of his men, and Master Sam, he met them down at the big spring," Otis would say. We shucked corn, throwing husks into a bucket, or his fist—the knuckles gray as if mud had caked there—whittled a piece of mesquite, his pocketknife curling thin strips into wooden bows. "Mrs. Houston wouldn't allow them to step foot into her house 'cause she never forgot about that princess of his."

Otis couldn't, or wouldn't, talk about Houston's previous years with the Cherokees in Arkansas, except to say that his hero had become a chief and had married the first wife. I imagined Houston, his face streaked in red and yellow paint, wearing a headdress, leading his whooping men down a ravine into battle while smoke rose amidst the shuffle of hooves. Years later, I read that the princess-wife had been Will Rogers' ancestor and that the general's adventure had apparently included a protracted drinking and peyote binge. Nothing in my research, however, reconciled Otis' devotion. Houston had been a colorful figure all right, but he'd refused to give my friend his freedom.

"After they'd smoked," Otis continued, "I brung Master Sam his foolscap paper, and a big pot of pokeweed ink, and his pen he'd made out of a eagle feather." Otis drew a large S in the air, for Sam, certainly, but I couldn't help but think, Sarah. "He sat hisself right there and wrote a letter to the folks in Virginia, telling how wrong it was for anybody to steal away them Indian boys." Lucky Otis, I thought, to have known such a person, a real live John Wayne.

The second story described Houston's death in 1863, when Otis was ten. "I slept right there on a pallet in his sick room," Otis said, his hands still. "At sundown, everybody was crying, and I was moaning 'cause the best friend I had or would ever have on this earth, somebody—'cause I was young, a little under what you are now—somebody I thought of as a sort of papa, he was dying. Even then, while I seen him all yellow and dragged down, I knowed my years working for Master Sam was to be the best of my life. Finally, he whispers, 'Margaret! Margaret! Texas!' and that great spirit lifts right off the bed like a light and flies its way out to the beyond."

Nothing could prepare me for the effect these words had—Otis, so close while he told the story, and slightly younger than I, so he said, when he'd watched his substitute father die. Some nights after I'd relived this scene with Otis, I had a dream. John Wayne, his face streaked red and yellow, held my hands as we danced around a campfire, until he, like Sambo from the racist book my mother gave me, turned into butter, melted into light, a disappearing star.

🌾

In May 1961, Otis was a remarkable 108, long beyond doing much except shelling peas, emptying the dishwasher, or wistfully telling stories. My mother's favorite story started on a morning that May when Ruby, Otis' wife, made a call from my grandparents' house to Mother, the only adult Pelton she could reach.

Sitting with her legs crossed, holding a cigarette, my mother would begin her performance by explaining that my grandmother had left earlier for Gatesville to lead some prayer group in a close study of Paul's letters to the Ephesians. Ruby, she said, had called, crying and "jabbering God knows what" over the phone. "After I figured out who the heck it was, all I could make out was Otis' name."

Even though they were relatively close in age—my mother was forty-one then; Ruby was fifty-eight—my mother, I should note, never liked Ruby, saying, "That trashy woman's just plain mean." The first part of her accusation hadn't been verified, as far as I knew, and the second part I'd seen demonstrated only once, on a Sunday morning after church.

Ruby had stood with Sam, who was eleven at the time, at my grandparents' kitchen counter. I watched while talking to Gran's parakeet, whose cage sat atop a pole in the hall by the door. With a gingham apron wrapped over his Sunday suit, Sam kneaded dough on a strip of wax paper, something I planned to tease him about later. Ruby smiled, plumping her girlish cheeks. She secretly reminded me of Lena Horne, a favorite singer of my mother's. Mother obviously didn't notice the resemblance, and would say whenever Lena appeared on TV, "She's the most beautiful woman in the world." Ruby patted her curled bangs and handed Sam a rolling pin with the teasing caution, "Best not to squeeze all the breath out, honey. These going to be biscuits, not bullets." When he grinned, sprinkling flour onto the linoleum, my mother walked in with freshly picked bluebonnets, needing a vase.

"Don't have a conniption," she said. "I'm only—" but she stopped, her face the shade of Mercurochrome. "Just what do you think you're doing?" she asked Ruby, who never liked her coming into Gran's kitchen. Mother yanked the ties to Sam's apron. "Go find your brother," she said, removing the gingham with a flourish. "You're not allowed to bother Ruby." Spotting me, she scowled. "You too, skedaddle. What's wrong with you children?"

Sam rolled his eyes, as if to say, "What'd we do?" and turned to go.

Ruby faced my mother, a slotted spoon in her hand. She held it high, like she did the Marlboros she smoked behind the hedge in Gran's backyard, her pinky finger crooked. "This be my kitchen, not yourn, and you been told to go."

"But," my mother said, backing toward the door.

"Just you leave me be."

Whatever the complicated source of my mother's resentment (maybe she simply resented a pretty, opinionated black woman), five years later, she said that on the afternoon Ruby had phoned, she'd sounded so upset, "I told her I'd be over soon as I finished my shower."

Forty-five minutes later, my mother went directly to the shack behind the main house. "I walked across that lopsided porch and opened the screen door," she said. She had to squint then she heard moaning. "There was Ruby, dressed in her uniform and lying on the bed next to Otis, her eyes all puffed and bloodshot." Ruby dabbed her cheeks with a handkerchief while she groaned. Her husband, wearing slacks and an undershirt, lay on his back "curled almost into a ball." His hands pressed against the sides of his chest. His elbows bent into points "like he'd been doing a chicken walk," my mother said. Leaning forward, she'd add: "His big eyes didn't even move."

Next, she said she asked Ruby, "What's wrong with Otis?"

According to my mother, Ruby sat up, lowered her handkerchief, sputtered, "He did some jumping and coughing, so I lay down here side him, thinking it'd calm him, you know. Next thing I knew…" Then, my mother said, Ruby shrugged, folded her hands across her lap, moaned. In other words, Otis—a person who'd told me about Sam Houston's spirit lifting off the bed "like a light flying its way to the beyond"—had died.

My mother had always made fun of the couple's age difference— "If he'd wanted a nurse, he shouldn't have married Miss Teenage Hormone"—so she couldn't understand Ruby's grief over the death of a husband that much older. To her, the situation—the marriage, in fact—was distasteful, embarrassing. That meant she could turn the tragedy of a woman she didn't like, for whatever reason, into a comedy. "How long ago did all this happen?" my mother asked.

Ruby pulled Otis' shirt down, covering her husband's exposed skin and underwear waistband. "Right after Mrs. Pelton left for her meeting."

Then my mother would describe how she circled the bed to the other side, her hands on her hips, a sour taste starting in her mouth. She said she remembered the son Otis had by another woman. Ruby had loved the boy, even visiting him and his family on her afternoons off. Both women as well as the son had scurried around Otis in his cottage, "getting him this, serving him that, always waiting for his final word, falling all over themselves with 'Yes, sir.' What in the world could Ruby have been thinking of, inviting that other woman and the boy into her home? And I don't even want to imagine what she and Otis said about that child to one another. Then this morning, *with me standing there*, she actually leaned over and plain as anything, she whispers, 'Husband, thank you.' I'll never understand those people."

Ruby watched her, she said, then pleaded: "What we going to do, Mrs. Norine?" Such trust didn't impress my mother as much as the hair on the right side of Ruby's head. Unlike her bangs or the rest plastered back, this was rumpled, with several strands, my mother said, pointing to the curled body of the husband.

My mother stared into Otis' face, but she didn't touch him. His lips turned down; his chin puckered. His skin reminded her of an old horse's jowl so she turned away. "I'm going to have to go to the big house and call an ambulance to come get him."

Ruby heaved across the body, grabbed my mother's arm. "No, please don't go, Mrs. Norine. We gots to stay here with my poor Otis or I knows something terrible will happen."

"Get a hold on yourself," my mother told her. "I'm making that call." She even patted Ruby's hand.

Ruby still gripped my mother's arm, but her head dropped forward, my mother said, as if a line had snapped. She squeezed her eyes closed, and "her lips wiggled, puffing and sucking in air."

"He can't stay here like this," my mother told Ruby. "Don't you see how all twisted up he is? If somebody doesn't do something, why, you'll never get him laid out. We've simply got to call for help."

"No, ma'am." Ruby started to sob. "He need us here."

So, my mother said, that was how she and Ruby came to be pulling on Otis' legs and arms, jumping and yanking on his limbs, trying to straighten him out. "We each pushed a leg at the same time, and I'll be darned if he didn't sit right up, like he'd pulled a chair to the dinner table." So they returned him to his back with his knees still bent, his arms at his sides, the fingers of his left hand permanently angled as though waving. My mother lowered Otis' eyelids and sat down on a chair next to the bed.

At this point, my mother would tell how all that straining had made her perspire, forming embarrassing stains under the arms of her flowered sundress. Even so, she never took off her high-heeled shoes. Ruby was so grateful, my mother said, that she mixed some lemonade— "Bless her heart,"—and after my mother had drunk a glass, they placed a sheet over Otis and waited for my grandmother to come home.

My mother told her story for the first time a few hours after it took place, as she sat in our kitchen with my father, Kurt, who was seventeen, and Sam, who was sixteen. Having slipped downstairs, I, then thirteen, knelt behind the hall banister. Earlier, she'd told the others to "Quieten down; this would upset Sarah," so I'd used the doorjamb to block their view of me. My brothers giggled when she imitated Ruby pulling Otis' shirt down over his underwear. Kurt laughed so hard he wheezed, but my father looked up occasionally from his *Texas State Journal of Medicine*, finally closing it, frowning as he gazed at her.

I can guess what he was thinking. Like Sam Houston was to Otis, Otis had been my father's surrogate parent. Dad and Ruby were also close, and I know what my mother must've thought of that. "Now, Mama, are you sure this is really what happened?" he asked. "You've been known to give your stories a little spice." He glanced at Sam, who snickered.

"I never exaggerated anything in my life," she said, then puffed her Winston.

"Better duck, boys. I think I see a lightening bolt." My father rarely stated his opinion. Teasing, proverbs, and questions were his primary modes of expression.

My mother stubbed out her cigarette in a saucer. "Are you going to let me finish?" She scowled. "I *was* in the middle of my story."

"Excuse me," he said, his palm in the air. "I was only saying Otis did a lot for my family." He opened his journal. "And I wonder, how should a good man be remembered?" *And Ruby*, I wanted to say. *Don't forget Ruby*.

My mother rolled her eyes. "A-ny-way," she droned, regaining her audience's attention, "that was when we started pulling on Otis' legs."

Sam listened, gaping, his sadness tempered by her theatrics and his fascination with the story's subject. He loved death or sex or any secret topic, the same way he ate a farm peach: examining stem hole, skin fuzz, coloration; savoring pulp, nectar; finally sucking the pit, knotty and wooden. Any less fervor was, for him, a sacrilege. So while my mother spoke of Otis' coughing and puckered lips, Sam kept asking for details. Once, out of wonder or uneasiness, he grabbed his stomach, shivering.

Peeking around the banister, I understood that something terrible had happened to Otis, but I didn't know exactly what. I only saw that, except for Hugh and me, everybody was listening to my mother; I'd purposely been excluded.

When I walked in, she was starting the part about Ruby making the lemonade, but she cleared her throat. My father held a human hand skeleton, its joints hinged with wires; weekdays, it lay with more bones inside a brass kettle in his study. Fingering the metacarpals like rosary beads, he was lost in his weekend ritual. I tried to figure how Otis could be a joke while those clicking bones were somehow holy. Kurt looked at me, his eyebrows raised. I smirked, hoping to make him feel stupid. Sam kept right on.

"His knees popped?" he said. "Like, you think something might've broke?" He leaned, squinted his eyes toward my mother.

"Sam, you're getting too carried away. Besides, your sister has joined us and now would be a good time to plan for Rockport." Each summer, we stayed at the coast two weeks in my grandparents' two-story with a screened porch facing a panorama of water.

"You sound like girls," I muttered to Kurt, knowing how to prick him. Then to her, "But what about all that stuff y'all were saying?"

"We were being silly." She straightened my collar. "Not 'stuff,' sugar. No such word, remember?"

I tilted my shoulder away from her.

She sipped her drink.

"But, Mom, you didn't finish," Sam said, scooting down the bench. "Come on, Sar." I sat beside him. "Tell her the part about Otis the first time," he blurted, "with his eyes stuck open."

"No, Sam." Her protectiveness was equal parts sympathy and a conviction that I be refined, not the ill-bred outcast she thought my grandmother had labeled her. "There are some things you boys are not to discuss in front of your sister. And that's my final word. Now, about Rockport…"

This was the same person who'd thrown a horse's reins into my grandfather's face, and that woman, not this parent, was the one I wanted to emulate.

"But you were the one telling the story," Sam said, "and *you're* a girl."

I leaned on my elbows.

My father's hand skeleton clattered. "That'll be all, boy. Remember that galled horse," he warned. "Rub him and he'll kick."

Sam glared, shook his head, and uttered a "Ga-a-ah" as he squeezed from between Kurt and me, then stomped upstairs. His bedroom door slammed.

My mother didn't know that Sam and I had already talked about death a few weeks earlier, on a day when he taught me how to hit a softball. He stood, pitching it in low, slow arcs. I had little trouble connecting, my target sometimes rising like a bottle rocket. He chased after my lobs and skinners while I ran around the bases.

Beside the house, Sam held the hose while I sipped, the water bubbling with its tinny taste. A spiked horned toad disappeared into the bushes. Sitting on the front porch steps with him, I hoped someone would drive by. Girls had crushes on him, and I wanted them to see him with me. He popped the softball in and out of his glove. As it hit the webbing, the thwap made him seem wise, handsome.

Our thoughts turned to our bodies, while, at the same time, our father stood in a sterile room cutting, suturing. A disorienting connection, like drinking *octli* then watching ritual sacrifice.

"Sarah, you know, we're all really just an accident," Sam said, holding the ball in his right hand, turning, rubbing. He glanced at me through a half-wink. "A minute or a second later, and you'd have been somebody else."

"Yeah," I mumbled, my mouth hanging open. Such talk felt creepy, but I loved it when Sam got serious.

He straightened his cap, pounded his glove. "But we made it. That's what counts, right?" His elbow nudged me.

"Uh huh," I said, hugging my knees. Again, a solid whack of leather.

"But the weirdest part is the other end." He pulled his hands, glove and all, toward his waist, rested his forearms on his thighs. He squinted at the sky, his cheek muscles twitching. "How, someday, we won't be alive."

I rocked, still holding my legs. The concrete felt warm, gritty. "I wonder if you dream when you die."

"Shh no." He rubbed his palm down his jeans. "Your body gets cold and clammy." He leaned toward me. "You don't feel nothing." His voice was husky, his breath like steam. "You don't even think. It's like, clunk, it's over, for good." He flipped the ball toward the mitt.

"But Gran says our souls go to another world so we don't need to be scared." She'd held my hand one night as we knelt by her bed, her knuckles a row of marbles.

"I don't know about any of that." Sweat dripped from underneath his cap, down the side of his face; he rubbed it into the shoulder of his t-shirt.

"You don't think there's such a place?" The possibility of Sam's disbelief panicked me. If he was wrong, he was doomed to burn forever. If he was right, I was doomed to rot.

"I believe there's just dead."

The ball smacked. My teeth pressed dashes into my knee.

The others stayed in the kitchen to watch TV while I sneaked to Sam's room. He sat on his unmade bed, holding his moss-colored, Chinese water dragon. A fluorescent light warmed its aquarium, bathing a branch and pebbles in a hazy glow. The lizard's tail curled across Sam's lap, the spikes along its back like miniature daggers.

"Come here. I'll let you hold her," he said, rubbing the top of its head until its eyes closed, sleepy.

"Uh uh." I took a step backward.

"Chicken," he said. "She can't bite."

He'd once made me touch a crawdad and, later, a fish. Light-headed, I sat on the edge of the bed. When Sam held out the lizard, it waved its front legs twice, froze. The spidery claws clutched my hand and wrist, its skin soft, not slimy.

"I'm sorry about what happened downstairs," I said.

"Mama's so stupid," he said, flopping on the bed.

"She must've had a reason."

"You don't know anything." He grabbed a tennis ball next to his bed, bounced it off the wall. He caught it, threw it again. Every time it hit, a gray smudge appeared. He tossed it into the corner. "Come on." He snatched his cap. "I've got something to show you."

He left a note next to the telephone in the kitchen: "Sarah and I have gone to play softball."

We trudged across yards, up streets, down an alley. "Wait," I whined, trotting. Dogs yapped along their fences; cars sped past. Downtown, an empty Woolworth announced "For Rent" in its window; boards sealed the double doors of the town's less popular movie theater. Over the years, each block's expanding quota of broken glass and graffiti had correlated with the accumulating window cracks and water-stains at the GC&SF station. Trains still lurched every day into its yard, then left again with an occasional passenger, grain-heavy hopper, log-filled flatbed. But most cars rolled along, their wheels clicking, their linked bodies empty.

The sky stretched a fading blue, cloudless; the sun inched behind First National. Half an hour later, we turned a corner to face Latimore Memorial Hospital, its complex of buildings and covered walkways sprawling.

Sam led me to the oldest wing, where my father taught anatomy. "Dad brought me here," he said, knowing I'd never been invited. "There's something you're not going to believe."

The construction was granite brick with Gothic oval windows, ledges of dark limestone, balconies on the west and north sides. The same architect had built the GC&SF station—ornate, clumsily reminiscent of European cathedrals.

The concrete stairs led to heavy front doors topped by a cut glass window inscribed "Nugent Sanitarium." An arch of carved Greek heads in profile bordered the entrance. Instead of starting for the entry, which was locked Saturday evenings, Sam turned toward a side doorway partially hidden by pyracantha bushes. He pulled it, motioned for me to crawl through the square opening.

We walked along the lobby to a double stairway. On the second floor, we found offices and exam rooms. The third floor was the top one, and when doors opened onto the lab, chilly air smelled of camphor, Lysol. The sun's last rays trailed through giant skylights, casting beams at angles across the floor, then up walls. I grabbed Sam's arm, pressed next to him. Huge jars lined shelves along both sides of the auditorium-sized room. The crocks were round or rectangular, with lids as big as my waist and human body parts inside, floating. One contained a leg with the outside layer of skin peeled away, the white tendons and bone and red muscle exposed, labeled with tags, spelling out long names ending in "ula" or "dorsi." A hand floated in another, the fingernails glistening silvery blue. The delicate ligaments looked as perfect as spider webs, the joints like intricate gears ready to whir. Next was a man from the chest up, his right side perfect, his left neatly whacked off through his ribs, past his nose, the top of his head. He wore a stony gaze, as though he hadn't noticed his condition. Farther down, I saw a brain, light gray, velvety, with its convoluted parts and purple veins, followed by other organs, rust-colored ones—a heart, lungs, a kidney, sliced and opened. Next to my shoulder, a baby's face stared from the single eye in its forehead, a tiny Cyclops, partially skinned. At the end of the room, a bookcase held more jars, these with tagged heads whose faces tilted, their swollen lips kissing the curved glass.

I stepped back, grunting. "Are they real?" No wonder my family didn't seem fazed by cruelty. What was it like to work here every day, where a body was only pieces tacked together? Robots. Zombies.

"Of course." But Sam was looking somewhere else. Two rows of coffin-sized metal boxes lined the floor. Over each, a light hung suspended from the thirty-foot ceiling. Sam stared at one of the caskets in back. "Come on."

Up close, the metal container reminded me of a torture chamber, of hunched clubfooted men pouring smoking liquid into beakers. Sam bumped me when he yanked down on a side latch. A clank echoed. One side of the lid slid back, and something rose on a plank inside. It was huge and must have been immersed in liquid, because there was a rush, like the sound of someone rising out of a swimming pool, dripping, splattering. A soiled sheet covered it; a sickly sweet smell flipped my stomach. Sam pushed the handle on the other side. Pulley ropes crept through their slots. The rest of the lid swung around, the plank rose again with a swoosh, the bang ricocheted.

Sam pulled the sheet back: A man, with flattened gray hair and a wide, slanted forehead with his eyes partially open. His face's left side pressed against the shoulder, wrinkling his cheek, puckering his crooked lips. His right calf and foot had been sliced, shredded—a scarecrow losing his stuffing. Above that lay the man's sagging genitals.

I knew what they were because I'd seen Hugh's—when he'd tear off his clothes and run down the street in front of our house— and Kurt's and Sam's too, as they each stepped out of the shower, before wrapping towels at their waists like skirts. Sam laughed at my accidental glimpses, but Kurt accused me of spying, yanked at my shorts until I screamed, then tightened his towel before walking to his room. I felt relief when those parts were covered, not only because my brothers usually spotted me watching, but also because I believed their bodies were too mysterious for careless exposure. Such marvels needed protection, secrecy, the bulges they formed in clothes hinting at something I didn't yet understand but longed to.

I stepped back from the cadaver, embarrassed but determined to watch whatever Sam might do. If the men in my family could look at a naked, plucked, dead man, so could I. But I moved around the feet, stood next to my brother.

Sam touched the arm, which rested on the chest. He tapped the skin in several places—firm as an orange peel. But its color was brown; even the fingernails had a tinge like muddy water. The man's eyes had sunk in their sockets, so Sam pulled a lid back until the black center, surrounded by its wrinkled, murky white, bulged. He turned the lid loose, and it fell, sleepily, to its original position. Touching, poking, he examined the man's ear and teeth; he even pulled lightly on the hair. Then he placed one of his hands back on the elbow and with the other, he tugged on the wrist. After several light jerks, he shifted his right hand to the man's waist, and with his left, he pulled hard on the forearm. Smoothly, as though sweeping through water, the contorted limb straightened. Sam rested it on the plank, and while he still held it, he stood there, nodding, gazing, nodding.

Here, I thought, in a place where everybody else hacked things apart, Sam pulls the body back together.

I remembered my mother describing Otis' curled body as looking like a chicken. *Terrible*, I thought. I heard him say, "...the best friend I had or would ever have on earth was dying," and I pictured him tracing a giant S in the air. *He's gone*, I thought selfishly, but I couldn't explain the emptiness.

"Hey, look," Sam said as he prodded just below the man's shoulder. "A tattoo."

A faded blue drawing of a hand holding a hoop with two keys draped across sagging muscle. The keys were the giant kind used for ancient locks. The hand, gripping the ring, curled into a fist.

"I don't like it," I said, tightening my chin, missing Otis: no more lessons about banana-peel starfish, and except for Sam, only my parents and people like them.

"He's a convict," Sam said. "The color's not right. See?" He rubbed at an obvious change in the tattoo's shading. "This father of a kid I know says they melt checkers or Bible pages for ink and can draw good but the color's never even."

"What'd he do?"

"Something bad, murder most probably."

I focused on his hand, the hair dark at the base of the fingers. "You think he had kids?"

"Maybe. A couple'd be about right." Sam took off his cap, ran his fingers across his stubble-cut hair. His biceps twitched; a whiff of sweat and orange soda hit me.

"Uh-huh. And one of them was kind of bad too, but his mom helped him all she could." I was thinking about how when he talked back to my mother, my father got so mad, sometimes he spanked Sam. My father was sad afterwards, but Sam never cried.

Sam stood close, his arm rubbing me whenever he moved. Each brush prickled, like something visceral moving through my pores, my blood.

He pulled on the tattoo again. "I don't think this is how the poor guy expected to get out." His gaze moved to the man's face, then the chest, the fists. With a hand on each side of the head, Sam gently turned it, facing it forward. But the cheek and mouth stayed crooked, so he tried smoothing the skin with his thumb; then, with his fingers, he worked the lips, touching them until the features softened, resting.

The dead man's hand lay across his thigh, the fingers slightly separated; the last nail, longer than the others, curved inward as though searching. Black hair swirled from under his breasts, across his stomach, finally thickening, soft and twining, at the nest of skin and parts between his legs. His penis had gauzy veins and a mushroom cap; it nestled against a divided sack covered in velvet. The area, with its shadows and central organ, signified earth shoots, fungus emitting spores like smoke.

I longed to touch such a place, to test the suppleness and tension there, to know, finally, my mother's most forbidden secret. I lifted my hand, but couldn't bring myself to place it on the dead man. Instead, without looking at Sam's face, I leaned my cheek against his chest, rested my fingers on the bulge in his jeans.

"Whoa," Sam said, jumping back, peeling my hand away.

I turned, startled, as he stared, his temple pulsing. *Please don't look at me*, I wanted to cry. Did I disgust him? I wanted to say I didn't mean to, that my touching him was an accident, that I knew it was wrong, *please don't tell, please don't…* I covered my mouth, squeezed my eyes shut.

"It's okay, Sar. Look." He nudged me. "Really, it's okay. Come on. I'll show you."

He pointed at the scarecrow's dark region. "This is a penis."

I hung my head.

"Sarah, hey. You need to know this." He put his hand on my back. "During sex it gets stiff, and semen from the testicles," he pointed again, "moves into the woman to fertilize her egg. Presto," he patted my head, "one more bratty kid for a brother to have to look after." He shoved me, knocking me off-balance.

I shoved him back, relieved, laughing. "You mean somebody for brothers to push around."

"Ungrateful," he sang, hanging his thumbs in his front pockets.

On the wall at the end of the shelf, I spotted the jar with the brain inside. "Look over there, Sam," I said, pointing.

"What about it?"

"What's that remind you of?"

"Huh?" He looked from the jar, to me, then back to the jar and its contents.

"Broccoli."

"That's good," he laughed. "Okay, now that one." I followed his eyes toward something round, puffy, faintly pink: intestines. "This, broccoli-brain, is one you'll never guess." He pointed at the guts. "Take a good look at the man in the moon, in a jar."

As our giggles rumbled around the room, I leaned back, catching the view through the skylight. Nighttime now, the sky an immense shadow. The moon's sullen beam had kept us from noticing the change. Two stars pinned the vast backdrop. Across the room, that half bust of a man perched in silhouette, staring ahead through the glass. Otis, I thought—more than flesh, limbs, body. Otis, the storyteller; Otis, the scarecrow; Otises everywhere, like lights lifting.

CHAPTER 5

As the Henry R. Fineman Endowed Chair of Mesoamerican Studies in the university's anthropology department, I teach a light course load each semester and never have to teach freshmen. That's fortunate because they make me jumpy (short attention span, practically illiterate), and they don't like me. It's not their fault. I'm not patient enough; the basics bore me. They wouldn't sign up, anyway. Word is out: *cranky*. Am I proud of this? No. Even my colleagues close their doors when I walk by (I get the hint). Can I change? I wish. But give me smart graduate students, and I'll turn myself inside out and enjoy every minute.

So when a baby freshman appears at my office door with purple eyes and a graceless stance, for a single slugging heartbeat I imagine Sam lurking nearby. I remember meeting Cornelia, Terezie's daughter, on the church steps after my mother's funeral. Her painted acrylic nails and pierced nose are perfect additions to her inherited allure.

"I hope I'm not bothering you," she says, though she's come during my office hours. She slides into the chair I've chosen for its discomfort; guests don't stay long when their seat wobbles and feels like pavement.

"How's your mother," I ask, afraid Cornelia's expecting special treatment. I can't help with financial aid or enrollment in a sophomore course without its completed prerequisite. Still, it'll be hard to tell Terezie Jr. no.

"As Grandma says, we're 'made from the same dough.' Which reminds me," she pulls a box out of her book bag, "Grandma wanted me to give you this."

A shoebox tied with grosgrain ribbon, from Albina. I haven't seen her in twenty years. Josef died a while back, but I can't remember when. "Does Albina live here?"

"Uncle Cyril set her up in one of those country clubs for old people. As she'd say, 'It is going on good so far.' *I* say, I'm going to miss *Babička* like hell when we move. Now, open it," she adds, pointing. "I'm starving."

I almost cry when I see the *kolaches*: prune, peach, poppy seed. People sell what they call *kolaches*, but I've never found any like Albina's: pastry somewhere between biscuit and pancake; butter, sugar, eggs, almond extract harmonious as a *Kachina* dance song.

Cornelia reaches for one of the poppy seed. "To your health," she says, and I almost drop the box. She closes her eyes while she chews.

I pick a peach one and picture Sam at the piano with Terezie, their songs this delicious. I take a bite and see Cyril swinging his hoe in a cotton field, then Sam knee-deep in the creek holding a gasping bass.

"Speaking of health," Cornelia says, "you've heard mine's on its final countdown?"

"Yes, and I'm sorry," I sputter. "But I understand you're getting a transplant."

"It's the only wish on my Christmas list. I'm being embarrassingly good this year."

"When are you and your parents moving to Rochester?" Is she still taking classes, I wonder. What's going on with Kurt and Hugh? Does she blame me for the hold up? Is that why she's here?

"We're hoping I won't turn blue before the semester's over. Then it's ta-ta to Texas."

"I'm sure you'll be fine," I say, standing, my discomfort obvious. "Please thank your grandmother for the *kolaches*."

"Mom's right," she says, grabbing her bag. "You're 'one tough customer'." She stands, throws a strap over her shoulder. "But I see why everybody likes you."

She definitely wants something.

"You knew Mom in high school. I'll bet she kicked ass, right?"

I picture Terezie in her brogans, clomping along the hallway. "Yes. Your mother was formidable."

"Afraid of you, though."

Me? I grip the desk, nudging my coffee cup, catching it as a few drops spill.

"*Legendary,* is what Mom says." Cornelia shrugs. "Fact is, you'd never pack a house, but I guess I could see that."

She moves to the doorway then turns, her amethyst eyes incredible. "Thanks for letting me crash your part-ay." She whistles, her raised eyebrows mocking. "Hey, I had to see what you were like, okay? Can I come back?"

"Of course. You're welcome anytime." I wave, trying to remember if I've ever said these words before.

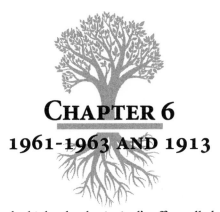

CHAPTER 6
1961-1963 AND 1913

IN SEPTEMBER, the high school principal's office called each time Sam was absent. Sometimes my mother lied, assuring the secretary that he was sick at home. Other times she said, "I have absolutely no idea where he is. Why don't *you* try to find him?" Sam always freely admitted where he'd gone, places like the Austin bat caves or my grandparents' house at Rockport; girls, of course, were involved. "You don't care what this does to me," my mother would argue, red-faced. My father's response was typical, another question: "What would happen if you needed Mama and couldn't find *her*?" Finally, one night he whipped Sam, then grounded him.

When my father called Sam into the master bedroom, I buried my face in my pillows. I could still hear everything, since my room was adjacent.

"Listen," my father said when Sam protested. "You're right." He cleared his throat. "You're almost grown. I don't have much time left to teach you." He sighed. "As for what I'm about to do, it's hard. But that doesn't keep me from doing what I'm supposed to." He walked several steps. "Let's say this has to do with the way you set priorities."

I imagined welts, my brother's flesh swollen, stinging. I counted five licks, then ten. Sam made no sound, and my father kept going—eleven, twelve, thirteen. Still, Sam was silent. After twenty licks, my father was panting. "Go to your room," he wheezed.

As Sam crossed the hall, my father closed himself in the

bathroom. The sound of running water couldn't drown out his weeping as I tiptoed past, toward my brother. But Sam's door was closed, so I stood listening, then I called him.

"Go away!" he growled. "Mind your own goddamn business!" Then something hit the door. I ran.

For the next two weeks, Sam dutifully obeyed the rules for his grounding, returning home after school, reading alone in his room. The last night, our whole family relaxed. At dinner, my father complimented him while he sat, watching.

But a month later, the high school called again. That night, when my mother told my father, he slumped, moaning, "Good God." He stepped backward, staring into the corner. "Even a dog learns after a while."

On each child's birthday, my mother walked us three blocks to a neighbor's front yard, and we sang "God Bless America" as we raised the American flag, its sagging stripes curled around the pole in the heat, a limp swirl of cubist patriotism. When Kurt, ignoring Sam, would tell Hugh and me to salute, my palm reluctantly rose to my chest, while Hugh would imitate a Boy Scout, three fingers pressing his forehead, his elbow a wing. Saturdays in the den, Kurt made even Sam stand during the national anthem when the television signed on, its circular test pattern an icon. Sundays were sacred, filled with enough ritual to appease any god. After church services, we ate lunch at my grandparents' (Ruby cooked, Otis served, early on), took an hour nap, then went to the farm: Jesus and Granddaddy ruled.

From the time Kurt, Sam and Hugh each turned twelve until the month they left for college, they underwent a puberty rite as pre-determined as a Coahuiltecan ritual. From the first Monday of summer vacation until the Friday before school opened in September, my brothers spent their days learning regimen and fortitude chopping cotton at the tenant farm.

Sometimes my mother allowed me to come when she dropped them off, their meatloaf sandwiches in paper sacks squashed under their muscled arms. One morning when Kurt told Sam it was his turn to unlatch the gate, Sam said, "You wish," and Kurt nudged him into the fence. On the other side of the creek, a rusty pickup sat parked next to the field. Cyril Cervenka, third generation of the family that worked the farm, stood at the field's opposite corner, his movements detectable only when his hoe's blade glinted a modified Morse code. As our car pulled away, Sam snatched Kurt's lunch and ran toward the creek. Kurt shouted, "You'll be sorry if I have to come after that." My mother, used to their bantering, grateful to drop them in what amounted, in her mind, to a giant playpen, shook her head as she turned onto the main road.

At ten o'clock, Sam sat against a huisache, his elbows propped on bent knees, plopping mustang grapes into his mouth. Kurt and Cyril worked their hoes along adjacent rows of cotton plants. Sam's right palm stung where blisters swelled with fluid.

On this, their second day, Sam and Kurt more than likely hadn't weeded as many rows combined as Cyril had managed by himself. It really chaps my ass, Sam thought, imagining the coming months. Slaving was for people who didn't crater in 115 degrees and could do the same goddamn thing over and over without puking. For a lousy quarter an hour! He'd complain, but the timing wasn't right. Kurt had started dating Miss Fuck-Me-Please, and even though Sam had been lying low, last week he'd gotten in hot water again. This time, he'd pawned Mom's Lalique bowl (found in a hall cabinet, like trash for Goodwill; how was he supposed to know?) so he could see Jerry Lee Lewis in Lubbock. Our father didn't whip him—Sam would gut up for that again only if he had to—but he got so mad during his responsibility speech (that and *duty*, his two favorite words), Sam had decided he'd go along again for awhile. Until now.

"Sam," Kurt yelled, "if your butt isn't next to these plants by the time I count to ten, this'll be…" here he shook his fist, flexed his jaw, "in your face."

Sam flipped a grape then looked up, catching it on his tongue. He shut his eyes, chewed, and positioned his shoulder blades among the huisache's angles of gnarly bark. This ought to be fun, he thought. Better than breaking our backs over those damn plants.

"One…two…three…"

Cyril's hoe swung up, down, hitting the ground in rhythmic clicks. A crow landed on the cedar fence, cocked its head, bobbed, cawed.

"Four…five…"

Sam squeezed a grape until the pulp popped loose, then sucked.

"Six…seven…eight…"

Cyril stepped forward, chopped, stepped, chopped, his straw hat's brim tilted against the sun. A dishrag's dripping corners hung below the hat, water and sweat beading in his eyebrows, soaking the shoulders of his long-sleeved shirt.

"Nine…ten."

Sam rose, smiling, to meet his brother; he raised his fists. As he deflected Kurt's punch, he skipped sideways; Kurt moved in corresponding steps. Each time their bodies rubbed, bumped, or jabbed one another, Sam's smaller frame swelled. He teased, winking, nodding between dares: "Come on."

Kurt's face reddened in blotches; his grunts and pants increased with Sam's taunts. The pummeling against Sam's stomach and cheek hurt but was expected. Kurt, taller, fifteen pounds heavier, usually won these bouts. As Sam was forced off balance, Cyril's elbows pumped at plants a few rows over, that hat's wet skirt the last thing Sam saw before he went down.

Afterward they stood, weak, breathless, until Kurt brushed at dirt clods stuck to his jeans, then walked toward his row of weeds and cotton. "Too bad," Sam shouted. "I was ready to chop again 'til you came at me like that."

Kurt reacted like Sam knew he would: He stopped, and he laughed. "You bastard," he said. He wiped his hairline with the back of his hand, flipped sweat onto the dirt. Sam wheezed his giggle, clutched himself, toppled onto his side.

Cyril dropped his hoe, ambled toward the '49 Ford pickup parked next to the fence. He reached over the lowered tailgate, unscrewed the top of his tin cooler, turned the spigot and filled the lid. He sucked gulps, filled it again, set it on the truck's fender. He removed his hat and the dishrag, drenched the cloth, bathed his face, his neck. He sat next to the cooler, his legs falling lazily open, and between more sips, he stared past the brothers at something invisible to Sam, something far away.

"Sam," Kurt called, "come back to work and I'll find a hanky for your head as cute as Cervenka's."

My biceps need work, Sam thought, and my chest could use some sun. He took off his t-shirt, draped it through a belt loop. He picked up his hoe, swinging at weeds with determined whacks, triceps straining.

"So, you think he's queer, or what?" Kurt said as he chopped in the row next to Sam. Each nicked root echoed: *tap.*

At the end of the field, Cyril stood, poured, drank, his head tilted back. Sam imagined his belly filling with sluicy coolness.

He remembered seeing Cyril two years before in the high school hallway, his textbooks carried in a ratty briefcase and no noticeable friends, even though there'd been other Czech students. Wasn't he in the band? The guy played basketball, for sure. Cyril's quick fakes had been legendary.

Cyril repositioned his hat, brushed his palms across his jeans then ambled toward his hoe, which lay in a furrow near Sam. His face turned toward the barn, then forward again. He moistened his lips, stretched his arms behind his head, then above it, finally swinging his hands. The guy made walking a sport, Sam thought.

"Or maybe," Kurt continued, "he'd rather screw one of his daddy's sheep." An eyebrow lifted; he scratched his head.

Sam knew Kurt wasn't comfortable around Cyril—all that aloofness and ease in this crop-and-animal place. But insulting Cyril not only might be dangerous; it wasn't right. "Shut up," he said. He was sure Cyril had heard.

Sam worked alongside the others for an hour, this time without talking, their hoes' clips and soil shuffling like soft brush beats. Sometimes one stretched, holding his breath, then released it, satisfying as a belch. Grasshoppers rattled free of the plants, chirring. Once when Sam tilted, arching his back, a buzzard circled three times, disappearing toward the railroad tracks.

The blisters on Sam's hands throbbed. Sweat dribbled down his forehead, burning his eyes. When his nose dripped, he sneezed, dropped his hoe, wiped his face with his itchy t-shirt. He walked to the truck for a drink, the water tinny in its metal lid, quenching. Then he soaked his head, the water stinging his neck, shoulders. Oh, he thought, and put on his shirt.

Cyril leaned toward the cotton plants, his hat shadowing his face, that dishrag protecting his neck, his shirt-sleeved arms pumping, his body drifting. Like a damn machine, Sam thought. Kurt, on the other hand, swatted weeds like flies, his body all strains and jerks, the sun roasting his arms.

In a minute, they joined Sam at the truck. Kurt got a drink then opened the door, stepped, grunting, onto the running board, and grazed his hip on the gearshift knob as he threw himself across the seat. Too much Budweiser and armchair football, Sam thought.

After Cyril doused himself, he sat beside Sam. He stared, unblinking, toward the field's opposite border at a silhouette of trees, a green mesa amidst the sky and scrub.

"See something?" Sam asked, peering.

"Great horned owl. Listen—"

"Shit, you can't see that from here." Crows—Sam had no idea how many—squawked like ducks. Another one appeared, plunked itself among the maze of limbs and leaves. "Those, genius, are crows," he said.

Cyril seemed not to notice Sam. "Look, in the top branches of that middle sycamore. Its face is heart-shaped."

Sam searched the center trees, each visible limb, trunk crook. "Man, there ain't nothing there." He shoved Cyril, who bumped the side of the truck.

Cyril waved a balancing arm, scowled. "The crows are diving at the owl because it eats their babies. I'd say there are five of them, gathered around him at the tank."

"Tank?"

"The caliche cow pond on the other side of those sycamores and poplars." He pointed, and as if commanded, the owl rose and flew, five crows darting, diving at its head, swatting with their stiff-legged feet, as it drifted forward.

Ten feet overhead, its body floated, a deformed moon swimming through blue. Its short wings agitated then stiffened, fluttering, then grew still.

Kurt stayed in Austin the next summer. When Sam arrived alone at the cotton field, Cyril might have already chopped a full row.

"How's it going," Sam would've said.

Cyril nodded then, his hat brim tracing a check mark. If he noticed Sam's change to a long-sleeved shirt and gimme cap, he didn't let it show. He clipped weeds again.

Sam got a hoe out of Cyril's pickup, chopped along an adjacent row. Flipping short taps, he almost kept up. By Nugent and Pelton standards, Sam thought, Cyril was strange enough to get talked about, picked at like his own parents harped at him. But Cyril's difference came from his foreignness, while Sam's *otherness* was tied to "unacceptable" habits like telling what he honestly thought, remarks others labeled "disrespectful," while he called them truths. "Sam's on another wavelength," our mother said.

Sam swung his hoe with minimum effort, having developed an instinct for where and how hard to chop. Each thump signaled a clip of Johnson grass. He squeezed a cotton boll, marveling that a bloom could be so soft, so fibrous, perfect as store-bought socks. An hour and three rows later, he took off his hat, wiped his forehead with his shirtsleeve; sweat beaded again. He aimed his face into a rustle of wind as a jet unfurled a smoky rope.

Thirsty, he dropped his hoe, strolled toward the cooler. Unscrewing the top, he heard a shuffling come from the uncultivated area beyond the fence. A scrawny jackrabbit, short-haired with jumbo ears, tipped forward off its back legs, lifted its head, stared. Ears flattened, it lurched then loped—back legs folding, stretching—fifty feet along the fence. Between posts, it stopped, raised its stringy ears, checked Sam a second time. Another frantic toss of limbs, then it bounded across the field.

Sam noticed small trails of worn undergrowth. Had rabbits made them? As if called, Cyril appeared.

"Are those some kind of animal trails?" Sam asked, pointing.

"Yeah," Cyril said. He took the lid, poured.

"*What* kind?" Sam flicked a grasshopper off his sleeve.

"Rats and field mice. They're all over." Cyril bathed his head and neck with his dishrag.

Sam drank, pulled a Boy Scout scarf from his hip pocket, copied Cyril's routine. "Saw a jack rabbit over there a minute ago." Cyril's eyes moved in close: telescopes. Sam shifted, his heel sinking into loosened earth. What was the guy thinking? Didn't he ever blink?

"You ought to see them at night while my father's plowing. Even the babies get at the loosened roots."

"You ever eat any?"

"They're too tough. But Mom and Terezie fry up cottontails with garlic and onions. For rabbit, we say *králík*."

Sam pictured Cyril's sister: tall, stomping, heavy-heeled shoes echoing, man's shoes, he suspected. Her eyes, the same near purple as poker chips, glared at anything daring to block her way. A scar stretched from beneath her nose through her lip, from falling off a horse, someone had said, but Sam thought "cleft palate?" then "no, of course not," and finally came to admire the lip's puffiness, its exposed underside. Once, she leaned, listening to a friend; then out of some primitive, childlike need for stimulation, she stroked the rosy mark, back and forth, up to the nose, down again.

Sam had overheard some girls at a football game giggling about Terezie. Apparently, her mother picked her up afternoons, kept her home on weekends. She was kept on a short leash. Except, she got a little on the side. According to the talk at school, Terezie was sneaking out with the band teacher.

"I know your sister," Sam said, his hands sliding into his back pockets, respectful. "Serious."

"Not particularly."

"Smart, though."

Cyril shrugged then shaded his eyes.

"I been meaning to ask," Sam said, picking up what looked like a piece of granite, specks flickering, "what'd happen if some guy called her? She go out?" He whipped the rock toward the tangled field of hidden animals.

"Depends on who's calling."

Sam wondered what that meant but wouldn't ask. Not yet.

As Cyril ambled toward the fence, his hat's weave cast striped shadows across his shoulder. Climbing, he called, "Over here."

Sam followed until they reached a stand of trees and brush.

"Remember this?"

Sam didn't.

"Last summer. The owl. This is where he flew."

Was Sam supposed to remember something from a year ago? "Oak?"

Cyril's eyes kept steady, a silent note.

"The tree," Sam said irritably, "here. Looks like oak."

Cyril pointed, "Wild primrose. My father makes pipes out of the briar roots."

"No way. What's that?"

"Hackberry," Cyril said, pointing, "mesquite, wild plum, and beodarck; over there, buffle, blue stem, and coastal bermuda."

Sam tried to memorize the names, noting the leaf and stem shapes, the textures, heights of grasses. The rotting stumps and broken limbs smelled dusty, the wildflowers spicy. He remembered Otis fertilizing with banana peels, splayed like starfish underneath topsoil. Then he spotted a green apple among flickering leaves, noticed seed heads on the grains. His nose itched, dripped.

"The creek's dry here, but my father left this place for quail and other animals." Pushing aside mesquite limbs, he stepped forward.

They found a spider web four feet wide and nine feet high. A dragonfly and a moth wriggled. The spider, six inches long, black with yellow stripes, crept upward.

"Wonder where the male is," Cyril said. "Their sex is really violent."

"Yeah?" Sam stepped back. "How?"

A whistle came from the left. Cyril answered in a duplicated skirl.

"A meadowlark. You interested in birds?"

Sam started to say something funny about peckers, but he couldn't. Cyril, he knew, got up at five every morning, liked his parents. "Yeah, I guess," he said.

"I do imitations on a violin. It's rough, but…"

The Cervenka farmhouse smelled strange. The odor came from garlic stalks set in drug store vases—Sam would later learn that Mrs. Cervenka added the cloves to everything from okra to catfish batter—and a pot of orange peels boiling on the stove. The family used garlic and orange water for home remedies— *domácí úlevy* Cyril later told him— to ensure a strong heart and relieve rheumatism. Sam knew what his mother would think of the air the Cervenkas breathed: unacceptable.

Cyril walked through the living room, and Sam followed. A sofa had a pillow and a folded army blanket stacked at the far end. Next to a pie safe stood a Victrola with a radio, doilies covering the top of its water-stained cabinet, and "The Czech Melody Hour," he'd later learn, tuned in most Sunday afternoons. Books on rocks and wildflowers, opera and symphony records, biographies from Truman to Caruso, and children's novels like *Green Mansions, The Sugar Creek Gang* series, and *Roy Rogers and The Rimrod Renegades* crammed an unpainted shelf that extended around the top of the room

Sam didn't usually notice furnishings, but when he thought of his home's chintz and marble, he longed to sprawl in a chair, to look.

Two paintings hung above the Victrola—bluebirds painted by Cyril, a still life of fruit by Terezie—their unembarrassed sentiment comforting. A tinted photograph of a stocky couple—grandparents, Antonín and Johanna, Cyril said—hung next to a doorway. "Howdy," he called into the kitchen.

Terezie stood across the room, slicing cucumbers on a cutting board at the tile counter. She wore a blouse and knee-length slacks. *Great ass*, Sam thought. The Chambers stove was metal-knob locomotion, a pinnacle of heat. "I brought somebody," Cyril said to his mother as she lifted a pot's lid then stuck in her finger.

"Naww," she said irritably, glancing at Sam. She replaced the lid and whistled, cradling her hand in her apron. "Just how did that thing got so hot? Tell me that." Her house shoes, strapped to her feet with rubber bands, slapped linoleum as she crossed to the Formica table. She slumped, sighing, into a metal chair.

Terezie reached into a cabinet for a bowl, set it down, and scooped in cucumbers, slices plunking.

"I'm showing him something," Cyril said.

"You the oldest one?" his mother asked Sam. He'd met her before, of course, and, along with his family, called her by her first name, Albina, a habit suddenly uncomfortable.

Cyril walked away as Sam answered, "No, ma'am. I'm second; Kurt came first." Behind her, Easter, Mother's Day, and birthday cards papered a wall, with a plastic framed print of "The Last Supper" in the center.

More of Albina's questions followed: "You boys, you mow that whole yard?" "Your grandma's big in some church; that is which one?" "Your father, he grows his own strawberries?" She confused the usual inflections yet enunciated precisely, the locals' sloppy slurs clipped, distinct.

"Leave him alone, Ma," Terezie said as she moved a pitcher and pastry tray in the refrigerator, then added the bowl of cucumbers. "Sam's got better things to do." When she closed the door, her blouse tightened across well-developed breasts. "Right?"

"Hey, Terezie," Sam said, imagining her—supple, forbidden—cupped in his hand.

"Sam," Cyril called, "back here."

Sam excused himself and, in a room off the living room, he found a bed with a swirl of sheets and a patchwork quilt. A Louisville Slugger, fielder's mitt, leather basketball, cork-handled spinning rod, and gray tackle box were spread across a dresser and two window ledges. A bathroom sink stood incongruously next to the open cedar closet. Cyril sat on a padded bench next to an upright piano.

He made Sam drag a bow across a screeching violin—spruce, carved and glued by his father, Josef—then he played what sounded like an exotic bird insane asylum. Terezie and Albina joined them.

"We come to hear you boys to play the duet," Albina said, this time with no discomfort. Exactly Sam's height, she stared straight at him. "My favorite, 'Rock of ages, cleft for me.'" She whistled perfectly pitched notes.

"No, I'm sorry," Sam said, raising his hands as though blocking a blow, feigning surrender. "I can't play."

"Aw sure, is an easy one," Albina said, motioning Cyril to let her sit, her fingers then moving over the piano's middle keys. "Rock of ages…" she sang.

Terezie handed the boys poppy seed *kolaches,* their aroma: sugar, yeast. She shrugged, an acknowledgment of her mother's nudging.

Cyril set his *kolache* on top of the piano then worked his bow again, following the odd rhythms of his mother's playing.

"You don't like music?" Albina asked Sam. "Is speech of your heart."

"Oh, yes ma'am. I just never learned."

"You draw, maybe, work with your hands?"

"Ma," Terezie cried, "please."

"So what you do at school?"

"Get in trouble mostly," Sam said. They talked about his year playing baseball, his dislike of sciences except for chemistry, his interest in Russian—only one semester offered—and Dostoyevsky.

"He's smart, Ma," Terezie said. "Not like the others." Instead of Chanel No. 5 and face powder, she smelled like grass clippings, cinnamon. Her hair was straight with crimped ends, yeasty from beer rinse. Occasionally her voice squeaked with cynicism. "*Všecko má konec*—Everything has an end," she said when Sam described the baseball coach explaining why he couldn't play anymore. "*Ale jitrnice má dva*—but a sausage has two," she added, anchoring curls behind an ear.

"Mr. Blazek, he could teach you," Albina said, and for a moment, Sam couldn't figure why she'd mentioned the band teacher. "He show Terezie good how to play important, Smetana, Dvořák, but also music for singing." As she guided Terezie onto the bench—"Now, one time round, 'Clementine,'"—Sam hoped Albina hadn't been lied to, that his friends had been wrong about Terezie.

He stumbled over words but sang along, corny songs he somehow knew. After "Clementine" they whined "Fraulein," and while Cyril's violin chirped, they remembered two verses of "The Tennessee Waltz." As Terezie stroked the keys, her fingers nimble, mechanized, her brogan tapping the pedal, she never looked at her hands, but watched for eye contact, head rocking. Her mother sat on one side, and Cyril stood on the other. They swatted their thighs, swaying with the rhythms.

"Naww," Albina interrupted, scowling. "Your father, home, and his table, it will be empty." She waved an arm. "Cyril, quick like *králík*, the barbecue. Naww." Her house shoes slapped toward the kitchen, while Cyril ran out the back, the screen door slamming.

Terezie shrugged, and they laughed. She didn't object when Sam scooted next to her. She even smiled when he took her hand.

I know the part about them singing is exactly what happened, because Sam told me. "Music," he said with a convert's enthusiasm, "is like that *kolache* I ate so fast, my lips left skid marks. Sweet, but a lot better if you make it last." We sang in his car after that, thinking we sounded like Patsy Cline and Johnny Cash. "A regular duet," he'd say. "Sure beats eating solo."

Sam practically moved in with the Cervenkas; their foreignness felt like hands pulling him through a door. He learned how to play dominoes and distill wine; he brought back three baby cottontails, round-eyed bundles with translucent skin. They stayed in a shoebox in his closet and he fed them with an eyedropper, but they lived only two days. His newfound attachment to the family was genuine, particularly his interest in Terezie.

He tried to get his girlfriend and me together, but I usually found an excuse. The last thing I wanted was to watch Sam with her. Finally he scowled, "What's your problem?" so I agreed to go. Since our cultural options consisted of movies, the Founders' Day parade, and the annual Lions Club minstrel, seasonal sports dictated social events; fall Friday nights meant Nugent High football. Sam played sandlot games, but in the high school bleachers, he grew restless. He shouted to friends, peered behind us, between the feet of a scowling couple. "Back off!" he yelled at a commotion under our seats.

"First down," the announcer bellowed, and the crowd cheered, cowbells clanging.

"You heard me," Sam shouted again. He knelt, bumping a man in front, then shoved his arm between the slats. The tail of his starched shirt came untucked.

Terezie leaned, searching the scene below, then pulled Sam's sleeve. "Hey," she said, "don't." When her head shook, crimped curls swished.

Sam shrugged her off, barking, "She was loud and clear, asshole."

The band honked "Everything's Coming up Roses." People clapped, whistling, while a player unsnapped his helmet's chinstrap, trotted off the field.

"Nice move, Chopin," Terezie said, her eyes stormy. "Please ruin this game for us. Sarah and I waited all week to watch you rag on those people." She kicked his leg.

Who's Chopin? I thought.

"You, too, buddy," Sam yelled, giving whomever it was the finger. "Punk," he grumbled, pleased. People around us glared, mumbling.

"C'mon," Terezie said rising, tugging his hand, her right brogan planted on the seat below. "We're hungry, right, Sarah?"

While he drove to Crystal's Cafe—specialty, chicken-fried steak; clientele, seniors—he and Terezie ignored me in the back seat. "Is that a chip I see on that muscley shoulder?" she said, a brow arched. "Let me take care of that." Brushing him, she batted her lashes.

"It wasn't my fault, George," Sam said.

She shook her head, mocking.

"Really. This girl was trying—"

"No, she wasn't."

"The hell you say. She was—"

"She was hoping her boyfriend would kiss her, until Superstud came to the rescue." She massaged the back of his neck. "So much evil; so little time."

Later over steak and fries, they explained their nicknames. "Chopin didn't copy anybody," Terezie said. Sam blew a straw wrapper skidding across the Formica. "He had a special sense of touch," she added, and Sam's hand disappeared beneath the table.

Terezie was George Sand, Chopin's lover.

Sam later shared a story that Cyril's father, Joseph, had told him.

Josef said that when he was a boy, his father, Papa Antonín, was swarmed while he smoked a hive toward a box he'd built for collecting honey. This image of Papa Antonín—bees attacking in black fits amidst swirls of poisonous clouds, with Papa's eyes glaring from behind checkered wire—was the one Josef saw whenever he thought of his *tatínek*. "A god, he was, next to them bees," Sam said, imitating Josef, "their stings, he don't care. Like when from the old country he first come, the Americans, they say things; they did not understand." The drama behind this myth established a family ideology extending to Cyril as he wielded a hoe. A dictum as lasting as my grandfather's inscription in the Pelton Bible, asking that our family be granted "the fortitude to stay the course we have been called to follow."

Sam told Josef's childhood story one Sunday over chocolate shakes at Dusty's drive-in; he described the old man sitting on the boxy sofa in his farmhouse, his beefy hands gripping his knees. Sam transported us to the farm at the turn of the century, a world of mules, cows, turkeys; cabbage, lye soap, potatoes rotting in the earth; Josef, his brothers, sisters, parents; and Otis, who worked beside Josef's father, Papa Antonín. That's where Otis had learned to fertilize with eggshells and banana peels. As Sam spoke, I knew he envisioned himself at the farm. So did I.

At first when the hive attacked his father, twelve-year-old Joseph thought it served him right, that Papa had cruelly disturbed the insects, and, as a result, many bees had needlessly died. Even so, the swarm was only a preliminary to the main part of Josef's story.

Several months later, at Papa Antonín's insistence, Josef had nervously driven their team of mules while his father guided the middleplow, busting the winter wheat field. But midway through a turn, a mule bolted. Whether she stumbled first or was bitten by a horsefly, Sam said Josef never knew. Because Josef had been looking at Papa when the beam snapped, he saw the yoke crack, the front piece tossing forward like splintered bone. His father thudded to the ground, the mules' straps still wrapping his waist. When the tri-cornered blade lodged on its side in front of Papa, Josef told Sam, "I see everything clear."

Papa stared but didn't move. Together, they inspected the arm. The gash, down the outer side, started at the wrist and ended near the elbow, the edges like jigsaw pieces. The blood, Josef said, flowed thick as prune juice, mixing with black earth, staining Papa's gloves, overalls, jacket. The wound's interior was slick, meaty as the pork hindquarters Papa hung in the smokehouse, except dirt, wheat shoots, and bone shards speckled the spongy layers.

Worst of all, Josef remembered, were the broken bones; the forearm bent in the middle at a right angle. The two bottom bone halves jutted through ragged flesh, their outsides white, their insides packed with red jelly marrow. Snapped cords of muscle surrounded the shanks.

Josef stared at the wound and his father's face. His own arms hung, clubs; his cheeks stayed cool, dry. Will he die? Josef thought. Have I killed him? When Papa grunted, trying to sit, Josef squatted, forgetting himself, lifting his hands.

"The blood," Papa said, and then, "your shirt," waving his good arm. Josef tore strips: one to stanch the blood, three to bind the wound, two to make a sling. Papa sat, his face wrinkled, scraped, and gazed at the blotched ground. Reluctant to humble his father, Josef leaned on his thighs as Papa, neck muscles rigid, struggled, stood.

Papa refused to see a doctor, so Mama tied strips of bacon at the incision's ends. She pressed cloths coated in heated cornmeal and salt over the leaking wound.

Months later, Josef dreamed his father died that day in the field, that the blade had cut Papa's neck. Wandering among bees, Papa became a nature god, stirring clouds, his eyes wild, resolute. That's when Josef knew that he and Otis should finish busting the field. Otis hadn't wanted to, but Josef insisted. "A question I am not asking," he'd said. "I must show this to Papa I can do." As Josef rounded the end of the second row, yanking and slackening the reins, he made a pledge: This Papa—the one whose devotion to the land crippled him yet he remained—this was the man Josef wanted to be. *Like Papa, the land, good and black, always I will work.*

Papa returned to work too soon. Mama's poultices prevented gangrene from setting in, but his tomato picking and hog feeding kept the bones from growing together. A new joint formed, and sometimes his hand and six inches of arm would flop to the side. Or when the whole arm hung straight, the segment would dangle. The nerve damage left his last two fingers limp against his palm; when the muscles atrophied, the digits froze. Papa compensated, his output about the same, the limb, for him, part of his makeup, his body mangled and transformed.

I wanted to say that I didn't like Josef's story about the wounded arm, that it was too gory, that it reminded me of our mother saying Otis' fingers had been "permanently bent as though waving." And I didn't understand why the old man wouldn't see a doctor. Sam, though, would think I was scared, so instead, I asked, "Did Cyril and Terezie know their grandfather?"

"Only through their father's story." He thanked the carhop, who took our tray. "Can you imagine what it must've been like coming here, not even knowing the language?" He steered onto the road. "People hated Czechs. That's why Albina quit third grade."

Sam had a habit of driving through unfamiliar parts of town. Now we found ourselves on the East Side, passing lopsided houses, three-legged dogs, cluttered yards—nothing like our neighborhood. I wondered if Otis' illegitimate son and former mistress lived nearby.

If so, then Ruby came here on her days off. When Sam waved to some people on their front porch, I asked who they were, thinking Ruby might've brought him. "Don't know," he said, "but it pays to be friendly." We didn't say anything else until we got home.

At our back door, he teased, "Thanks for the date, cutie." He twirled the keys. "Cheap and quiet—the way I like them."

"Jerk," I said. I wished our strange afternoon wouldn't end.

I caught Sam in his room on a Saturday morning before he left to take Terezie on a date. This would be our last private talk before he moved to Austin.

"Where y'all going?" I asked.

He peered over his shoulder while brushing a shoe. The second shoe and an open can of polish lay on his chest-of-drawers. "To Taylor for a Cervenka reunion," he said.

"Is Terezie making you go?"

"They have great food, and a band." He glanced at his hands but watched me. "And I get to take her home." His eyebrows did a Groucho Marx.

"So, how does she feel about you leaving next week?" I hoped they'd decided to date different people.

"It's not like she and I won't still see each other." He started brushing the other shoe, the first left beside the can of polish. "I'll come home most weekends." He flipped the brush then buffed again.

"So you'll be spending that time with her? I mean…"

"Don't you like the Cervenkas?"

"Why do you always want to talk about them?"

Sam stopped brushing. "Are you mad at them, or at me?"

I bit my cheek. "It's just hard, you know, to see you go."

He tilted his head, leaned on one hip.

"O-ka-ay," I sing-songed. I wasn't going to embarrass myself. At least my father wouldn't be giving Sam anymore whippings. Besides, the Cervenkas' contrast to our country-club life was probably what attracted him. I guiltily wondered if they, in turn, welcomed him because his mother was their landlord. Still, when Sam helped me take a closer look, even I was curious. I'd recently talked to Josef about keeping a hive at the farm and sharing the honey. Unlike Sam, though, I thought he and Albina were stricter than our parents. "Exactly how are Dad's rules any different from Josef's?" I knew that Terezie had a nightly curfew and daily chores. Cyril still worked on the farm every summer.

"People are respected in that house. Everybody can say what they think."

I remembered my father's straight back as he said "Yes, sir" to my grandfather and my mother's rules about being a lady. In fact, we weren't allowed to say a lot. But there was one thing Sam couldn't argue with. Josef had told Sam that for as long as Papa lived, whenever that arm cocked backward around a hoe or shovel, the three-fingered claw clamping the handle, he'd thought of *earth's minerals and moisture, its depths, odors and texture, its hidden roots and worms.* "Josef's story about his daddy's arm, that claw and the worms—it sounds like he's a farmer because he's guilty."

"He may feel guilty, but nobody blames him. They don't feel sorry for him, either, or for Papa Antonín. They see everybody the same. Nobody's better *or* worse." I wondered if he'd heard Dr. King's speech on TV two days earlier. "The truth's all that matters. There's no secrets. The Cervenkas just get on with it. Life, I mean." He dropped his shoes on the floor, and stepped into them, scuffs erased, ready to go.

I nodded, thinking, What secrets? What truth? "You hear Martin Luther King at that rally?"

He shrugged. "Of course." He shoved shoe polish in a desk drawer. "Why?"

"Just wondered what you thought."

"Be faithful to whatever exists in you," he said, his brow a question mark. "That way, you become indispensable."

"Huh?" Had he heard that in class? Was he making fun of Dad?

"Oh. Nothing." He flipped off the light switch by the door.

"The Cervenkas are like family," I blurted, deciding to tag along, if he'd let me.

His snicker cut a seam in the dark. "A person can make his own family."

"So I'm not your sister?" I blinked, and his silhouette emerged from shadow.

"You can't get rid of me that easy."

When I turned on the light above the stairs, he started down, his shoes gleaming. Glancing back, he winked.

Instead of coming home in October for my birthday dinner, Sam sent a postcard. The cover photo showed the Jets and Sharks from *West Side Story*, along with the caption, "Play it cool, boy." On the other side, Sam wrote, "Breeze it, buzz it, easy does it." Next to his signature, he wrote, "Your badass brother," and sketched a torso in blue jeans, leaning casually against a wall.

CHAPTER 7

SPIRIT DAY IS THAT awkward few hours during the opening of the fall semester when a parade of student-decorated floats winds through the campus, ending on a back lawn where contests and general mayhem commence (dunking booths—ugh!). Since classes are called off, faculty members are expected to attend. I usually appear just before the parade begins, wave to any administrators I see, then sneak my way back to the side door that leads to the staircase across from my office.

I'm standing on the mall, twenty feet from the floats, trying to catch my dean's eye, when someone calls my name. "Dr. Pelton, yoo-hoo," she sings. "Hey, *yo*, over here."

Behind me, no; to the side, nothing. I try again, no one.

"Dr. Explorer-Who-Can-Find-Anything, *this* way. Up *here*."

Cornelia is standing in a pickup's flatbed with a group of girls wearing green t-shirts and throwing pieces of hard candy into the crowd. A hand-painted banner reads, "Kappa Delta Chi." Cornelia waves: not hello, I realize; she's calling me over. "We saved you a spot," she shouts.

Now, the dean is watching. He claps and nods, laughing, poking the Vice President of Academic Affairs with his Brooks Brothers elbow. She points her accountant finger and smiles.

I shake my head, no. I wave to the truck.

Suddenly, the girls are chanting, "Doc-tor Pel-ton, come on, get on."

I scowl my most ferocious scowl. I glare.

"Doc-tor Pel-ton, come on, get on." They're bending, twirling their arms: cheerleaders. Three sweet-faced devils, not Cornelia, hop down and skip over. I'm lifted forward, limp, sputtering.

On the truck, Cornelia is wearing yellow flippers. She smacks her right foot three times, and music pounds from someone's speaker. Candy is shoved into my hands. So I throw the handful, pieces pelting the air like bullets, a cherry sour ball ricocheting off the dean's shiny forehead.

When I was thirty-four, an oncologist told my mother that she had multiple myeloma. Kurt said the only difference between her situation and ours was that she didn't have to wonder how and when she'd die, a prophecy that unfolded twelve years later. Her surgeries and cycles of medications began thirteen years after Sam was gone. At the end, stoic as her hero Dorothy Parker, she slumped in a wheelchair, a silk scarf serving as a sling for her broken arm, a glass of champagne in her free hand. During her final months, I drove home most weekends, and we lay on her bed, talking. Although she didn't ask about my work, I once heard her say into the phone, "She's an authority on the indigenous people of Latin America."

When my father had a heart attack two years later, Kurt, by then a celebrated surgeon, inserted a calf's aortic valve, and following recovery, Dad broadened his contemplation of the spiritual. During weekly phone calls, he'd make some reference, like "avoid the tunnel," or "exponential diminishment," or "the Gnostic self as compared to the Buddhist self." I visited him on Christmas and his birthday. He never asked me to stay, but occasionally he'd call me Mama. His hand squeezed my elbow, bruising, when he walked me to my car.

He drove to Austin for acupuncture treatments and began a regimen of vitamin therapy. He'd been visiting me monthly since my mother died. Over vegetarian lunches—his acquiescence to my new habits—he asked questions about other cultures' medical theories. I hoped he'd incorporate some of the more conservative ideas into his own practice, but my brothers, of course, wouldn't have approved. He arrived most third Mondays at 11:00 a.m., once asking a waiter to take a picture of us sitting at our table eating geranium ice cream, our dishes topped with blooms. Two weeks after his funeral, as my brothers, their wives, and I walked through the house, Hugh, who'd slept in a recliner at the hospital, held out the framed photograph, our father's smile straight from my youth, genuine. "Here," Hugh said, "this is yours."

CHAPTER 8
1964

DURING THE FIRST MONTH after Sam left, I pretended he still lived upstairs. The second month, although he skipped my fifteenth birthday, he came home to see Terezie. That weekend, he slept at our house, but he spent his days with her parents or fooled around at the farm. After he left again, I tried to figure a way to visit him in Austin. He shared an apartment near the campus with Kurt, who spent most of his time at the ΣAE house. In November when President Kennedy was shot, the school sent us home at exactly 1:42 that afternoon, and I phoned Sam. I didn't care if I got in trouble over the long distance bill. I needed his reassurance, but, instead, *he* cried. After that, I made myself wait until the Christmas holidays, thinking we'd have time to go to the movies, to talk. Instead, he spent his two weeks with a few friends and, again, Terezie, then Kurt drove him back to school. He hadn't mentioned the torso on the postcard, but to tell the truth, he was already somewhere else. By February, I turned my attention to my father.

On a Saturday morning at the end of spring break, I stood in the upstairs hall ironing a blouse on a contraption that folded out from the wall. From my position, I could see Hugh's back as he stood in our parents' bedroom. Together, we watched our father sitting on the bed, tying his wing tips. I imagined his hands gloved, holding a metal tool, blood daubed with cotton by an attentive nurse.

Routine circumscribed my father's life. Saturdays, he met my grandfather for golf. He used an old set of clubs, the bag limp and faded, its crudeness, for him, advertising his sacrifice. "My P.G.A. rabbit's foot," he'd say before he left, holding out the stained canvas, hoping someone would comment on its ragged condition. At the end of the match, he'd privately tip the course starter so he could return at 5:30 the next morning and practice a shot he'd hit poorly. He stayed most Sundays until just before church, where he taught a Bible study class, its members the same eight men for fifteen years.

Most of the hour they talked sports, each game a contest between good and evil, the key players God's acolytes. The last twenty minutes, the men discussed Bible chapters my father had researched in books of historical and textual analysis. He'd become a scholar, the individual figures, especially reluctant, ill-fated Moses and devout Paul, his friends, their doubts and talks with God described as family anecdotes.

"After guiding two generations through the desert," he liked to say, "barely any food, his people squabbling, sinning, Moses wrote his five books, then took a break at the Water of Contradiction. And for just one second"—he'd snap his fingers—"he wondered whether God could actually get them out of this mess. And what do you think he got for that?" Here, my father would search the faces of his audience. "He got to stand on Mount Nebo and watch everybody take off, leaving him to die by himself. One mistake," my father would add while raising an index finger. "One."

Hugh, who'd just turned eleven, had a different passion—music— and that Saturday morning I had a clear view of him tilting his head, pretending to hold a horn. "I was playing this big ole saxophone," he said. "Big, big as a tuba." He hopped then drummed his feet.

"Can't usually remember *my* dreams," my father said, standing, sliding his wallet into his back pocket. "Try not to, in fact."

"Playing, you know, that one from July Fourth. But the notes were bubbles." Hugh punched the air as his bare feet slid across the carpet. "Like clouds, except kinda shark-shaped."

My father clapped teasingly. "Shark clouds from a tuba, huh Hugh?"

Hugh grinned, shrugged twice.

"I hope you'll be sure and tell that to the guys at school on

Monday. They ought to get a real kick out of it."

"Aw, Dad, it's only a dream."

Hugh walked, dragging his toes, toward the doorway. "Did I ever tell you," my father said, "about my patient whose foot had been eaten by a shark?" They stepped into the hall, and my father lifted his hand to pat Hugh's head then returned it instead to his pocket. His keys clinked; I smelled coffee, Vitalis.

Hugh's eyes widened. "You're just kidding, right?" He grabbed the banister when they started down the stairs.

I unplugged the iron, followed. The only way I'd learn details about my father's work was by overhearing him with one of my brothers.

"Said he'd been working for Texaco off the Houston coast," my father said. "Can't remember exactly how it happened, but with his prosthesis he got around pretty good."

My father's patients often called, tongue-tied, or sent gifts, some expensive, but he discouraged visits. Mr. Gueldner, muscled as a weightlifter, his voice like a radio announcer, had come anyway, right before Christmas—he, his wife and three children, one an infant. They brought a Swedish ripple coffeecake baked by the patient himself. "Bless you," he kept saying while my father mumbled something, shook hands with one of the older kids. They sat on the sofa, and when my father said he'd leave some cake for Santa, they all blinked, nudged one another. After they'd left—Mr. Gueldner thanked at the door, the baby needing to be changed—my father mentioned the leg.

"What's a prosthesis?" Hugh asked when we reached the downstairs landing. My father checked his watch. He pushed Hugh toward his study.

"Can I come?" I asked.

He nodded while we walked. "It's an artificial limb."

"What's it made of?" Hugh leaned close, tripping on his toes, grabbing my father's sleeve.

"Various man-made materials are—"

"But how does it stay, you know, on the leg?"

I sat on a stool in the corner while they walked over to the copper kettle filled with bleached human bones. My father picked out a fibula, a tibia, a talus, then one of the feet, its sections held together with wires. Pointing, working the joints, he helped Hugh memorize the names, explained the procedures for making and wearing a prosthetic foot. Hugh assumed I'd already been given the lesson, and my father seemed to forget I was there. Hugh asked questions ("Does it hurt when you walk?" "Can you swim in it?"), and my father answered, using medical terms ("mechanical device," "supplement the function," "*extensor digitorum longus*").

"Are these real?" Hugh asked. "Did you know…him?" He tried to walk the foot across the desk, anklebones limp at the joint, toes skidding.

My father folded a section of newspaper, stuffed it in a wastebasket. "He wasn't anybody. Granddaddy calls him Beaner."

I laughed, thinking the name sounded silly. Now, knowing how close my father was to Otis and Ruby, I wonder how he reconciled his father's racism. Years later, he'd try to explain. "It was common in that generation."

"Cause he's like a bunch of beans?" Hugh asked. He turned the foot over, its segmented parts flopping.

"No, it's just his name."

"Crazy," Hugh said, balancing the sole on his hand, toes like claws, dangling. Then, appalled: "Granddaddy knew him?"

My father slumped in his chair, his elbows on his thighs. He wiped one side of his high-boned face, tugged his nose. "No, of course not. I didn't say that."

"But where'd the name come from? You said—"

"Granddaddy told me the story."

"Tell *us*," Hugh said, peeking over a scapula, "please."

My father ruffled a book's pages. "I don't think so," he said, looking at his watch, then surprising me with a wink. "I'm awful late. Couldn't possibly."

"Awww, Daddy, please?" Hugh's forehead wrinkled; his mouth fell open.

"Are you big enough?" My father caught Hugh's arm, pulled him like a crane hook—Hugh's feet barely kept up with his body. "This is serious, now."

"Yeah."

"Yes what?"

"Yes, sir."

My father glanced at the carpet. "The whole thing started when a farmer and his family were killed, and the sheriff arrested a man who had swum across the border from Juárez. He was wearing the farmer's pants, and the farmer's wedding ring was in the pocket." Folding his arms, he seemed to go into a trance.

Hugh blinked, then stared, receptive as Sam must've been at the same age.

"Know what?" My father slapped his thighs then leaned on his hands, serious. "I really don't like this story much." He studied his watch, sucked his teeth. "I really do have to go. Granddaddy's waiting. We'll have to finish our talk later."

"But you can't quit now," Hugh pleaded, not realizing that our father wasn't teasing anymore. He wrapped one arm around Dad's neck. "You already started."

"Hugh," my father said, exasperated. He rolled his chair toward the windows, stared at a pecan tree in the yard. "Those days, you see," his words uttered by rote, as if counted off a list, as if dredged then reported, "Nugent was a wild place with things happening we'd never stand for today." He faced Hugh again. "And, with everybody so mad at the man for killing their friend, a big crowd got together and, oh, they hanged him. And since nobody knew who the guy was, Granddaddy thought, well…he brought the body home." He stood, then swatted nervously at a grease stain. "Anyway, that's Beaner."

"Uh, Dad?" I interrupted, unable to stop myself. "You mean it was, ah, a lynching?" I couldn't think about my grandfather and the dead body yet.

"Times were different then, Sarah."

"But what happened to the skin and hair and all?" Hugh asked, his face puckered as the one he imagined.

"I know—" my father started.

"No, excuse me," I said, nervous but determined. "Could you tell us anything else about it, the lynching, I mean?" I'd heard about such things, but the men were always black and the hangings happened around the Civil War, on plantations. Not in Nugent with my grandfather in the crowd.

"I don't know anything, Sarah. I told you, it happened a long time ago."

"But Granddaddy was there?" I wondered if he'd helped slip the rope around the Mexican man's neck. "What did he say happened? Did he know anyone who did it?" I was getting scared.

My father sat again. He rolled his chair over to my stool in the corner, pulling Hugh with him. "Sarah, you're right to be upset. What happened was terrible." He looked into each of our faces. "A man was murdered by a mob. True, he probably committed a crime, but that shouldn't matter. He didn't get a trial, so we'll never know."

Hugh bounced the foot skeleton on my lap.

"Stop!" I shouted.

He leaned back, stricken.

My father set the foot beside him in his chair. "The important thing," he said, "is that Granddaddy didn't have anything to do with the hanging. I don't know who did, although I'm sure there must be some kind of record." He turned to me. "If you're interested, you might look that up. In fact, I hope you will, because you won't find your grandfather's name there."

"But I don't know how." I wouldn't be placated. I pictured my grandfather describing Otis as "a good and faithful servant." I wondered if Otis knew how the man from Juarez had died.

"Where do you think you might find such a record?"

"I don't know...the library is the only place I can think of."

"Good. When you get to the library, where will you go?"

"Old newspapers?" My father always seemed to be testing. Why couldn't he just take me to the library himself?

"Sarah, you can do this; you don't need anyone's help. As I recall, the hanging took place during the summer of 1915. That's all you'll need to get started."

Buoyed by his rare expression of confidence, I pledged to go to the library as soon as possible. I didn't know what I'd do if I recognized any of the names, and I prayed he'd be right about Granddaddy. "But he took the dead body?" I was still innocent enough to hope that my grandfather had deserved a professional claim on someone's son, brother, friend, regardless of whether the man was guilty. Otherwise, how could my father keep the bones in our house, encouraging us to touch them?

"I know it's hard for you to understand," he said, rolling to his desk. He began placing the bones back into the kettle as Hugh joined him, "But he was used in Granddaddy's research." He glanced at me, cleared his throat, coughed. "Hugh, you'll learn more about anatomy when you're in medical school."

Suddenly I had to know why he didn't expect me to be a doctor like my brothers. "Can Hugh and I go with you to your lab sometime?" I walked toward him.

"Mama might have something to say about that," he said.

Before I could answer, bones clacked, rolling. Hugh leaned over the kettle, reaching in.

"Hey, be careful." My father used both hands, checking. He stacked the bones in their usual order.

"Grandaddy's what *kind* of doctor?" Hugh said, resting his hand on my father's shoulder.

"Internist. He operates on the organs." My father sat back, looking at Hugh.

"Is he, I mean, he's good isn't he?"

"Son, your grandfather is the best doctor I know. Do you realize what he's accomplished, the number of people he's helped?"

Hugh shook his head, no, his face an empty plate.

I thought about my father meeting with hospital residents every morning, about his patients' gifts and letters, about his trips to conferences, his work with Boy Scouts, PTA, and his Sunday class. Had my grandfather done more than that?

"Great minds must be ready not only to take opportunities, but to make them." He wiped his jaw. "Come closer, Sarah. I want to tell you both something."

We huddled. "About Granddaddy?" Hugh asked.

"Once, when I was a few years older than you, he decided a sore on his lip was cancerous, so you know what he did? He stood in front of a mirror and cut it off. Just like that. 'Somebody had to get it out of there,' he said. I remember the blood but not one complaint. Then he had me sew it up."

"Were you scared?" Hugh chewed his thumbnail until my father pulled his hand away from his face.

"Yes, very." He sounded out of breath. "But my job was to do what my father expected. He needed me, and it was an honor to help, even though it was hard." He patted Hugh. "Let men laugh when you sacrifice desire to duty. You have time and eternity to rejoice in."

Sam appeared, standing sideways in the doorway, gazing at the far windows. He tongued a wad of gum while he held out his hand. "Ready, Hughie?" he said. Kurt was still at the coast for spring break, but Sam had arrived last night after spending his holidays in Laredo. As usual, I'd barely seen him. "We got to go, guy. Cyril and Terezie will be waiting."

Hugh jumped up, his face a commercial for little-brotherhood. "Where are you off to?" My father scowled at Sam, and I wondered how two people who looked alike could stay so mad at each other.

Sam's chewing stopped. "Hugh says he wants to look for arrowheads, is all. I said I'd take him."

"That's right, Daddy," Hugh said. "Sam found a midden. We're gonna look for a Clovis point." He leaned sideways.

"A midden?" my father said, catching Hugh's shoulder.

"You know, a trash mound." Hugh edged toward Sam and the doorway. "Okay? So can I go?"

I knew what my father was thinking. During the Christmas holidays, I'd talked nonstop about Texas Indians, so Sam, who'd been friends since high school with a West Side brother and sister, Jaime and Mariana Cardona (I wondered if they were descendants of Geronimo), brought me a book on Aztecs. "Read this if you want to know who had the smarts over here," he said. Later, when I told my father that during the Wichita deer ceremony, a newly initiated shaman ate a coral bean so he could be unconscious while the leader scraped him with a garfish jaw, he said, "If you're interested in the supernatural, think about Paul's conversion on the road to Damascus."

"Why is it," my father said to Sam, "you're so interested in the very things the rest of us try to avoid, and you avoid what we hold important?"

Unfair, I thought. I stepped around the desk. "Dad—"

"Your thinking is somehow off track," he continued. "Don't you want to be happy?" He stroked the side of his face. "What attracts you to so much that's ugly? Pinpoint it, be specific. Please, I need to know."

"What'd I do?" Sam looked at Hugh and shrugged, trying to reassure him.

My father's features softened; he slumped. "Sometimes, I wonder if there's *anything* we can agree about."

Hugh frowned, confused.

"Embarrassing, huh?" Sam said, his expression open as a child's. "Or maybe I just remind you of something you'd like to forget?"

My father flinched, leaned forward. "You're my son. But I don't like the trouble you take pleasure in causing."

"Why do you care so much what people think?" Sam's gaze soured. He leaned close, whispering, "Even I know you're too good for that."

"Now that I think about it, your problem must have something to do with me."

"So there wouldn't be a *problem* if I acted like *you*?" Sam looked away, as though he were thinking it over. "Then we could both follow our dads around," he said, his voice shaking, "forget what *we* want."

"That's called responsibility."

"No, sir," Sam whispered again. "You know the name for somebody like that, but I don't think you want me to say it."

"Exactly what I mean. No respect," my father said. "Some things a man does, son, without question, because they're morally right."

"You think demeaning yourself is a way to show respect? You really want me to do that?" They stared at each other. "And is it morally right for a kid to be hit twenty times with a belt if he doesn't?"

My father tapped Hugh. "You've got something more important

to do this morning," he said. "Go get your shoes. I need you to caddy."

"But, Daddy, Sam—"

"Arrowheads will wait. Go on. I'll meet you at the car." He steered Hugh to the doorway, then faced Sam.

Sam nodded at Hugh, who turned to leave. Then he nervously popped his gum. "Why don't you just give it up? Tell the truth, for once."

My father reached to snatch the wad from Sam's mouth. But as his fist clenched, he caught himself.

I thought, If he hits Sam, will Sam hit back? What truth is Sam after?

"You're on your own today," my father said, inches from Sam. Then he clutched the keys in his pocket, watched Hugh cross the hall.

"Don't worry," Sam said, grinning, "I'm used to that." He shook his head. "When we do go, though," he flinched, looking sideways, "I hope you'll come with us."

"Son, scratching will only get you raw. The way to stop your itching is to pat someone else's back."

Sam said he had to talk to somebody, so I agreed to go with him to meet Cyril and Terezie. At moments like these, increasingly predictable times prickled with disaster, I was sadly eager for him to go back to Austin.

He began talking before I could close the door of the second-hand Corvair. "Did you see that?" he said, starting the engine. "Could you believe it?"

I was afraid to say anything. I hoped he'd explain.

He shoved the car in gear. "Our father the hypocrite, scared to death." He headed toward the road to the farm. "Sad."

A sharp turn pressed me against the door. I grabbed the handle. "What's he scared of?"

"Anything outside the rulebook in his head. *Duty*, what a joke."

I shrugged, confused.

"Dad's got wires for brains. Zing, this is how you work; zing, here's what's good and bad; zing, these are the facts. Easy—one, two, three, life makes sense. Guy's a robot—no emotions, no imagination. You push those buttons, he blows a fuse."

Our father had a jazz collection, and he'd built a tree house with elaborate shelves and a stirrup pulley for raising us to its floor. He'd recently explained that Buddha and Jesus were alike in their teachings about compassion. "If you could just talk to him without getting so mad."

"Me? You were there, did I do anything?"

"Something about—"

"Look, I know he's a good doctor and you look up to him and all. But you got to see past that. For instance, tradition." I nodded. "It's just a habit without a reason. The opposite of truth. Nobody remembers how the thing got started, but it's sure as hell sacred. How stupid is that?"

I thought about Sundays at our grandparents' house and the farm, about my brothers chopping cotton, about church.

"He doesn't even know what a midden is, for Christ's sake." Sam shook the steering wheel, so I didn't confess that I didn't, either. "He sees me, he thinks he hasn't done things right. I'm like Joseph after his brothers drop him in that well."

"I know," I said, not really understanding.

He rolled down his window, and the wind whipped his ear, ruffled his shirt. "Whatever's left out of that rulebook might as well not exist."

"Like what?"

His scowl got scary; then he sighed. "Like, you think he's eaten baby eel?"

"No," I moaned, repulsed.

"See? You never even tried it."

"Gross…why would you?"

"To see what it tastes like."

"Not me."

"Why be born then?" He hung his arm out the window, slapped the door.

He'd told me to face the truth, no matter how ugly. Why was our father's search for facts any different?

"I say if there's something to know, bring it on. You going to tiptoe around like Dad, afraid, only eating baked potatoes?"

I had a general sense of what he meant. "I guess not."

"Smart girl." He squeezed my shoulder, but I could see he was still upset.

We drove without talking. If Sam was expected to be like Dad, I thought, was I supposed to emulate our mother? "But what about Mom?"

"Who? Madame Loafing Meat?"

I giggled, remembering an afternoon her younger cousin, a girl we rarely saw, had come to visit. They acted like girlfriends, chatting, and I was the outsider. "She never listens; I'm like nothing to her."

He turned, rested his arm on the seatback. "Don't you know the story about her grandparents?"

I did, but I'd sworn not to tell where I'd heard it. Aunt Lynette had said their parents died in a train wreck on the way to a friend's wedding in Galveston, so their grandparents had raised them. The grandmother had had a temper, sometimes crawling under the front porch to ambush them when they came home from school. I pictured a crone like the witch in "Hansel and Gretel," but Aunt Lynette laughed when I said that. She showed me a wallet-sized photo of a woman, her hair parted in the middle, holding a wide-brimmed straw hat, standing in a garden of vegetables and daisies next to a white clapboard house. The girls fended for themselves unless their grandfather fried a platter of squirrels. "Might as well've been rat," Aunt Lynette had said.

"Now," Sam said, "Mom's a gourmet cook, and everybody thinks we're perfect so she can forget about when she was a kid."

"Really?" I said, looking out the window. A stand of mesquites bordered a fence in the distance next to the highway. Straight ahead, the sky's edge seemed only a few miles down the road, its blue abutment a vast backdrop to the familiar stretch of concrete. "But, you know, sometimes Mom acts like it's my fault," I said. "And it's not," I added. "I don't like that."

Sam turned onto the farm road, stopping at the gate, and a covey of bobwhites fluttered from the hedgerow. He latched the gate behind us, then crossed the cattle guard, drove over a wooden bridge, and parked in the corral next to the Cervenkas' house. He leapt out of the car, whistling as though he hadn't just fought with our father, as though we'd entered a different world. Maybe we had.

We walked to the barn, where Cyril and Terezie were saddling four horses. I had to admit Sam's girlfriend was pretty. Makeup would've made her look like everyone else. Faded workman's jeans clung like kidskin. Would Sam tell her what had happened at our house? "I thought you were bringing Hugh," she said, buckling a girth strap. "Everything okay?"

Sam kissed her. "Peachy," he whispered. "I brought our Indian expert instead." He aimed an index finger at me, his other arm draping her shoulder. He nodded at Cyril. "I.Q., my man," he sang.

"Dad needed Hugh to caddy," I said, stroking a mare's neck, still worried about Sam and relieved I wouldn't have to explain. A hog rooted noisily at a trough in its pen. "I hope it's all right…" My plan was to hang back, try not to be noticed.

"Sure, it's all right. Now the numbers are even," she said, handing me the reins. "I've been on testosterone overload." She was getting harder not to like.

"You interested in Indians?" Cyril said, swinging himself onto a saddle. He squeezed with his boot heels, and his palomino trotted into the barnyard.

The three of us joined him, galloping along the path to the creek. "Well?" he said.

"Yeah," I said, and he nodded. He'd been on a university archeological dig, and I hoped he'd talk about it. He would graduate soon in political science with plans for law school.

Eight cows meandered toward us, on their way to the afternoon pasture. "Hello," I said, leaning to pat a dusty back. In between a cluster of live oak and agarita, I glimpsed a newly planted cotton field, the furrows raised like groundhog tunnels. Hugh would work there next summer alongside Cyril.

Sam led us into the creek, my horse leaping off the bank from a flat-footed position, rocking me forward as I clutched the saddle horn, soaking my jeans. The mare paddled, so I slackened the reins, allowing her to maneuver forward. Her breaths echoed off the water.

Sam steered us up a gently terraced incline on the other side. He dismounted near a spiny hackberry then tied his and Terezie's reins to a limb. Cyril and I tethered our horses and followed Sam to a grassy mound in the open. It had to be the midden, and I wondered if my brother, as Hugh claimed, had actually found it.

Cyril produced a canteen, two small picks, and a hand shovel, which he passed around. He assigned us each an area and started digging with a hunting knife he had attached to his belt. We peeled back grass and poked through a top layer of dirt. Sam attacked the midden like he did everything, digging toward its heart. A few yards away, bluebonnets peeked through buffle, mountain laurel smelled like cider, and an owl hooted in a littleleaf sumac near the horses.

"You think Dad might come if we tell him what's here?" Sam said, shoveling. "I mean, he's a history buff, right?"

"Sure," I said, wanting to hug him. Maybe they could somehow work everything out.

"Don't get your hopes up, Chopin," Terezie said, wincing. "He's awfully busy." She arched, stretching her back.

"Maybe," Sam said. "Sarah could bring him some Sunday." He lodged his shovel in earth, wiped his forehead with the sleeve of his shirt.

I nodded.

"He's not going to believe this," Sam said, breaking apart mud clumps. "I hope I'm here to see his face."

"Look for rocks that are fist-sized, that have right angles," Cyril said, holding one for us to see. He tapped its corner with another rock, and it flaked, brittle as glazed candy. "Burnt rock," he said, showing its pink inside. Then we began finding them among a dark gray mixture of ash and charcoal. Terezie uncovered fossilized clamshells, laying them in the grass.

"What's burnt rock?" I asked. "Are they arrowheads?" The stone I held didn't have the triangular shape I'd expected.

"Tonkawas camped here," Sam said. "This was their campfire, and before that it was where their ancestors butchered animals and scraped the hides. Any tools we find here could be 10,000 years old." Squatting on one knee, he sifted more soil through his fingers. "You never know."

He'd given me the book on Aztecs at Christmas, but we'd never talked about local Indian history. "Where'd you hear that?" I asked.

"From I.Q.," Sam said, motioning with his chin toward Cyril. "But when you bring Dad, you'll tell him I found the midden, okay?"

Terrezie shook her head. "Sam…"

"What?" Sam said, irritably sailing a rock at the trees. "He'll want to know how we got here. What's wrong with that?" He shrugged, daring her to disagree.

"Nothing," Terezie said, digging again. "Not a damn thing."

"Sam found this place," Cyril said, "because he knew what to look for. He doesn't need anybody's help."

We worked for twenty minutes without talking. Every so often, someone sipped from the canteen, the water still cool in spite of the heat. Sam inched toward Terezie, finally pretending to fall, his head resting in her lap. "Sorry, George," he said, and she laughed. "No, really," he said, gazing at her face.

"Can you cut the crap about your father?" she said, cupping his cheek. He kissed her; then, side by side, they combed the mound again.

Cyril hadn't said anything for about an hour, and I wondered how anyone ever got him to talk. Lunchtime was nearing, and I still hadn't asked him about his university dig.

"Bingo," Terezie sang, cradling something in her palm. She stood and gave her prize to her brother. "What is it?" she asked, rubbing her scar.

Leaning on his haunches, his hat shading his hands, Cyril inspected the flint while Sam watched from behind. "It's a dart point," Cyril said, "either a Nolan or a Pandale. Beautiful." He brushed dirt loose with his nail then turned the stone over.

"Way to go," Sam said, massaging Terezie's back. "My girl, She with Beautiful Dart Points."

Terezie shrugged, smiling.

Cyril stretched across the midden, holding out the arrowhead to me. A narrow heart-shape, it almost measured the length of my palm. Still damp, its flaked grooves were dark as charcoal. I gave it back to Cyril, who put it in a cloth sack, then scribbled something in a small notebook.

Sam and Terezie took a walk, their voices only mumbles. Was he finally telling her about his argument with Dad? Cyril and I kept digging, he sometimes holding rocks up to the sun then setting them aside. I didn't say anything when I found my dart point, instead carrying it over to the trees near the horses. Fatter than Terezie's, it looked like a goldfish as it lay in my palm, its tip pointed to the side of my hand, its fin tail next to my thumb. Beveled along the lateral edges, it could've been a cutter or scraper, but more than likely it, too, had been hafted to a spear. Scalloped grooves chiseled the rim. Made with what? Another rock? Or a knife improvised from a deer antler? Could a girl have carved the flint? Had it been used to kill something, an animal, or even a man?

Cyril said it was a Marcos point. "The core," he said, "is the piece you hit with a stone hammer, and the flake is the piece that comes off." He showed me some flakes he'd just found. Women, he said, cooked, cut leather, carved wood; so, yes, surely they must have also made arrowheads. He wrote a description of my Marcos in his notebook then told me to keep it.

That night, I gave it to my father, who took it to his office on Monday. I showed him the midden the next weekend. He squatted, inspecting our excavation, the rocks we'd left behind. "If Sam didn't notify the authorities," he said, his arms opening over the mound, "he's stolen from his own heritage." Half of me was hurt for Sam—I never told him about it—while the other was impressed that my father recognized our connection to these early Americans.

CHAPTER 9
1964

I FOUND A NEWSPAPER ARTICLE about the lynching. The murdered man's name had been Gregorio Diaz. The story said he'd waded across the Rio Grande the year before and then lived on the streets, a "transient." My father was right: Someone killed a farmer, his wife and two children. Even though Mr. Diaz was wearing the farmer's overalls—the name printed inside in ink—he claimed two men had given him the clothes. Once the sheriff had arrested all three, a crowd of one thousand gathered, prompting a deputy to hide the prisoners in an upstairs courtroom. My grandfather, a minister, and the newspaper publisher took turns standing on the balcony, trying to calm the mob. Men with rifles forcibly took Mr. Diaz, so the sheriff let the other two run down the back steps. As my father had said, after the hanging someone found the farmer's wedding ring in the pocket of Mr. Diaz' overalls. I recognized two names in the story—my grandfather's and the publisher's—but the fact that they'd tried to stop the lynching didn't alleviate my suspicion. If my grandfather later took the body, was he the "someone" who'd claimed to find the ring?

People of the Clovis culture were thought to be the first inhabitants of North America. Until recently, the standard theory was that they crossed the land bridge over the Bering Strait from Siberia to Alaska during the Ice Age period of lowered sea levels, then made their way southward through an ice-free corridor east of the Rocky Mountains into present-day western Canada as the glaciers retreated. In 2000, working with three archeologists from Texas A&M University, I recovered over 74,000 pieces of debitage and over 1,300 artifacts, mostly Clovis, at the Gault site near several springs in Central Texas. First investigated in 1929, the site had almost been destroyed over the subsequent six decades by relic hunters. But in 2001, at the Debra L. Friedkin site in Buttermilk Creek, Texas, we uncovered artifacts that pre-date the Clovis by 2,500 years.

The way some boys become obsessed with car models or Civil War battles, I memorized the names of Texas Indian tribes, their diets, tools, rituals. Casual remarks at school or the dinner table elicited details about the sixteenth-century Coahuiltecans as recorded in the journals of Cabeza de Vaca, or the Tonkawas, *tickanwatics,* as they called themselves, *the most human of people.* I used tribal behaviors to illustrate facts during history and government classes. The Choctaw and Cherokee immigrated from the East, and—surprise!—the Cherokee tried to help throw off Mexican rule during the Texas Revolution. During English, I wrote essays based on accounts by soldiers, missionaries, explorers. The children of a married Tonkawa couple, I noted, belonged to the mother's clan, which meant that, to them, men and women were equal. Parents, I added, did not spank their children. Shamans took care of the sick, rubbing the skin with medicines, calling the gods for a cure. Spirits of the dead became owls and wolves, which made me wonder if a farm owl could've been Antonín Cervenka. When I told my father that reservations were like concentration camps, he said, "Check out Sam Houston's involvement. Otis used to tell stories you might run across." The history teacher invited my parents for a conference. My mother told what happened while she drove us downtown to a shoe sale.

"She thinks we should find you a special tutor."

"She said that?" Working with an ethnographer was suddenly all I cared about. "What'd you say?"

"She said she didn't know anyone."

"Can't you check around?"

"I'm proud of you, Sarah, but tutors are expensive, and the whole thing sounds extreme, if you ask me."

I clutched the dashboard, turned toward her. "Mom, please. I promise you won't be sorry."

"I didn't say I wouldn't try to find somebody." She pressed the lighter to her cigarette. "But I can't imagine who that'd be." As the car filled with smoke, I lowered my window.

My father asked me to stay after supper as Hugh thumped up the stairs. My mother sat looking sidelong at him, then loaded plates and silverware into the dishwasher. Water sprayed into the sink.

My father linked his fingers, leaned back. "Have you thought about a college and a major?"

As I suspected, this was going to be my rite-of-passage chat. Kurt and Sam had had theirs the spring semesters of their junior years. I believed they'd give good advice. Not only had my father counseled patients and given speeches at high school graduations, his questions and proverbs, although frustrating, had introduced complexity and its rewards. "Don't think about education as something you *have* to do," he'd say. "Learning should be a pleasure." I hoped they'd know which schools specialized in ethnography. Anthropology was supposed to be a popular major. "What do you and Mama think?"

"Your mother's always dreamed of you going to a girls' school. You've worked hard, you've earned it."

"Why a girls' school?"

The spraying stopped. The dishwasher door clicked shut. "Because girls are appreciated there," my mother said, sitting. She wiped her forehead with a cup towel. "Since you've had to grow up with these monkeys, a girls' school could show you what you've missed." She folded the towel, hugged herself.

Kurt was following their prescribed path to Latimore Memorial. Sam had resisted and was studying Russian literature, not knowing or caring what he'd eventually do. Now it was my turn. The result of this conversation would dictate the rest of my life. "Are you worried that I act like a boy?"

"What a silly…of course not," my mother said. "Just think of it as a house full of sisters."

"Great. More gossip. Can't wait." The dishwasher hummed. "I don't need to have sisters to find out about being a girl."

"What are you talking about? That's exactly why you—"

"What if I don't want to go there?"

My father cleared his throat, walked to the sink. "Then we won't make you," he said. He filled a glass with water. "But would you visit one?"

"If I have to."

"Wonderful," my mother said. "You'll see; everyone's just like you."

"Apply to at least three places," my father said. "Talk to your counselor. But what should you study? You've always done well in science."

"You, of all people," my mother turned to him, "know how badly they treat women. Besides, Sarah's life doesn't have to be that complicated."

"You're right." He nodded. "If she left, it wouldn't be fair to the boy who could've had her spot." He drank, watching my face. "What do you think of nursing?"

"Nurses are important, but isn't it like being a maid?"

He flinched. "Nurses are indispensable, and the profession happens to be…"

"Good," my mother interrupted. "You're not the thermometer and squeaky shoes type." She squeezed my hand.

I didn't know how to respond to what seemed like insults. How could my parents be so wrong? I pulled my hand loose and swirled my finger in a congealed gravy puddle, squashing bits of roast, pepper.

"Okay, then anthropology," my father said. He returned to his chair at the end of the table. "Isn't that what her history teacher recommended?"

Finally, I thought, my stomach unknotting. "I've always—"

"Yes, but—" my mother interrupted. She waved a hand at my father, shook her head.

"She should choose something she excels in," he said, "and Sarah is an exceptional student." He faced me. "What's your favorite subject?"

"I've *always* wanted to study ethnography. You know that."

"What in the world?" my mother asked. "Is that some kind of water science?"

"Didn't Mrs. Sconstance explain it?"

"Oh, that," she said. "Have you thought about what it would mean? Traveling to God-forsaken places, primitive conditions. It's just not normal. Trust me, life is hard enough."

"Now, Mama," my father said, "you're better at these kinds of questions than I am, but she seems genuinely interested in the field. Don't you think she could make it work?"

"Are you prepared to risk your only daughter's future?" She wiped her nose with a napkin. "We have a responsibility, and more than anything else I want her to be happy."

"But Mother," I pleaded, "we're not the same person. This really *is* what I want."

"Diseases," she said, "no stability." She blew her nose. "Owen?"

"Can we agree," he said, looking at me, "that this needs more discussion?" He glanced at her as she put her hands in her lap. "Do we have to decide this tonight?"

"Could we at least think of some options," she said, her chin quivering, "just in case?"

He looked at me then back at my mother, and she nodded. "I don't see how that can hurt. After all, events are only the shells of ideas." He rubbed his palm down the side of his face. "Let's say, Sarah, that, hypothetically of course, you had a second interest. If you did, and only if you're comfortable sharing it, what do you think that would be?"

"Haven't a clue," I said, this time dipping two fingers in the gravy puddle. The people who claimed to know me best apparently didn't know me at all.

"We've heard about your first choice, and I don't want you to feel pressured. This is certainly your decision; we're only here to give advice." He held his chin. "But what about a degree in education?" he asked hopefully. "You could go anywhere with that."

"Anywhere," my mother said, folding her napkin. She put it in her skirt pocket. "And she'd have something she could always fall back on."

"Besides," my father winked, trying to lighten the tension, "teachers make good whistle bait."

I placed my palm in the gravy and pressed until liquid oozed out. My hand, *me*, I thought. Neither of my parents saw as I reached and flattened it again, this time against my mother's seersucker shoulder.

During one *Mexihcayōtl* festival, women made *ātōlli*, a thick maize gruel, poured it into gourd bowls, and let it cool until, records state, "it spread quivering." The congealing gruel and human flesh were thought to be the same, a Eucharistic demonstration of consubstantiation. When parents then feasted and encouraged their children to eat with them, no one was surprised later when a sacrificed *ixīptla's* thigh bone was shared. How responsible is a parent for the adult child's decisions?

CHAPTER 10

IN ORDER TO LOWER his tax liability when Gran died, Dad signed a disclaimer refusing acceptance of the Rockport summerhouse, so that property came directly to us. Sam and Terezie didn't know this, since Sam died a few months later and Gran's estate was never closed. They did know that Dad would leave us equal ownership of the farm. In other words, Sam's scrawled message bequeathed to Terezie not only his share of the farm, which she now expects, but also his portion of my grandparents' coastal property, valued recently at above a million dollars.

"If you bring yours, I'll bring mine," I say to Kurt when he phones, "and I don't think you want that." I pinch the inside of my arm.

"The hearing's day after tomorrow, which means you're going to have to grow up, Sarah. Instead of being the problem, help us solve one for a change."

"I tell you what," I say, relieved by his usual candor. "I'll help you fight Sam's will if you'll come without your lawyer."

"Terezie's bringing hers."

"Cyril may be a lawyer," I say, "but he's also a friend. I suspect he'll be more accommodating if you approach him from that second position."

"Don't be stupid. That hearing's his way of showing how devoted he is."

"Then what do you want?"

"What do you mean?"

"Are you going to try to persuade Cyril to cancel the hearing?"

"The only way we won't have that hearing is if Terezie signs the agreement."

"That's my point. Who's she going to do that for? Us or an attorney?"

Cyril meets us in his office lobby on the top floor of a downtown bank building. It's the last chance to avoid a probate hearing over Sam's will. He's wearing black Tony Lama boots with a navy cotton suit and a bolo tie. "Sarah," he says, surprisingly animated, "it's been too long." We shake hands; then he does the same with Hugh and Kurt. "Terezie's already here. This way, at the end of the hall."

When we walk in, Terezie rises from a wing-back. My brothers and I crouch like interlopers on a sofa between her and Cyril. The office is opulent. Between us stands an antique mahogany display case filled with Texas Indian artifacts, their flint bodies like incubating infants.

"Nice collection," I say, spotting a tanged Crescent blade. "Where'd you get them?"

"This Pandale," he says, pointing, "came from our midden on the farm."

I wonder if it was the one Terezie found. Where was the Marcos dart point I gave my father? I picture him standing over the evidence of our search, his arms raised, accusing Sam.

"Most of the others I found in a burnt-rock spring mound near the Gault site." He looks at me. "I've followed your work there. The midden helped people research the area's water history."

"I know that spring. I'd be interested in reading the report."

"I'll send you a copy."

My brothers are embarrassingly disinterested.

"You married?" I ask, nodding toward a photograph on his desk.

"Mariana. Sam introduced us."

"Cardona?" Kurt asks, the jolt of his voice a warm compress.

"Her brother's Jaime. You remember, right?"

"Yeah, sort of." Kurt slides his eyeglasses on.

I glance at the picture again but can't find the girl I knew. I've always wondered whether she and Sam were more than friends. She's Terezie's sister-in-law now. Imagine: the three of them together, talking about my brother.

"I don't mean to be rude," Terezie says, her purple eyes still luminous, "but you understand why I need this money."

Hugh sits forward. "We heard about the transplant, and we want you to know that Cornelia's been in our prayers."

"I appreciate that, really I do. But right now, prayers won't do diddly squat. Both of you've got kids. Think about it. My baby's dying." Tears drip from her chin onto her percale lap.

"Of course, we sympathize," says Hugh while a buzzer beeps in the next room. A door slams. "But Cornelia's doctors are convinced they can stabilize her condition so she'll be optimal for surgery."

I don't ask about the ethics of him getting details about Cornelia's case.

"No, let's get to the real issue, here," Kurt says, pulling a piece of paper from his inside pocket. "We've got a buyer for the farm, and Terezie can have Sam's share. All she has to do is sign this waiver saying she won't come after anything else."

"That's it? How soon could I have the money?" Terezie's husband has already sold his used bookstore and taken a job as manager of a Barnes & Noble in Rochester, where he finally gets health insurance. Ironically, he'll lose it again when he donates his kidney. With the state of public education, Terezie's part-time job as a music teacher is tenuous, at best, and Cornelia's shortness of breath, aches in her side and back, urinary tract infections, and headaches are forcing her to drop out of college.

After reading the single-page document, Cyril says, "There's no way she's going to sign this."

Arching an eyebrow, Kurt grins at Hugh.

"And why not?" Hugh asks. "The sale could go through tomorrow. Everything's ready. That's what you want, right Terezie?"

She swallows, her chin tight.

"Tell him, Terezie," Hugh says. "Explain it to Cyril. Go ahead."

"I know exactly what my sister wants," Cyril says "and she's not signing this piss-ant agreement."

"Please, Cyril," Terezie says, "it's okay, really. All I want is Sam's share of the farm. What's that, eighty thousand? That's right, isn't it, eighty thousand?" She glares at Kurt, who nods. "Then that would do it. I couldn't afford to pay you back yet, Cyril, and I hate that, but we could pay the bank's fee to keep the house and, please God, not have to file bankruptcy. We'd have just enough for surgery. Hand me the paper. Let's get this over with." When she reaches forward, her handbag topples to the floor.

Cyril grabs the document. "You're not going to sign this," he says. "It's an insult. Don't you see what they're doing? Sam's will is legal. I can prove it."

"But I don't want to have to—" She covers her face with her hands.

"That prostitute's signature makes it ironclad. No way a judge'll throw it out, especially if I can get her to testify." A shaft from the window creeps onto our feet.

"You're not actually planning to have that woman talk about Sam, are you?" Hugh says. Footsteps click in the hall. "I mean, that wouldn't be good, you know what I mean? I mean, Kurt?"

Terezie says to Cyril, "I don't have any choice."

"Stop and think. What about the credit cards? How're you paying them off? And you think Cornelia's not going to need medical care after surgery? Where's that coming from? You don't even have a job yet. A share of that Rockport house is legally yours. These guys know that; they're just greedy. Their own brother wanted you to have it, but they don't care. Typical. Remember how they treated Ma and Pa? Sam was the only one who was decent. You're not going to sign anything."

I picture Sam feeding his cottontail with an eyedropper, then sitting in his car pretending to be Johnny Cash.

"But we can't wait for a trial," Terezie says. "How long would something like that take?"

"About a year," Kurt says. "Because we'll contest that will. People do it all the time. Your brother knows that. We have a good chance of winning, too."

"Debbie and I talked about the surgery," Hugh says, "and we're willing—"

"Either you sign this agreement now," interrupts Kurt, "or we'll see you in court. Nothing else is on the table. We're willing to give you what you've asked for, and then you'd have what you need for the surgery. I think that's fair. What do you say?"

Hugh leans back, his top lip folding under. He hums "Amazing Grace," rolling his head side-to-side.

"Cyril's right. You don't care about us. You know we need help, and you're doctors. How do you live with yourselves? I'm glad Sam's not here to see this."

Or Dad, I think. "Hugh," I say, "you made a promise. Wouldn't you like to share your offer with Terezie?"

Hugh's fingers play imaginary keys on his legs. "That saved a wretch like me," he whispers, tapping.

I want to shake him, bully him into saying he'll help her.

"Kurt knows something about Sam," I blurt, "something that could have a bearing." My chest fills with incense someone's burning.

Our heads swivel toward Kurt. "You son of a bitch," he says. Then he smirks, chuckling.

"If you have any pertinent information," Cyril begins.

"I'd tell you," Kurt answers, "believe me. Look, contrary to my sister's opinion, I'm not a crook. Her accusation says more about her than me or Sam. Her so-called secret is actually a personal matter, the kind that really yanks her chain."

"What about your fistfight with Sam right before his accident," I say. "Go ahead; tell Terezie what you said."

The trickster snaps his switch, and *Xipe Totec*'s patio forms in the window's glare like a developing photograph. A conch trumpet wails. *Please. No.*

Kurt stares at Hugh. "Okay, so I'm an asshole," he says, and, thankfully, the image wavers, shimmers, faded, leaving what feels like an arrow lodged in my right eye socket. "But I'm not hiding anything," he says.

Cyril raises the document, and before passing it to Terezie, he tears it in half. Then he tears it again. "I'll pay for the surgery. But I expect to be paid back, and that means you have to agree to fight this. We're taking these bastards to court."

CHAPTER 11
1964

THIS ISN'T THE ONLY TIME my family has had a legal problem. We had two during my junior year in high school: the first was Sam's; the second, mine.

A month after my parents tried to give me advice about college, Sam was thrown into a Mexican jail. He'd gone back to Laredo with Mariana and Jaime Cardona for the weekend, and all I knew was what I'd overheard my mother whisper to my father a few days later in the downstairs hallway. "Thank God Mariana had enough foresight to call," she said. "Otherwise, Sam would still be in jail. I knew those children were trouble, especially her. What else would make Sam shove a policeman?" I didn't care about the Cardonas, only Sam's unexplained push. I was sure the guy had deserved it.

My parents' reaction fit a pattern that had begun to bother me—proof of my new maturity, I assured myself. My mother spent most of her time at the stove and the grocery. She drove to the beauty shop twice a week, same ten o'clock appointment, same back-combed chignon. Her neighborhood friends arrived for wine and gossip each afternoon at three then left each evening when my father walked in and gave her a kiss. He, on the other hand, went to work, played Saturday golf, taught his Bible class, and watched whatever sport event was on TV. Sundays, we ate at my grandparents' even though we didn't picnic at the farm anymore. Hugh and I could've checked our watches at any hour and named the location and activity of each parent, a phenomenon that was suddenly appalling to me.

They instructed us to adhere to prescribed routines, too. Deviation predicated disaster. No wonder a "service-oriented" profession was what they'd recommended; conventional opinion was their plumb line. I'd have to find my own way out of their prefabricated life.

Sam came home two weeks after his Laredo trip for a meal and the use of the washing machine. That afternoon, he brought me a mask. "What you think?" he asked, standing in the doorway.

A hanging bulb blazed over the closet shelves I'd been straightening, and when I turned, shadowy spots made me blink.

Wearing a checked shirt Albina had made, Sam leaned against the doorframe. Head tilted, one eye shut, he anticipated my reaction to his present. His standing there was gift enough. I hoped he'd tell me what happened at the jail and then describe Mexico, a place I wasn't allowed to visit. Were there really tequila bottles with worms in the bottoms and nightclubs where women danced naked, trumpets blaring? Did people eat barbecued goat and grow roses and carnations, the patches of red or yellow next to dirt and cactus, brown, then football fields of color? Would he please please take me?

"What we have us here," he said, pulling something toward his face, muffling his voice, "is an Aztec warrior mask." A tooth appeared at one of the holes; an eyelash fluttered. The image was a reversal: outside, Sam's spirit; inside, his body.

I bumped the clothes rack.

"Thought you might wear this to church."

I smiled, picturing myself in our second-row pew, sharing a hymnal with our grandmother, surrounded by neighbors pretending not to look.

He leaned the mask close. "Too bad they can't see the magic." His lips barely parted. "This is for somebody who's not afraid to look." He blew a gray bubble, chomped. "It must be for you."

Painted rosettes spread like a rash from low on the mask's forehead, getting larger and more detailed, finally circling the neck. Folded leather flaps formed the nose and ears, innocuous as a kitten's. The eyes were indentations with pinhole centers, the mouth a jagged slice, leather tongue hanging.

"Had a chance to read that Aztec book?"

Since I'd only been interested in Texas Indians, I'd stuck it on a bookshelf in the study. "Sure," I lied.

"They had a kind of club called Order of the Eagle and Jaguar Knights," he said. "The battlefield was a sacred place," he tapped the light bulb, sent it swinging "and if you died fighting," his eyes moved left then right, "you rode the sun across the sky then turned into a hummingbird."

The jaguar's nose and cheek felt curved, bony. I held the mask up; with my other hand, I caught the bulb. Light shone at the eyeholes, the mouth.

"Anyway," Sam said, shifting away from the door, turning, "I thought it was a good story."

Was he leaving? Already? "And what about you getting thrown in jail?"

"Who told you?"

"Mom said you pushed a policeman."

He pulled his wallet out of his back pocket. "What a shithole," he sang, laughing. He unfolded a newspaper clipping then pointed. "Look at this." The article was in Spanish, its headline, *"El Gringo Golpeo al Guardia."* A photo showed Sam in a cell, his left eye swollen, his mouth open, his arm reaching through the bars. "I almost killed that S.O.B. before his buddies jumped me."

Now I noticed the remnant of a bruise at his cheekbone. A Band-Aid at his hairline hid stitches. "What *really* happened?" I checked his cut, imagining sadists taking turns beating him. Maybe he'd insulted them, or defended somebody else. I'd heard Mexican police were crooked; now I understood what that meant.

"You should've heard the guy next to me. Screaming—it was that cold." He folded his arms, bent over, laughing. "So I started howling. He'd scream, I'd howl." He wiped his eyes. "I was a goddamn coyote. One of the best nights of my life."

Was he howling because he was mad or happy or scared, or what? And how was that funny? "You still haven't said *why* you got thrown in jail."

"I was on my way out after paying a hooker eight dollars, and this creep at the door says I owe him five more. No way I'm doing that." He spat a puff of air. "I didn't see *him* with us upstairs. It's a clear matter of principle."

"You were with a prostitute?" Where was Mariana? Did Terezie know?

"When Jaime told Mariana, she called Mom."

"Did Mom come to Mexico?" I didn't remember her being gone, but now I'd believe anything.

"Dad had to pay fifteen hundred dollars to get me out." He folded the article and slid it back into his wallet. "What a rip-off."

"Was he mad?"

"The great man of principle, and guess what he says?" He lifted his hand in a mock plea. "*Just once, couldn't you try to do what's right?*"

The term "Aztec" usually refers incorrectly to the founders of *Tenochtitlan*, now Mexico City; or it refers to one of several other possible definitions. *Aztecah* is a *Nahuatl* word that means "people from *Aztlan*," the mythological homeland in Northern Mexico from which several tribes migrated between the 12th and 13th centuries to south and central Mexico. The group split, and the members who moved into the Basin of Mexico named themselves *Mexihca*. In other contexts, "Aztec" includes inhabitants of *Tenochtitlan*'s principal allied city-states, the *Aculhuaque* of *Tetzcohco* and the *Tepanecah* of *Tlacōpan*. Other times, "Aztec" includes all city-states that shared the *Mexihcayōtl* language, history, culture. This definition was originated by the German explorer Alexander von Humboldt in 1810, but these "Aztecs" are now referred to as *Nahuah*. In 1843, William H. Prescott spread acceptance of Humboldt's definition, resulting in its use by 19th century Mexican scholars to distinguish modern Mexicans from pre-conquest Mexicans. Although "Aztec" is consistently misused or misunderstood, it's still common. As a high school student, my uneducated use of the term and misinterpretations of the culture were logical. But society's repeated misuse of these terms only illustrates history's continual evolution.

The mask's magic, though, didn't feel tied to one time or title.

Monday, I switched stations on my bedroom radio, alternating between sentimental blues crooned to three strummed chords and a band of joyfully ironic Brits hooting in minor keys. I did the frug while I sang "A Hard Day's Night." Sam's mask hung on my papered wall.

By Wednesday, shadowed patches showed through its openings. Lying on my bed, the fan ticking, the image of my gravy-covered hand against my mother's shoulder made me laugh. I remembered Sam wearing the jaguar face.

Once during his senior year, he'd stomped the car's brakes as we'd passed the vacant lot behind Phillips Food Mart on our way to school. "What?" I said as he jumped out, the door ajar. A group of boys shouted, one shoved, while some barked accusations at two others: Emil Kulhanek, a known bully, and Wade Nyank, a watchful boy who was sometimes spotted with Sam. Whacks thudded and twice Sam went down, but his concentrated expression never altered. Weepy, I called him, wondering if I should phone the police. After Wade turned, staring, he pulled Sam toward the car, and they got in. "Are we late?" Sam said, steering the Corvair away from the curb, rolling his sleeve to hide a tear at the elbow.

Sam slept with at least one prostitute, a revelation surprisingly inconsequential, but had he been with his girlfriend? Sure, a few of the girls I knew were having sex, but we didn't talk about it. I'd seen couples necking on *As the World Turns*, a show I watched furtively while eating lunch. Sam's hand would slide like a soap star's under Terezie's blouse, rubbing its way to her pursed nipple. He'd kiss her then, and maybe she'd touch him, pressing, as I had in our father's lab—did he remember?—against the bulge in his jeans. But Sam wouldn't push Terezie away. He'd probably moan like they did on TV, moving his mouth down her neck. "No," I said to myself, turning my back to the mask on the wall.

The next morning, I heard what sounded like someone speaking a foreign language, a looping of vowels with tongue-clicked endings, words I somehow thought I could translate. *Beat your breath. Be a cornstalk. Be possessed of eyes and ears.* I didn't know what it meant, and, worse, it manifested what I'd secretly feared: a parent-like god-spirit. I pulled my knees to my chest. Sam's eyes had fluttered behind the mask; his voice had been muffled: *for somebody not afraid to look.* I pictured his hands, kicked free of the sheets, walked to the dresser.

"Sarah," my mother called. "Breakfast."

I searched through drawers, in a chair's stack of clothes, in my phys ed bag for my favorite bra but couldn't find it. I yanked my blouse from its hanger, poked my arms through, buttoned. No one will notice, I thought. Why do we have to wear those things anyway? I pulled on a half-slip, brushed my hair.

"Sarah!" my mother called.

I wiggled into my skirt, ran down the stairs, breasts bobbing, then slid into my chair at the table. Not until I swirled a last bite of toast in egg yolk did I realize I'd forgotten to put on panties. I tightened my hem across my knees, then remembered being a girl, swimming, sometimes naked, in the farm creek. No one, especially me, had been bothered.

"Missy, Mama needs help with the dishes," my father said, nodding toward her at the sink.

"Sorry, can't today," I said, ducking. "Latin club meeting." I climbed two stairs at a time, thinking, *a nurse would never go without underwear.*

At school, I hugged my books or folded my arms as I pictured my nipples flopping. Later I forgot to hide myself, and by lunchtime, my blouse felt like a pajama top. I threw my shoulders back, ignoring glances. Wind puffed up my skirt, and I shivered, sweaty, a sensation that reappeared when I realized I wasn't embarrassed.

For my last class, tennis, I had to change into a gym suit. The girl I shared a locker room cubicle with belonged to an orthodox religion that outlawed makeup, boys, and knowledge about bodies. She stared, shocked by my total nakedness.

"Once in a while," I said, "girls have to let their breasts and vagina breathe." Her gullibility was irresistible. "If you don't, the natural bacteria will mutate into an infection that looks like mold. And it can spread. See?" I showed her a mole on my chest. "When I saw this, I knew it was time."

Frowning, she turned, unsnapped two buttons, and inspected herself. I hung my skirt and blouse on a hook, thinking maybe I would/ maybe I wouldn't tell her the truth when we changed clothes again at the end of the hour.

I wasn't part of the 2006 archeological team that discovered the twelve-ton, pinkish andesite monolith of *Tlāltecuhtli* near the ruins of the sacred pyramid known as Templo Mayor. Broken into four pieces, it squats to give birth while drinking its own blood, devouring its own creation, a symbol of death perpetuating life. But I was part of the team, led by Leonardo López Luján two summers later, that found a deep pit beside the monolith. When Leo and his assistant pulled off a stucco block in the plaza floor, we stepped back, startled. Twenty-one flint knives painted red—teeth and gums in the open mouth of *Tlāltecuhtli*, the earth god—positioned to receive the dead. Underneath, in a shaft eight feet deep, we uncovered a stone box. Leo allowed me to open it, but when I took off the lid, my gloved hands shook like an amateur's. I retrieved, avoiding all but the slightest pressure, the skeletons of two golden eagles, twenty-four knives wrapped in fur, and the remains of a dog or wolf wearing a collar of jade beads, turquoise ear plugs, and gold bells on its ankles. The objects had been arranged according to a certain logic, re-creating the *Mexihcayōtl* cosmos.

After dinner, I searched my father's shelves for Sam's Aztec book. The cover image, a marketplace, reminded me of Otis and his stories about Houston's years with the Cherokees in Arkansas. I'd told Sam that East Texas Comanche had once kidnapped a girl, Cynthia Ann Parker, and that when she was returned to white, germ-free order in Navasota twenty-four years later, she'd died of heartbreak. He gave me the book the next day, but I didn't understand how he'd gotten from Comanche to Aztecs, so I'd stuck it with my father's orthopedic journals, dog-eared copy of Thomas Merton's *Seven Storey Mountain*, and the *Bhagavad-Gita*.

I turned to a chapter titled "The Eagles and Jaguars." *Men*, it said, *earned knighthood by capturing four prisoners for ritualistic sacrifice. The knights kept concubines and drank* octli, *an alcoholic drink. They worshipped the warrior sun god with cannibalistic feasts.*

Archaeologists had discovered a life-sized pottery statue of a jaguar knight at the entrance of the order's private hall inside the Great Temple. A photograph covered two pages, its background black, the terra-cotta figure with detailed features. Crouched, the warrior bent his sinewy arms upward; his fingers curled, ready for battle. He wore the animal's speckled skin, complete with sticklike tail, his human feet magically attached at the ankles.

Reaching for a lamp switch, I glimpsed my father's desk topped with bills, pens and pencils in a jar, a copy of *The Journal of the American Medical Association.* My silhouette reflected from the glass-fronted bookshelves, superimposed over rows of colored bindings. I pulled off my socks and Weejuns, twisted the lamp knob.

The knight wore the jaguar's head like a helmet, the small ears pointed, the eyes black-rimmed, the whiskers jutting. Here was the marvel: Fanged jaws were unhinged, spread impossibly wide, the man's face protruding as though he were being swallowed. His lips parted; he frowned, his eyes wide, focused on some distant sound. Was he man or animal? Was the jaguar animal or man?

If I could, I'd slide my palm around his killing arm. Together we'd catch fish with our hands, tear white flesh, eat it raw, each slick morsel a gift from *Tlāloc*, the rain god. We'd drink *octli* and rub oil into each other's hair.

I carried the book to my room, took down the mask, set it next to the picture: same rosettes, same leather tongue. Pulling the jaguar face to my face, I looked in the mirror. The pin-sized eye holes worked like binoculars. I moved closer, crouched, raising my arms, curling my fingers. "Night hunter, maguey dust," I said.

Later, lying in my nightgown, breasts pressed against the mattress, fan cooling my legs, I read: *Eager to join the gods, some captives sprinted up the temple steps, then bent backward over the sacrificial stone so a priest could scoop out their still-beating hearts with an obsidian knife.*

Then Hugh walked in, his bare feet slapping the carpet. "Where is it?" he asked, glancing at the top of my dresser, my desk.

I couldn't believe he was almost a teenager.

"Sam told me," he said, his brows lifting, clownish, a kid again.

The mask lay next to me, and when I held it up, he ran over. "Oh, man." He tapped the nose and tongue then put it on. When I reached for it, he shoved my arm.

"Hey, be careful," I said as he strode around the room, the mask an obvious attachment, unable to transform someone so young. "Sometimes an Aztec wore a dead man's skin." I leaned on an elbow, wiggled my feet.

"Yeah, right." Hugh took off the mask and studied it, rubbing the eyes, peeking inside the ears.

"Really. Every spring they had a holiday, like Easter. They cut out prisoners' hearts, and then jaguar warriors wore the skins."

"Gross," he said, frowning. He sat on the bed. "How come?"

"It's their religion," I said, sitting, marking the page with my finger. I longed to show Hugh that he, like Sam and I, should be unafraid to look. "The first guy died for this god, *Xipe Totec*, and the second one wore the dead guy's skin to honor him."

Hugh positioned the mask over his face as he stepped to the mirror. "Can I have this? Please?" he said, hunching, pretending pain.

"Let's say it's ours together."

"Yeah!"

"But it stays in here."

That night, I dreamed a muscled boy lay across a bloody stone. The dream started with him whole, brawny one minute, then limp, mutilated the next, his eyes glazed, his mouth open. As a priest held up the heart, his cowl slipped back. Cuts surrounded his eyes; his mouth puckered, a mashup of teeth and skin. I saw myself—next to the body, across from the priest—dip fingers in a bowl, smear blood on my lips. Hands appeared then, rubbing, oiling me: slithery. As I grunted, pulling on the skin, I thought, Why don't men have to wear these? When I woke, I remembered the stench, the itching, the faint pressure of a daisy garland on my head.

ꓽ

Most of the weekend, I sat at my desk studying the book. Its cover was a picture of Diego Rivera's "Great City of *Tenochtitlan*": a marketplace of bodies draped in colored tunics, cloaks, some people tattooed, others wearing animal skulls or tusks hooked into their noses. One man in headdress held a silvery white arm hacked at the shoulder, the damaged joint, muscles and ligaments, marbled, purple. In back of the commotion, an archaeological detail of the ancient city spread to the mountains, its pyramids grand as castles, the layout an aerial view of a metropolis.

Monday night, I paced in circles next to the windows, my shoulders casting shadows across the pages:

> *Can it be true that one lives on earth?*
> *Not forever on earth; only a little while here.*
> *Be it jade, it shatters.*
> *Be it gold, it breaks.*
> *Be it a quetzal feather, it tears apart.*
> *Not forever on earth; only a little while here.*

My glance drifted to the ceiling. The people I knew thought of death as a clinical diagnosis, its fatal aspect signaling that the doctor's work was done. I pictured an Aztec funeral, the man's face painted white, his mantle covered in macaw feathers, his body surrounded by a gourd-and-stick rattle, a turkey, six frogs, a bowl of ant eggs. The image of him lying on a stone altar like the cadaver and half bust of a man in my father's anatomy lab. I remembered looking through the skylight, and, earlier, Sam saying that I should face everything, no matter how ugly. Maybe, if I focused on whatever made me uncomfortable, Sam would notice. Self-righteousness, naiveté, those were now sins. Sin, in fact, would become my specialty. Not the petty, dishonest kind, but the kind my parents seemed to fear most: impropriety.

My English teacher sent the class the next afternoon to the library to research the existentialist interpretation of *Hamlet*. Instead,

I found a book on Aztecs. I'd been looking for references to their women, and although I'd found descriptions of birth rituals and the moon goddess, who'd been overpowered by her sun god brother, such typical females were not what I was looking for. I was looking for, and found, *Tlahzolteōtl.*

Wearing a flayed skin, its hands hanging at her wrists, precious raw cotton on her headpiece, black painted on her nose and mouth, a man's head emerging from between her spread legs, *Tlahzolteōtl* was outrageous, beautiful. "The Goddess of Filth," a caption read, "both absolved sin and inspired it."

The bell rang, chairs scraped against linoleum, somebody whistled, another shouted, a few squealed, an elbow jabbed my shoulder. But I leaned closer to the photo, examining each feather, embroidery thread, the easy way the goddess squatted, the expression on that man in profile (broad nose, large, round eye) as he slid out, like some full-grown baby in headdress, from…? Was he coming out or going in? I touched the picture, wondering whether the extra hands had fingernails, then glanced up, seeing Harold Drumm standing at a shelf but staring at me. I noticed that my skirt was hiked when a breeze traveled up my legs. Moistness prickled, but I didn't move.

That image of *Tlahzolteōtl* is found on page thirteen in the Codex Borbonicus. She presides over the fourteenth day (*Ōcēlotl,* jaguar) thirteenth *trecena* (*Olin,* movement) of the sacred 260-day year and most likely originated as a *Huastec* goddess from the Gulf Coast. Some doubt that, from the Mesoamerican point of view, she inspired transgressive behavior. Still, noted scholars think she represents a male-dominated society's Freudian fear of femininity, becoming both life-giving and cruel, an instigator of depravity, even insanity, yet an administer of forgiveness. Before his death, Diego Rivera pleaded for her intervention. Patroness of adulterers and physicians, her most noticeable feature is the black on her mouth and chin, left from chewing bitumen, a byproduct of decomposed organic materials. *Tlahzolteōtl* is the Eater of Filth, the Eater of Sins.

After school the next day, I made a beeline for The Hair Boutique. I was tired of looking like a Pelton. As I stepped onto the shop's pine floor, a bell tinkled. Shampoos and rinses, permanents, electric curlers, brushes, and hair dye covered carpenter's racks. My mother had told me I was too young to frost my hair. I grabbed a bottle of peroxide, headed for the cash register.

Once home, I locked myself in the upstairs bathroom, punched holes with a screwdriver into a rubber bathing cap, put it on, coaxed hair clumps through the slits. I followed the bottle's directions, and when I took off the cap, my head was a rat with polka dots. What will I do? I thought as I looked in the mirror, about to cry. When I held up a strand, I remembered feathers like corn stalks in *Tlahzolteōtl*'s headdress. "Wait a minute," I said. The goddess wore cotton in her hair. "Nurses never bleach it white." The second time, I soaked my head, no bathing cap.

After a shower, I towel-dried, then leaned toward the mirror again: beady eyes, angular face, chalky hair. I fluffed the top. This new person was wild, possibly unbalanced—a pre-seventies punk, absent cachet.

"Is something wrong, sweetie?" my mother said, knocking. "Are you okay?"

"Yes, ma'am," I said, smoothing frizzle.

"Hurry up, then. Supper's ready."

I knew what Sam would do. "Hey, Good lookin'," he'd say and walk me to the kitchen.

Downstairs, I sat at my usual place next to Hugh. My father didn't notice, but when my mother turned to ask me to serve the plates, she froze, her face slack. "What is *that*?" The spoon in her fist shook. Who knew kids would soon body pierce, neon hair a given?

"What?" I said nervously. "Are you talking to me?" My fingers slid underneath my thighs.

Hugh leaned back, blinked.

"It's not permanent, you can wash it out?" my mother said,

lurching, shifting the spoon to her other hand. She pinched a strand. "It's some kind of game your friends cooked up?" Her face blanched; perspiration flecked her lip.

"Mama, I'm trying—"

"Peroxide. Owen, this child has ruined her hair." Her breaths jerked; she stumbled to the sink, fingers pressing her brow. She tossed the spoon, which bounced and clanged against the porcelain.

"You dyed it?" Hugh said, eyebrows raised.

Still facing the sink, my mother shook her head, shoved her palm at the air.

"I bleached it," I said. "It's no big deal, really."

"Your hair?" my father said. He lifted his hand, covered his mouth.

"I just wanted something different," I said. Maybe I was about to learn how Sam felt.

My mother turned, pointing. "A haircut, a new dress, *that's* different."

"Do you know what you look like?" my father asked in monotone.

My mother sat at the end of the table, next to me. "I could have helped you. There are ways to go about this, and bleaching your hair is not one of them. What you've done is just plain stupid."

I winced. "I didn't like it the other way, that's all." I stretched my arm toward her.

"Who talked you into it? Owen, I don't know if I can fix this." Her chin wrinkled, a rubbery patch.

"Won't anybody listen? I'm trying to tell you I had a reason." I clutched the table edge, closed my eyes. I remembered sitting together at our Rockport summerhouse. "This family's impossible," I said, but I wasn't sure. It was something Sam might've said.

I didn't hear the lecturing. My father's face contorted as he picked up his glass then set it down. My mother paced, throwing out her fist, shoving it at her waist, while Hugh scooted low in his chair, his eyes peering over the table like periscopes.

The next day at school, at a junior class assembly, I spotted Mary Jo LaFoille and Diane Kressbach sitting in the corner on the last row. Mary Jo slumped; Diane chewed a curl of her hair. We'd sometimes bumped shoulders in the hall and spent a friendly semester together in American History. I slid down the row, sat next to Mary Jo.

"Seat's taken," she said, digging in her purse, looking me over. "Nice do, but that ain't getting you into this club." Diane peered in my direction, her pageboy blanketing all but a snout-like nose and freckled mouth, as though she'd bent over and brushed her hair forward.

Mary Jo lived by herself, for all anyone knew. She was always with Diane, whose father owned a downtown gas station. Diane was a member of the honor society, but she never went to meetings. They played in the band—Mary Jo the drums, Diane the clarinet—because everybody had to take that or speech. They never appeared in organdy formals at the dances or at Service Club car washes, only at the Friday night football games, dressed in their blue-and-white uniforms with gold braid, talking, glancing distractedly at the field. Rumor had it they put their bodies first.

I kicked off my Weejuns, balanced my heels on the seatback, rubbed my thighs.

Mary Jo shifted her mannequin legs. Her figure rivaled Ann-Margret's, but her face didn't match, the nose puffed, veiny as a boxer's. That plainness canceled itself out, leaving the effect of that body, its implications.

"Ain't she cute," Mary Jo said to Diane, who leaned, poking her cheek with an index finger. "Miss Josephine College, over here with her white hair, slumming."

Like Sam, who'd befriended Jaime and Mariana at least in part to needle my mother, I wanted someone like Mary Jo. She had good cause to be suspicious. "Look, if I make you nervous, fine." I hoped curiosity would convince her to overlook my good-girl image. "But if you're game, my car's outside."

Mary Jo scratched her arm, worked her tongue at the side of her mouth. She turned to Diane, the gawky sidekick. "What do you say, Graceful? What we got to lose?"

"Mary Jo, I can't miss anymore class. My dad'll kill me."

Mary Jo stood, facing me. "Okay, genius, lead the way."

Diane's knees bumped the seatback as she brought her feet down with a thud. She grabbed Mary Jo's purse, followed.

While I coasted past the old Avalon Theater, now the First National Bank, Mary Jo stopped two soldiers from Fort Payne, the nearby Army base. "Y'all are cute," she teased, leaning out the window. Diane dipped her head; I smoothed my cotton hair.

"What about a ride?" one asked, his khakis like pressed copper.

"Sure," Mary Jo said. "Hop in." They slid into the back with Diane, who hugged the door, her mouth an open pocket.

The USO was only a few blocks away. Inside, men ate sandwiches and played cards. As Roy Orbison crooned "Blue Bayou" from a jukebox, a couple danced, their foreheads touching, their pressed bodies barely swaying.

Walter, from Nebraska, hated the heat. "Pardon my French, but it's like fucking Arabia down here," he said, wiping his shaved head.

I covered my surprise by looking out the storefront window, seeing street, an occasional car.

"How do you stand it?" he said.

Pulling over an extra chair, we squeezed around a small table. The shy one, Tyrone, brought sandwiches on a tray from the buffet next to a wall. He had the longest eyelashes I'd ever seen, and when he smiled at Diane, she fidgeted, crossing her arms. She grabbed a pimento cheese on white, bit, chewed, swallowed.

Is he flirting? I wondered. Our high school was still segregated, so I'd never sat with a black boy before, but maybe Diane had. A guy at the other table turned, glared. Tyrone stared at his hands in his lap. He frowned at Walter, who smiled.

"How long you been at Fort Payne?" Mary Jo asked, leaning on her elbows. She tilted her face toward Walter, her veiny nose mesmerizing.

"Six weeks," Walter said. "Might as well've been six months." His glance dropped below her chin then lifted again. "But we hadn't met nobody before now."

When "The Days of Wine and Roses" started playing on the

jukebox, Diane moaned, "I love that song."

"Me, too," Mary Jo said, pulling Walter toward the dance space. They rocked together then twirled. Walter said something; they laughed.

Diane glanced at Tyrone, who looked toward the table of men. I'd never seen an interracial couple, and even though the idea bothered some people, I wanted to watch one now. "Diane, why don't y'all dance?" I finally asked.

Diane shook her head, her face hidden in ringlets.

Since I'd always heard that Diane, like Mary Jo, enjoyed men, I wondered if she'd refused because Tyrone was black. "Then Tyrone," I blurted, "will you dance with me?" I held out my hand.

"Please, ma'am," Tyrone said, scowling, "you know I can't do that." He stood. "I'm sure you're a nice person," his jaw flexed, "but I won't be somebody's joke." His shiny shoes clicked across the floor, then out the door.

On our way to Dusty's drive-in, Mary Jo laughed when I told her what had happened. "But why did he think I set him up?" I asked.

"You acted like he's from outer space. Besides, what in hell did you expect?" She slapped her forehead. "Don't you know what those other guys would've done?" She rolled her eyes.

"How come he sat with us then?"

"'Cause Walter made him."

I ordered three lime Cokes and two fries. I couldn't explain that Tyrone's accusation had made me think of my mother's theatrics about Otis, and that Mary Jo was right: I had seen Tyrone as somehow different. "Why didn't you stay with Walter?" I asked Mary Jo.

"Didn't feel like it." She craned toward the dashboard, checking cars several rows away. "Soldiers are all over you."

"What do you mean?" I knew I sounded stupid.

"God, another virgin!" Mary Jo said, disgusted. "I thought Diane was the only one."

Diane shrugged.

So Diane *had* been too shy to dance with Tyrone. "But you've done it?" I asked Mary Jo, feeling like a gawking neophyte.

"I been balled," Mary Jo sprawled against the door, "twice."

"What'd it feel like?" I said, unable to stop myself.

Two weeks later, I told them it was my turn. Mary Jo had taught me how to tease, so I'd let Harold Drumm rub my breasts, stroke down *there* until, huffing, he'd reached to unbuckle his pants. "I can't," I'd whined. "I really want to, but it's just not right." His whack at the steering wheel had been my favorite part. When he walked away, the bulge in his jeans had been a testimonial. My interest, though, had recently shifted toward Antonio Mendoza, a somber boy with dark, unflinching eyes.

That weekend was communion Sunday. Over the choir loft hung a Christ figure in a loincloth, limp, bleeding, nailed to a wooden cross. I fingered the silver cross I wore on a chain and recited the Lord's Prayer by rote. This man, the son of God, had allowed himself to be arrested, beaten, crucified so I could get into heaven. At least, that's what I'd been taught.

Twelve hundred years after Jesus' death, Aztec captives had sprawled backward over a waist-high sacrificial stone. A nearby clay vessel had held still-beating hearts, that energy moving sun across sky. Gore, sacrifice to assure life. The gods had entered their statues like Christ's Holy Ghost. Were the similarities between Baptist doctrine and Aztec theology coincidental?

Aztecs believed souls of the drowned went to a separate part of paradise. In return, the rain god required blood and tears, so they built a special chamber for him. When archaeologists uncovered it three hundred years later, they found children's skulls, ribs, limb bones.

Sam had sacrificed a creature, its intestinal sac, instead of a heart, held toward the sky.

Maybe, I thought, adventure brought knowledge. Sam, who'd

recently watched the Saturn space launch, would say risks cause change. Extremes alter the future. Before he moved to Austin, he'd quoted something about becoming indispensable by being faithful to your true self. I hated my parents' prefabricated life. *Tlahzolteōtl* was supposed to inspire sin. My friends would help me coax the goddess into doing her magic.

Mary Jo, Diane, and I were in my car, watching *Hud* at the drive-in. "You don't care about people," Hud's father said after Hud and his nephew staggered home drunk. "You don't value nothing." The old man's voice was calm as he stared at his son. "You live just for yourself, and that makes you not fit to live with."

I'm the one Dad ought to worry about, I thought. The movie was almost over. I had to work fast.

"I thought of something to do," I said, turning, draping my arm across the seat back. "This is different. Big." They had to come. It had to be like church.

Mary Jo scowled, squinted toward the screen.

"Yeah, what?" asked Diane, giddy at the hint of trouble.

"A ceremony for Tlazoltit," I said. Mary Jo had thought of the nickname. "For inspiration. Then I'll have sex with Antonio."

"How stupid," Mary Jo said, wrinkling her lumpy nose. She pursed her lips, snooty. "Oh, yeah, and let's have a parade too." She groaned. "You're pathetic. Just go fuck the guy."

Diane stroked a curl, wrapped it around a finger.

"Mary Jo, *you're* stupid," I said. I turned toward Diane. "I'm a little nervous—okay?—and this'll help." I slapped the seat back. "I'll pick you up at nine tomorrow night. Bring your flashlight and a Bible."

"Yeah, all right," said Diane, leaning forward, hugging herself. "But we can't get hurt or anything...?"

"No, Diane," Mary Jo said, exasperated. "She's talking Girl Scouts. Sunday school."

"Come on," I coaxed Mary Jo. "She protected prostitutes."

"Aztec Chicken Ranch," Mary Jo sneered.

Diane laughed, spewing Coke.

"If you come, I promise you won't be sorry," I said.

"But nothing scary," Diane said. "No sacrifices or anything."

"Forever the wimp," Mary Jo said, shaking her cup of ice.

Hud came through a banging screen door, shouting, "This world is so full of crap, a man's going to get into it sooner or later whether he's careful or not."

I knew I was supposed to like the nephew, but Hud was visionary. Indispensable.

"Fun," I said, thumping Diane's head. "I promise."

Each school day, I'd driven past the train station with its arches and stained glass window. A steam engine stayed parked on a side track visible from the street. A group of women had rallied the community to "save a piece of Nugent history," so the engine had been restored, visited by elementary schoolchildren and the occasional tourist.

While stepping over the tracks on Sunday, I remembered something I'd seen a week after I'd hidden my grandfather's money clip inside a pyramid of stones. A man had leaned against the rail of a caboose as it clicked over the trestle, away from the farm. When his white shirt merged with sky, a cow had meandered toward the barn.

Now, standing inside the steam engine, I ran my hands over the metal levers, knobs, figuring people cleared the area at night. Somebody could stoke the furnace for light and ceremonial effect.

I drove to a store owned by Mariana and Jaime Cardonas' parents and bought mescal, a clear *octli*-like drink distilled from maguey leaves. When I set two bottles on the counter, they said Sam had recently been by to celebrate Jaime's birthday. I pretended he'd also come to our house, and then I got busy trying not to wonder why he hadn't. Three hours later, Mary Jo, Diane, and I each drank a Styrofoam cupful, the liquor stinging our throats while we drove to the station.

Three lights banked the main tracks, with none near the engine. Even in shadow, its giant wheels, bolts, towering sides seemed Herculean, cabalistic. I imagined it rumbling past, its mountainous metal frame crushing everything.

I'd loaded the car trunk with firewood. We each carried an armload as we crossed the tracks: me first, also holding a flashlight and lighter fluid, Diane last, clutching her monogrammed Bible. A stepladder boosted us into the engineer's compartment where we threw our firewood into the furnace.

"This is fuckin' stupid," Mary Jo said, slapping dust from her shorts. "I can't believe you talked us into this." She checked her arms for scratches.

"This'll help," I said, pulling the second bottle of mescal from behind two pedals in front, near the corner.

Mary Jo sat cross-legged on the steel flooring, facing the furnace, the dash of dials and levers her backdrop. She swigged a gulp. "Okay, now what?" she said, passing the bottle to Diane.

Our bodies almost filled the cramped cubicle. Was this how my brothers felt while they chopped cotton together? "I need to light the fiery pit, of course," I said, squirting logs with lighter fluid, adding twigs, newspaper. I lit two grocery sacks with my Zippo, threw them into the furnace. Flames and heat shot out. I slammed the steel plated door shut.

"Shit, we're going to cook," Mary Jo said, waving her hand in front of her face.

"It is hot," I said, unbuttoning my blouse, dropping it on the floor. I unhooked my bra, even though I hadn't planned to. Had *Tlahzolteōtl* made me do it? Diane blushed, hugging her legs. Mary Jo happily removed her top and bra, then baited Diane until she, giggling and covering her face, did the same. We leaned against our knees, pretending we weren't hiding our chests. While they jabbered, I gathered our camisole, blouses, bras, used one as a glove when I unlatched the steel plate, and, picturing Antonio's sinewy arms, threw everything into the blaze. The flames lapped teases of light over my friends' lurching bodies. Diane said, "No!" Something popped, logs shifted, rumbling, and sparks snapped.

"Hey," Mary Jo said, pushing my shoulder. I stumbled backward, my breasts bobbing, and Mary Jo blinked then pointed, laughing.

"Titties," she spread her arms, "in the temple of Tlazoltit." She cupped her own, shook them at Diane.

Whimpering, Diane covered her mouth. Her snivels turned to cackles then she copied Mary Jo. "Tlazoltit," she said, aiming her peewee breasts at me.

"*Tlahzolteōtl*," I corrected, scared and half-naked, lost in metal, flames. "We're beautiful," I said, thinking, *Yes, this is who I am.* When I poured mescal on their heads, saying, "I anoint you," they laughed and lapped the spill-off.

Diane licked Mary Jo's cheek. "Gross, keep away," Mary Jo said, bumping her head on a gearshift.

"Where's your Bible?" I asked Diane. After she pulled it from underneath her leg, I turned to Psalm 100. "Make a joyful noise unto *Tlahzolteōtl*, all ye lands."

Mary Jo howled; Diane joined in.

"Serve the goddess with gladness. Come before her presence with singing."

"*Tlahzolteōtl* loves me, this I know," Mary Jo warbled.

"For Mary Jo tells me so," sang Diane.

"Enter into her gates with thanksgiving and into her courts with praise. Be thankful unto her, and bless her name."

Another thump of logs, a burst of sparks.

I turned to Ecclesiastes, where I'd pieced verses together, knowing I could make the Bible mean anything. "There is one event to the righteous and to the wicked; to the good and to the clean, and to the unclean. The heart of the sons of men is full of evil, and madness is in their heart while they live, and after that they go to the dead."

I pressed the book to my bare chest and reached toward a corner of the dashboard for another sack. As I peeled cellophane off a calf's heart, Diane's hand went to her mouth. "Eeeew," she squealed. I held up the heart, and Mary Jo frowned, rolling her eyes.

"Go thy way," I read, "eat thy bread with joy and drink thy wine with delight, for *Tlahzolteōtl* now accepteth thy works." I closed the book, shoved the Styrofoam tray at Mary Jo. A steam engine shaped like a woman, three half-naked girls, a Phillips Food Mart calf's heart:

no blood sacrifice, but close as I'd get.

Mary Jo's eyes widened; she cocked a fist at her hip. "You're crazy," she said as flames popped, fizzed.

Blood dribbled onto my wrist. I dabbed, coating my finger, then smeared my mouth, my chin. Did I look like the goddess? Would her spirit, like the Holy Ghost, move inside me?

Diane gaped, her expression a gargoyle's face.

"Unbelievable," Mary Jo said, pulling her hair back. She shoved her fingers into her back pockets, forcing her chest forward.

I imagined mine pressed against Antonio, his skin rubbing, our movements synchronized, rhythmic, his breath on my neck. Then I dipped into the blood, this time aiming for Mary Jo's nipple.

"Damn!" she said, knocking my hand. She grabbed the calf's heart. "Get back!" She tossed it, a red lump on its flimsy saucer, into the pit.

We leaned toward the furnace. Our flesh grew sticky, familiar, while the meat sizzled and smoldered, smelling of barbecue, turning crisp. Metal plates, knobs, and rims flickered, a room of mirrors, as a whistling rumbled, surrounding us.

When the furnace exploded, none of us died. Flames filled the compartment and knocked us backward off the train; smoke spiraled upward into the night.

From gravel several yards away, Diane whimpered. The fire now burned inside my ankle. Bones, I realized with relief, thinking of my father. I crossed my arms over my chest and rolled to the side, wanting to cry. Instead, I limped toward the voice.

Diane was alive, sitting sprawled between the tracks, her curls caked, matted. A gash ran from her scalp to her eye, the skin folded back, exposing raw underside. Welts, where skin had shaved off, covered her body, but nothing looked broken. I swallowed, tasted blood. "What happened?" she said as though I'd planned the explosion. "It's like we...I guess we made her mad." She hiccupped, wiped dirt from her knee.

"Where's Mary Jo?" I asked, and Diane wailed, fingering her

bloody head. I grabbed her shoulder. "Help me find Mary Jo."

She tapped her cheek then noticed her uncovered breasts. When she fell chest forward, searching the station and street, I knew she was looking for her father. I hobbled across the tracks, calling Mary Jo, firelight guiding me.

Mary Jo lay in weeds beside the tracks, arms oddly twisted, perfect breasts exposed, legs ironically bent into a *Tlahzolteōtl* crouch. My hands moved from her neck to her mouth, checking for breathing; I hated myself for not knowing what to do. Her still, naked body reminded me of the anatomy lab cadaver, and I thought, *She needs a nurse.* My father had called them indispensable, the same word Sam had used when he told me to face my true self. Now I wondered who that person could be. Mary Jo's chest rose, but her eyes glared. "I'm sorry," I whispered, choking, wondering if I should drag her to the station platform. Instead, I leaned, protecting her from view.

Smoke floated above us. The engine smoldered, its iron side gutted, misshapen, its compartment squashed, sheets of steel flapping inside flames. I'd tried to do what Sam said, and now look.

Before we had anything to cover us, people gathered on the station platform to watch firemen douse the flames. When he faced me, Antonio Mendoza tipped back on boot heels, his finger raised, pointing.

Two emergency aids rushed over, but I insisted that Mary Jo and Diane be treated first. I raised the collar of my borrowed coat and sat, leaning against a light post. Later, a technician strapped a temporary cast on my leg. As he propped my foot on an empty packing box, two uniformed men stepped forward.

"Miss Sarah Pelton?" one said.

"Yes."

"Would you come with us, please?"

I hobbled to their car with its flashing light, then sat in back behind a wire screen, throbs searing my ankle. I remembered that Sam had shoved a Laredo policeman and found myself thinking how stupid that had been.

"This won't take long, Miss Pelton," the driver said, pulling onto the street. When he lowered his chin, a fleshy pouch framed his jaw.

The other, younger man had a receding hairline; comb tracks exposed more strips of scalp. My view of his mouth fit between the screen's rungs. "You and your friends had some big party," he said. "Are y'all lesbos?" Static crackled from a dashboard box, its microphone dangling like a toy.

"Let the lady relax," the driver said, his profile a mug shot. "Downtown says go easy on this one." His partner's face materialized, crisscrossed by wires, then turned back toward the street.

Gusts from the front windows whapped my face, ears. The seat covers smelled of unwashed bodies, of "altercations," of coffee, salt, grease. I thought of my room at home: its desk with a secret compartment where I kept a note from Mary Jo; its bed with a mattress molded to fit my shoulders, spine; its second-floor windows framing views of neighbors in their backyard. Shivering, I bent over, shifted my legs, but I couldn't stop shaking.

"Have you talked to my parents?" I asked.

The radio barked, "Five-twenty-one in progress, Sixth and McAllister." The officers exchanged comments, oblivious. Static rattled, then again clicked off.

I pictured my father holding the phone, being told about the explosion. He'd frown, and then his eyes would widen, not out of anger, but fear. His disappointment would come once he and Mother knew I was safe. Then I'd be like Moses, who made that one unforgivable mistake. "It was my fault," I said.

"Yeah?" the young cop said, turning, wire framing his parted lips.

The driver nodded, "Won't be long we'll be at the station. We'll take your statement there."

Neither man touched me as we walked into the building, but the creaking leather felt like a pistol at my back. "I made my friends do it," I said, suddenly weepy. I hoped taking the blame would somehow ease my guilt. Jesus rode into Jerusalem on palm leaves knowing what He faced. Aztec warriors climbed hundreds of steps to bend backward over the sacrificial stone. Sam fought gangs with no chance of winning when someone needed help. My father had bowed his head when Mr. Gueldner, his patient, placed coffeecake in his hands. "I'm ready," I said, praying that jail was one of Sam's experiences I'd somehow escape.

My parents brought the district attorney Blair Corcoran, a neighbor and long-time friend, with them to the police station. My mother, her face oily, flushed, came through the door first, huffing, checking the room. She glanced at me sitting on a chair in back, then approached a slab-jawed woman in uniform, who sat at a desk by the door. "Someone tell me what's going on," she said. My father and Blair appeared. "Pelton," my mother insisted, tapping a stack of forms.

"Yes, ma'am," the woman said, swinging her chair to the other end of the desk, "your daughter's been charged with destruction of public property." She pointed to a chair as she picked up the phone. "Take a seat."

"But what does that *mean*?" My mother stiffened, her floral handbag squashed against her chest.

The woman mumbled into the receiver, then hung up and opened a desk drawer. "Restitution and a fine, possible jail time," she said, pulling out a piece of paper. She began to write. "Would you sit down, please?"

"Blair," my mother said. "What's going on?" Behind a counter, another phone rang. A shadow flitted past. Someone laughed.

My father stood nearby. He stroked his tie, buttoned and unbuttoned his suit jacket. "Mama?" he said, his expression like the engine's metal: hard yet broken.

My mother walked over, slid her arm under his, then patted. "Blair's going to explain," she said. "Sarah's all right, see?" She nodded. "Right, sweetie?" Immediately, he approached.

"I'm okay, really," I said as he checked my eyes, my cheek, head, neck. Removing the temporary cast, he pressed and turned my swollen leg. If a limb could have a migraine, mine had one, the nerves electrified, merciless. A throbbing shot to my groin, almost making me faint. "Oh," I moaned, clamping my teeth.

He re-wrapped everything, tightening the straps. "I don't want you to worry," he said, his eyes watery. "Your mother and I are here to help." He straightened, his back rigid as ever, then rested his hand on my shoulder. "Now, try to relax. I'll take care of your ankle as soon as we're finished here." Then he walked to Mother, who stood, hand on hip, talking to Blair. "Is there any way," my father said, "to pay for the damage, whatever those charges come to, and not have to put her through anything else? This, of course, was a terrible accident. Sarah's always been a good girl. You know that."

Blair looked at the linoleum then slipped his hands into his slacks pockets.

"I apologize for putting you in this position," my father continued, "but I don't know what else to do. Certainly, we want to do whatever you decide is right."

Mumbled shouting came from the entrance. An officer wrestled a stumbling soldier across the room and into a large cage in the corner. "I want a phone," the soldier wailed, his words wobbly as a loose wheel. "I know my rights."

The officer strode to the counter. "Call the M.P.s," he said, leaning close to the glass. "Tell them to come pick this guy up." Then he tugged at his waistband, repositioning his pants, turned, and left.

Blair looked at my father. "Let me make a couple of calls," he said. Suddenly he stood next to a phone on the slab-jawed woman's desk. Putting on his reading glasses, he watched while she helped him find a number; then he dialed. Following the usual courtesies and a summary of what had happened, he said, "So you don't have any problem with a fine for damages and some community service? We don't want to step on your toes, here." He listened; we waited.

"I'll call him now," Blair said into the receiver, plugging his other ear. "I appreciate your cooperation, Willie." He hung up, adjusted his eyeglasses, and checked on a second number. Again he dialed and relayed a summary of events. "The sheriff says as long as you go along, he's agreeable." After a pause, he added, "Then I'll go ahead and make the plea bargain for you to approve in the morning. Thank you, Judge." Nodding at my father, Blair asked the woman to prepare a personal recognizance bond. Afterward, he turned to my parents. "You can take her home in a few minutes," he said.

"Blair," my father said, reaching for a handshake, "I don't know how—"

"But what about her record?" my mother snapped. "She can't have a record. She's just a girl. Can't you—"

"Nothing will appear on her record," Blair said, dropping my father's hand.

"Mama…" my father said, almost touching her shoulder.

"But," Blair explained, "she'll have to come to court Monday morning."

"Court?" my mother whined. "You said that—"

I stood. "Daddy, I'm so sorry. I was trying to—"

"Sit down," my mother said, dropping her purse on the woman's desk, toppling a cup.

I did as I was told, relieved. Tell me when it's over, I thought. My mother's sharp voice had an oddly relaxing effect.

My mother followed in her station wagon as my father drove us in my Corvair to the hospital so he could set my ankle. He helped me hobble to the back entrance then pushed me in a wheelchair to his examination room, my mother walking alongside. After seating me on a table, he swiveled his chair between a bowl of plaster on a metal tray and my leg. He squinted; his jaw locked. His strokes and taps made me weepy. I couldn't remember if he'd touched me since we'd squeezed together on a saddle at the farm.

"What has gotten into you?" my mother said, pacing. "First your hair, now this." Her nylons swished with each step. She coughed, then turned, lip trembling. "You could've been killed."

I was as baffled as she was. The fact that I'd reasoned myself into trouble made me numb. I'd had fun with my friends—yes, was that so terrible?—had felt the presence of something—I knew I did—and look where that got me. Now, my sweet, ridiculous parents seemed right. Was I the only one confused? I remembered my face in the reception room mirror: cut, swollen, like the priest's in my dream. "What now?" I said.

"A man is what the winds and tides have made him," my father said, wrapping my leg with plaster covered gauze. "Circumstances form the character."

"Owen," my mother said, pressing her forehead, sinking into a chair.

"Sir?" I said, afraid not to respond. More than ever, I wanted to understand what he was thinking. I hoped he'd keep talking until I did.

"If you were a jury member hearing this case," my father said as he layered the dressing, his ritual creating a firm support, the result clean, reliable, "how would you judge the situation?"

That's when I cried, sobs that shook until my parents helped me lie back, a prostrate offering.

I decided to go with my father and Hugh the next morning to church. Even though people would stare, I could listen to music, think. The familiar rituals, ecclesiastical stained glass, assurance of a loving God, and compassionate crowd were the comforts I needed most. First, though, I had to find out about Mary Jo and Diane.

"That goddess of yours knows how to throw one hell of a tantrum," Mary Jo said into her hospital phone. She'll be fine, I thought. Diane said, "I'm grounded till the year 2000." Good-bye, I'm sorry, I thought.

Dressed, my head in a scarf, I took the mask off the wall. I fingered the earflaps, tongue. When I remembered the looped, clicking voice, I covered its mouth with my hand. I needed a clear definition of Sam's idea of truth, a description of who he thought I was.

"What happened to your face?" Hugh asked, sliding his socked feet across my floor. His shirt, a hand-me-down, stopped at his belly button.

"Nothing," I shrugged. Dad had stitched a cut on my chin. "I'll be all right."

"Is that a cast?" he said, trotting over, rubbing the plaster. "Can I touch it?"

"I guess so, sure."

You in trouble?"

"Not any more." I put the mask in a cabinet underneath my bookshelves.

"What'd you do *that* for?"

"What?"

"The mask. How come you took it down?" He picked a pen off my desk, threw it into the air, caught it. "If you don't want it," he said, stepping forward, "can I have it?" He clasped his hands in a mock plea. "Please? Come on, Sar, do this one thing."

I remembered telling him about ritual sacrifice; I'd thought I was saving him. "I can't," I said.

"Crud," Hugh said, wilting.

"Wait," I said, forcing him to face me. "Something happened last night."

His eyebrows arched.

"Trust me, Hugh. You don't want that mask."

Be a cornstalk. Beat your breath.

That afternoon, while I lay on my bed surrounded by homework, Sam appeared. "What are *you* doing here?" I asked. He wore a t-shirt and faded Levi's, the row of copper rivets like antique coins. Now, I thought, I'll get him to explain what he meant when he said I shouldn't be afraid to look, that I should become my true self.

He walked around the bed, leaned against my dresser, aiming his glance. "I came to thank you," he said.

"For what?" I propped myself higher.

"For taking the heat off." He started to smile but stopped. "Mom and Dad must be royally pissed."

"They're mad all right," I said shoving books, thumping, onto the floor.

"Yeah, what you did was stupid. For once, I actually agree with them." He crossed to the bed. "You okay?" He leaned, checking my leg, stitched chin.

"How'd you find out?"

"Who *doesn't* know?" He laughed, walking back to the door.

Was he leaving already? Why did he always do that? "How come you're here?"

He looked at his feet, his thumbs in his front pockets. Dad coughed in the next room, waking from his Sunday nap. "You ever seen Caley Creek?"

I shrugged, confused as usual, waiting.

"Can you ride in a car?"

When I reluctantly agreed to go, he drove to the Holiday Inn on the main highway, singing along with Bob Dylan and the Beatles on the radio. "Sam?" I said as he parked next to a pickup at the end of the motel lot. A woman wheeled a cart of supplies to a room, knocked, then disappeared inside.

"Creek's in back," he said, helping me out. If we'd stayed at home, we could've talked.

Sure enough, the creek meandered across the vacant lot behind the building's wings of rooms. With three-foot banks and a foot of water, it was more like a ditch. Weeds, Johnson grass, and rogue cedars dotted its edge. Behind the open acreage, a chain-link fence bordered Nugent's tiny airport. Sam helped me walk to a marble slab near the creek. Attached was a metal plaque that read:

CALEY CREEK BATTLEFIELD
Named in Honor Of
CAPTAIN HOGARTH CALEY
Who Lost His Life Here
May 26, 1839
With Only 34 Texas Rangers
He Met 240 Indians At This Point,
And Routed Them.

"I never knew this was here," I said. "Not much to look at, is it?"

"A mile up is a cave and 32 Bluffs."

"What's that?"

"Jaime, Wade, and me used to climb the bluffs, exactly thirty-two. So that's what we called it." He picked up a rock then turned it, chips sparkling. "Once when he was near the top, Wade put his hand out and there was a rattlesnake." He threw the rock. "When he fell, his ear almost got cut off."

"Gross," I said, picturing a hole in the side of Wade's head. "He doesn't have an ear?"

"It was hanging. The doctor sewed it back on." Sam looked up. "But you've been to the bluffs before. We caught that crawdad with string and bacon, remember?"

I nodded, feeling its pinchers, the pressure of the jumping after he'd placed it in my hands. "Did you ever go inside the cave?"

"We tried, but somebody would've had to dig a bigger tunnel."

"Did you take a flashlight? Could you see inside?"

"Sure."

"What?"

"Springs must've been in there." A car started; a plane rumbled overhead. "It was dark, damp. Smelled like mildew."

How could I not have heard what happened here? "What tribes?"

"You mean in the battle? Caddoes, Kickapoo, Comanche. Their leader, Chief Buffalo Hump, got his head stuck on a pole somewhere out there."

I reread the plaque. "'Routed them.' What does that mean?"

"I wonder," he said, refusing to tell. But I thought I knew.

"I was trying to do what you told me," I said, not looking at him, but hoping he'd say where he thought I'd made my mistake. If the best night of his life was when he'd gotten beaten up in a freezing Mexican jail, our little ceremony couldn't be so bad. Then again, Mary Jo and Diane were in the hospital, and I could have gone to jail. "Sam?" He squatted next to the water, rolling a branch down the bank. "Sam?" I called. He turned then walked me back to the car before I could say anything else.

On the drive home, I tried again. "When you told me not to be afraid to look, what was it I was supposed to see?" I refused to give up 'til I got an answer.

"Did I say that?" He slapped the side of the car in time to the radio's "I can't get no, sa-tis-fac-tion."

"When you gave me the mask." He'd imitated an animal that, in turn, disguised him. "You told me to be my true self, remember?" As usual, he wasn't going to make this easy.

"No. But sounds right. Absolutely," he said, bouncing his head to the music's rhythms.

"What does it mean?" I said, clutching the armrest. What if I never found out where I belonged? "Are you saying it's a good thing to get in trouble? Mom said she thought life was hard enough, even if I was careful. Are you saying she's wrong?"

"What do *you* think?" he said, drumming the steering wheel. "I try, and I try, and I try," he sang. He quit drumming, blinked. "Did I ever say you shouldn't be happy?" He turned down the radio. "I don't think so."

"It seems like whenever you see everybody going one way, you notice what's wrong with that and go the opposite. If you're always watching for what's ugly, doesn't that make you sad? How do you know, when you think something's ugly, that you're right?"

Sam snapped off the radio, stared. "I'm listening." His fist made loops in the air. "Keep going."

"You said being in that jail after getting beaten up was great, but it sounds awful. Screwing around with my friends in that engine was fun, but it sure got us in trouble. I see ugly stuff: people hurting other people, animals, kids—terrible—but I can't stop any of it."

Sam stared at the road and nodded. "'Routed,'" he said. "To defeat, demoralize, conquer. To massacre. Thirty-four against two hundred forty. Impressive, don't you think?"

In court Monday morning in front of my parents and other waiting defendants, a man announced my name and a case number. My father and Blair helped me hobble on crutches to the front bench, its mahogany bulk an altar. The judge checked his notes; then, in a smoker's rasp, he rattled off my charges. He asked whether I was guilty, and the rest happened like Blair had said it would. "We've entered a plea bargain, your honor," he said.

"What do you plead then, Miss Pelton?" the judge rumbled. An inky hyphen smudged his cheek.

"No contest, sir," I said.

Blair explained that the city park manager had estimated the damages at fifteen hundred dollars. Any excess my father would also pay. I'd work eighty hours assisting city staff during children's park programs. I didn't add that I'd probably work five times that.

Never again would I see my father's broken expression. Trouble: a mirage, a curse. Here it was—wavy, soft; there it went—slinking. Gone. Its only remnant, the memory of my one mistake. Like Moses, I was ready to pay for that.

As Blair thanked the judge and I hobbled out of the courtroom with my parents, the fact that my fine was the same amount as the bribe my father had paid to get Sam out of jail seemed more than a coincidence.

Chapter 12

By Cornelia's next visit, I've quit checking for a scar on her lip or marveling at the mother/daughter resemblance. I try not to notice how pale she's become or how much slower she moves. She's been turned down a notch.

"Knock, knock," she says, walking in. "You're under arrest. Stop that," she says pointing to my computer, "and follow me."

"Excuse me?" I say, trying not to smile.

She grabs my arm, lifting me from my chair. "All work and no play makes the professor cranky."

I hesitate then realize I have an hour and a half before my next class. "Where are we going?"

"We need some vitamin D. Don't take this personally, but it wouldn't hurt if you left this cave once in a while. Even moles pop up for air."

When we get outside, she winces, holding her side while she sits on a concrete bench facing the grassy mall. "Here you go," she says, patting the seat. When I join her, she pulls another shoebox from her bag, takes a *kolache*, and hands the box to me.

A couple is lying under a gnarly oak. The boy is propped on an elbow, talking.

"What did Mom used to be like?" Cornelia says, wiping her mouth with a Kleenex. *Albina used to do that*, I think. "I mean, she married your brother so she must've been way different."

I picture Terezie digging with Sam in the midden, then dressed in her *kroj* for their wedding. "She wore men's shoes," I say, "and nobody cared, not even in high school." I laugh. "Her nickname for Sam was Chopin." I want to add that they almost had a baby.

"Chopin, the composer? Why?"

"I don't remember," I lie. "You have a napkin?"

"Did he play the piano? I guess I didn't picture him like that. What was he like?"

How to capture a life, his life? Impossible. "He was, well…we were…close."

"Yeah, well, what's not to love about you, Doc?" She hands me a Kleenex and wraps her *kolache* in another. "Grandma says he spoke Russian."

"He took some courses, yes, but he wasn't fluent." I wipe my mouth, hands. "If you don't mind, I'd rather not talk about this." A toad crouches in my throat, ready.

"Mom says I'm a lot like him: rude, pushy. I wonder who else that sounds like. Maybe a fancy smancy professor we both know?"

"I beg your pardon?" I say, my scalp tingling. This interview has ended. I scowl, scoot forward ready to stand.

"Okay," she says. "I shouldn't have said that. Sorry." She barely taps my shoulder then squeezes her hands. "Please don't leave yet. I have something to show you. It'll only take a minute." She arches her brows, pleading. "Will you come?"

She takes me behind the building to an untended area of wild grasses, pecan trees surrounded by rogue sprouts, discarded Styrofoam cups, cigarette butts, and other trash near a locked tool shed. A hydrant with a dripping faucet has left a circle of damp earth, a full bucket of water nearby. A black cat and two red tabbies stroll over, one whining in chirpy Morse code. Then three more appear: a tri-color with an orange nose, two more rubbing heads while they walk. They gather at my feet, squalling.

"Come to mama," Cornelia says, grinning, holding her side. "They act like they know you."

"Every campus has strays. They're a nuisance and a health hazard.

Now, thanks to you, I'll have to report these."

"Too late," she says. "You've been caught."

"I don't know what you're talking about." I shove the black one that's rubbing my ankles. "I've got to get back."

"Everybody knows you feed them. We've got bets on whether you take them to be spayed and get their shots. My guess? Heck, yeah. 'Cause you've got a gorilla-sized heart. Secret's out: You're nice."

"If you're so interested in these cats, why don't you and your friends take over? Be constructive instead of spying on your teachers."

"You forget: I'm leaving. But you know what I'll do?" She walks behind the shed, pulls back grass, twigs. "I'll show this to some of my friends." A cross made from scrap lumber is stuck in the ground, a pile of white stones surrounding it. "Somebody's bound to volunteer."

"If you think I had anything to do with that, you're wrong," I lie. "Now, let's walk back. We're both tired."

"You're right. My side hurts. Thanks for noticing."

"Would you like to lie down in my office?"

"Why, Doc, is that a pass?"

"Don't be ridiculous." I take her arm while we walk. "You're not my type."

CHAPTER 13
1965-66

I WAS ALMOST EIGHTEEN, a senior, when I chose what seemed to be the safer path: religion. Even now, my educated understanding of the natural world has not rendered my sense of the holy obsolete. So attuned am I to this dimension that when I first saw the Lower Pecos cave rock art at the White Shaman site, I witnessed a mystical manifestation. I'd been sketching the headless spirit shaman floating from its shadowed physical self when the amorphous shape materialized briefly at the end of the cave. Although this illustrates my welcome connection to the spiritual, the episode precipitated my uncontrollable hallucinations.

Now they're escalating, and I can't stop them. I'm terrified that I'll drift off while driving, or worse, during a lecture or conversation with a student or colleague. I try to resist them by practicing a tea ritual that involves ceramic dishes and an uninterrupted hour. My backyard rose garden teaches humility and an appreciation for acidic soil. I meditate. I sit, legs crossed, focusing on the Noble Truths, praying to end my need for escape.

The high school assistant coach was talking about the moral dimension of athletics to my Wednesday night First Baptist youth group. I was not, let us say, riveted. When the speech ended, a man whispered, "Are the meetings routinely like this?" The week before, he'd passed out fliers, but I'd left mine on my chair. Except for a few strands sprouting from his receding hairline, he was bushy as Omar Sharif, with a mustache and hair covering his forearms like a veil of thread. He looked wounded at the implication of his question.

"No. They're sometimes…better." I wanted to defend the group, but the majority was a clique of girls, gossipy, heavily painted. I couldn't decide if they were just shallow or shallow and scary. No one talked to me much, which was fine. I didn't come for the people.

He leaned, whispering, his gaze making me flinch. "This world-denying type of faith has been rejected by Christianity." He checked the room, but no one noticed us talking. "The most extreme forms of dualism are simply not good theology."

"Really?"

He suppressed a smile.

I wasn't sure, but I thought he'd said I shouldn't accept a simplistic view of good and evil. At least, I hoped that's what he'd said. "Who are you?"

He squirmed, a fidgety highbrow, like me, a misfit. "My name is Saul. I'm visiting my friend, Fay." He nodded toward one of the women who took turns bringing punch.

"You don't live here?" I asked.

"No. The School of Jericho Prophets is in Palestine…that's Texas, about a hundred miles from here." He pulled a pamphlet from his briefcase. *Heritage and Children's Craft Fair*, a caption read above pictures of women quilting, a man sanding one side of a tin-fronted cabinet.

Weird didn't capture it. "What kind of school is it?" The women wore aprons, kerchiefs; the men sported beards, cowboy hats. They smiled a lot.

"A place where the gospel is for everyone, including Jews, because God is faithful to His covenant with them."

"A Bible college like Oral Roberts?" I asked, even though Jews weren't allowed there.

"People say we resemble the Amish, but our teacher is Elijah, the new prophet."

"Sounds like a cult," I said. I was looking for answers to questions like, Was the God who commanded Abraham to kill his son the same one I had to worship? Or, Why weren't any of the disciples women?

"Ours is a place where dialogue is a means of appreciating the difference of the other." He folded his arms then picked at his sleeve. "Our homestead fair is in two weeks. Will you join a group I'm taking?"

At the craft fair, I learned that members made soap, planted rice and alfalfa with teams of draft horses, even refused birth control and medical care. Their complex of bungalows stood at the end of a dirt road in a pine forest clearing. It seemed like another planet, but I tried to reserve judgment.

At the fair, children spun wool and pressed apple cider. I stood with Saul, who responded to greetings with exaggerated acknowledgments, bowing, repeating himself; no one stayed to talk. A woman was shaping a vase at a potter's wheel when Elijah joined us. His appearance seriously tested my composure.

He wore what looked like a striped bed sheet draped over his head, swirled around his body. A leather strap wound across his palm and wrapped in loops up his forearm. He was tall, brawny, a fullback in a toga.

"Good day, good day, father," Saul said, twitchy.

"Good day, Saul, brothers and sisters," Elijah said. Men and women answered in robotic counterpoint. When a child took his hand, he patted her head. "I'm grateful today for this bounteous display of love and talent. God has surely blessed us." When he tightened the fold of sheet at his neck, his leather armband squeezed flexed muscles.

If this had been a movie, I'd have laughed. Picture John Wayne in *The Robe*.

"Father," Saul said, his glance darting, "this," his hand jerked in my direction, "is Sarah Pelton. From Nugent."

"Welcome." Elijah noted my matching skirt and blouse, my bubble haircut. "Are you considering joining us?"

"I...this is my first visit," I stammered, appalled, fascinated. Who could possibly think I belonged in this la-la land?

"Wherever you go, my dear, may your spirit, like leaven in dough, shape you into good light bread." He rubbed the sign of a cross on my forehead then walked toward a home-school display.

Later that evening while Saul led me to the cabin where I'd spend the night, he told his leader's story. Two years before, Elijah, whose real name was unknown, had visited Israel with a tour group. While strolling the Via Dolorosa, he'd heard a voice say, "If the Lord be the true God, why not follow him?" The same words spoken by the biblical Elijah. That night an angel appeared in a dream, reproducing a visitation to the ancient prophet. The next day, the new, emerging Elijah spent most of his time bathing, purifying. His last afternoon in Israel, he wrapped in a hotel sheet then chanted "Amazing Grace" while walking the streets. Back home in Alpine, he read in the newspaper about a neutron star that had torn through a gaseous cloud, creating a ram-shaped nebula. Sure this was a sign, Elijah traveled to the MacDonald observatory. The image, when he viewed it through the telescope, recaptured for him God's act of burning a sacrifice to disprove the power of Baal. So Elijah assumed his new name, took his life savings, and, like his mentor, opened a School of Jericho Prophets.

Saul wasn't stupid. He knew I'd see Elijah as a zealot, maybe a schizophrenic who should be institutionalized. "It seems fantastic, I know, but our culture is too quick to reject the mystic. I'm sure you're familiar with Native American shamans, and Sufi teachers in Morocco and Senegal practice a mystical expression of Islam. Opening yourself to such possibility can expand your appreciation of the world."

Now, he had my attention. "Does Elijah think he's been reincarnated?" I asked as we stood outside the cabin door. Window light spilled onto our feet; an odor of pine, mint-sweet, tannic, sanitized the compound.

"No. He feels a spiritual connection much like a husband and wife who have stayed fifty years together. But holy." He'd met Elijah, he said, ten months earlier. The prophet had been distributing School of Jericho fliers at the entrance to a Waco rodeo.

"At the what?"

"Just listen," he said. The two men had talked under the bleachers while loudspeakers blasted and bulls and broncos tossed their riders.

"Only in Texas," I said.

A mother and teenage daughter walked past, and Saul nodded. "Hello, hello," he said, ignoring their sneaked glances as they stepped into the cabin. I decided to save my questions about his religion. "Did he wear his sheet to the rodeo? You must've thought he was psycho," I said, impressed with Saul's brainy talk and age of, I guessed, about thirty.

"You should watch, decide for yourself, little girl."

I didn't mind when he wandered off. But the next day, he'd know that Sarah Pelton was nobody's little girl.

I visited the Jericho School four more times with Fay. The school's general population most resembled the cross section you'd find inside any grocery store. I attended chapel services led by Elijah, his Episcopalian-style ritual accompanied by robust Baptist hymns. Meals included sugary pastries and garden-grown vegetables; anyone could pick blackberries in a cultivated patch behind the barn. During one of the daily adult classes, a hunched older man said, "For Christians, suffering is inevitable," and Saul actually snorted. Fay rolled her eyes, and I began to feel at home.

A week later, when Elijah offered me a job in his office, I searched Bible verses for guidance and stumbled through the compound's prayer routine. When I told Sam I might go, he called me Sister Judas. "Religion's an illusion," he said, scooting his chair back. Disagreeing with Sam was hard, not only because it hurt, but because I didn't know enough to sound convincing. By my graduation day, he took for granted that I'd decided to go. "This Jesus stuff can get pretty sticky," he said. Still, I knew he thought quoting scripture was proof of being brainwashed, his teasing remarks painful reminders of our changing relationship. "Faith, hope, charity, these three," he said, "roads advertised but less taken."

I'd been accepted at Sophie Newcomb College in New Orleans, and my move was the family's topic of conversation at dinner the night after my graduation. Kurt had already driven back to Austin, but Sam was staying for the weekend.

"I can't wait for you to see the campus," my mother said, spooning piccalilli relish onto her greens, "and that city."

Sam sat back, crossing his arms, but I kept silent. "Mom, Dad," he said before I could stop him, "Sarah needs to tell you something, but she's worried that you won't like it."

My mother's head cocked.

"Thanks, Sam," I said, furious.

"Tell them," he said. "What's the worst that can happen?"

"I don't exactly know how to say this," I began, squeezing my eyes shut. "I've been thinking about joining the School of Jericho Prophets."

"The what?" my mother said.

"The group I've visited in Palestine? You met Saul, the assistant director, at church." They'd been introduced in the parish hall at a wedding reception.

"Let me get this straight," my mother said, folding her arms. "You're giving up college to join a cult?"

"Please don't get upset," I said. "If I go, and I haven't decided yet, I'll work as their secretary and bookkeeper. You won't have to pay for anything."

She gripped the front of her dress. "This absolutely takes the cake. Ho-nest-ly." She shook her head. "Could you pick *anything* further removed from this family? What'll it be next—Martians? Owen, aren't you going to say something?"

Hugh leaned over his plate, chewing, watching Dad.

"This is the first time I've heard anything about a school of this sort," my father said, "and before I make any decision, I'd like to hear Sarah tell us what it is and why she wants to go."

"Ever since the explosion," I said, "I've needed some answers, not the kind you get in a classroom. I believe the Jericho Prophets can help. Please, I have to try this first, then I promise I'll go to college." As I talked about the school, Elijah, Saul, Fay's family, and the Amish-like way of life, I made my assessment sound more acceptable and my decision sound more definite than I felt.

"Sam, did you encourage this?" my mother asked.

"She told me she was thinking about it," he said. "I, for one, say as long as she's no Jesus freak, if it's important, she should go."

"Oh, you do, do you?" my mother said, squeezing her hands. "No college education, no future. Just pack her off to a nut camp." My mother's opinion of organized religion paralleled Sam's; in fact, many of their views were similar, an ironic source of the tension between them. "Typical. You'd support anything that upset us."

Should I go, I wondered, even if they tell me not to? I pictured the school's chapel, its purple-draped altar.

"Wait, wait, Mama," my father said, pushing his palm against air. "I'm hearing that Sarah is interested in religious study."

"Yes, sir," I said, relieved but unsure.

"It seems the least we can do is visit this place."

"But how can you—" she interrupted.

"All I'm saying," he said, raising his palm again, "is that we'll look at Sarah's school, then we'll talk again later. Nothing's been decided."

Hugh slumped, almost invisible.

"But let me caution you, young lady," my father said, pointing his fork. "The Peltons don't make commitments lightly."

During their test visit, my father was so fascinated by the draft horse cultivation that he guided a team and plow himself, his leather-strapped shoulders and waist tilted against the tugging reins, his Florsheim wing-tips plodding forward. When he met Elijah, though, he almost balked. That evening, after a sermon on the Christian ethos of compassion, he sat in Elijah's book-stacked office, and they debated the philosophical underpinnings of Paul's conversion and the theology of his first Athenian convert, Denys the Areopagite; my father didn't mention the sheet again. Later, at home, I overheard him telling Hugh while they watched a Cowboys game on TV: "Elijah is like Moses. He's a mystic who's witnessed the symbolic presence of God."

Saul's master's degree in divinity, his observation that scientists (and doctors), like prophets, "confront the unpredictable realm of uncreated reality," and his conversion parallels with my father's hero, ensured my father would find him acceptable. My mother, I knew, was confident I'd be leaving for New Orleans in January. But in the meantime, she liked Saul's manners: the way he opened a door as though someone were sleeping in the next room, and his habit of resting his fork then folding his scrubbed hands while he chewed his food. She ridiculed the kerchief-covered women, imitating what she described as their cocker-spaniel expressions, so I steered her away from people on the fringe. The facilities ranked three stars: mopped floors, sanitary, semi-private baths, sufficient air and heat. Once I'd promised to see a doctor if I broke a bone or felt feverish (no one worried about me not having birth control), we made a deal. I would try the school until Christmas, then we'd renegotiate. I moved in on a Monday in August.

I posted checks, placed orders for alfalfa seed and notebook paper, typed letters. As for enlightenment, Elijah and Saul were the only sources, and while one was busy, conversation with the other was like deciphering algebra. I gave up trying to find a boyfriend.

New Year's Day came and went, and I played the *commitment* card. Of course, I explained, breaking in a new bookkeeper mid-year would be difficult, and after all, I'd promised. My father convinced my mother to let me stay the year.

In February, Saul volunteered us, together, to make the new supply of soap, a chore passed, in turn, to each person in the compound. I didn't understand why he'd chosen me, and I dreaded spending the next hours with someone so odd he might inadvertently deliver an insult.

Once we'd hung the kettle over a bonfire in the usual clearing, we melted sixteen pounds of hog lard and beef tallow. Smoke scorched my eyes, and grease, in thickening layers, slicked my face, arms, cotton sweater. My hair stiffened into wet clumps, the air thick as paste. All the while, Saul fanned the coals or stirred the kettle's vile contents with a long wooden paddle.

"Why are we doing this?" I asked, raking a finger across my cheek. "I mean, what's the point?" I stepped out of the smoke's grimy path. "I'd be glad to pick some up at the store."

"Sarah, I know this is unpleasant. It's filthy and exhausting and—"

"And it stinks." I covered my nose and mouth with my sweater.

"Yes, I know," he said. "Instead, would you bring me a bowlful of pine needles?"

"What for?"

"Just go."

I admit that I stayed longer than necessary in the kitchen, boiling needles. The next day, according to his instructions, I mixed the cooled pine water with four cans of lye, a mixture that to my delight grew hot, the odor: Christmas trees. While I stirred with the wooden paddle, he poured a thin stream of our lye solution into the fat, all the while describing St. Therese of Lisieux, the Little Flower of Jesus. "To ecstasy," he told me she wrote in her autobiography, "I prefer the monotony of daily toil."

"The girl was seriously deranged," I said.

Later that month, Sam came to check things out. Walking along the pathways, I had to keep glancing to make sure he was actually beside me. While we toured the main buildings, I introduced him to whomever we passed, enjoying their expressions when I said his name: *Sam. My brother, Sam. The one I told you about, Sam.* Then we sat on a bench in a clearing at the edge of the woods. He asked about my classes, my job, the food, the people. When he asked about Saul, I described my ordeal making soap, and as if summoned, Saul appeared.

"I hope I'm not interrupting, but I wanted to welcome your brother." He extended his hand. Sam stood and shook it.

"What a great place," Sam said. "Man, you've got it made." He glanced at me then returned to Saul. "You can actually breathe out here."

Saul kept dipping his head. "Yes. It *is* peaceful."

"And you get a great view of the stars, I bet."

I stood between them. What was Sam up to?

"Yes, quite," Saul said. "We've got a group that studies them, in fact. I'd be happy to introduce you to the members."

"Outstanding," Sam said, nodding then taking a step back,

looking at me.

"I have to get back to the office in about twenty minutes," I said, thinking he'd signaled a request for rescue. "I thought we could sit here awhile then you'd go with me."

"You don't mind, do you? I'd really like to talk to these guys," he said while looking at me, nodding again, then turning to Saul and back. "Why don't I meet you at the office in about an hour? Saul can show me." He looked serious.

I sat on the bench, watching them disappear. While Saul talked, his index finger tapped his left palm. Sam shoved his hands in his jeans pockets, looked at his feet, listened.

I didn't talk to Sam until the next morning when he came to my office. The night before, he'd invited me to join them, but the stargazers' talk was longitudinal/latitudinal gibberish. Now, it was Saturday; I worked until noon. "Hey, stranger."

"Sorry about yesterday," he said. "When are you through here?"

"They told me I could leave early. What do you want to do?"

"Breakfast?" He gave me his arm.

While he ate his fried eggs in the cafeteria, he asked questions about some of the people he'd met. We laughed about the guy with Elvis sideburns who had two Chihuahuas and a marijuana patch, and the four-foot tall woman who sang country music like a pro and used to be a Siamese twin. He described a teenage girl with braces, who quoted Marianne Moore: "The whirlwind fife-and-drum of the storm bends the salt marsh grass, disturbs stars in the sky and the star on the steeple; it is a privilege to see so much confusion."

"You're making that up."

He said, "How long are you planning on staying?"

"I haven't decided yet. Why? What are you thinking?"

"It's a cool place," he said, pushing his plate away. "Don't get me wrong. I'm impressed, and the people are interesting. I like Saul, too. I know that's important."

"Come on, Sam. You don't like it. I can tell." A week before, I'd been a complainer. Now, I was being defensive. Which was it? Sarah, the whiner; Sarah the Christian. Sarah, the baby sister.

"Okay then, here it is: This place scares me. It's too comfortable, too easy. It's like falling in a rabbit hole. *Alice in Wonderland.*" He leaned into my face. "You *got* to get out of here."

I held his hand. "I know why you think that, and it makes me feel good that you're worried. But don't. I'm not going to stay here forever, but for now, it's where I belong."

"Just so you know: I'll be checking."

"Noted."

"Now, can we get out of here and find a movie?"

In March, I went to the Sunday service as usual. The sanctuary was a one-room hall with floor-to-ceiling windows behind the altar. As Elijah, draped in a purple and maroon cloak, spoke and gestured from the lectern to our congregation of close to two hundred, pine trees swayed, snippets of lambent shadows stroking the glass. Saul sat like an android propped on a folding chair, nature's commotion behind him.

"I am the wife and the virgin. I am the barren one, and many are her sons. I am the silence that is incomprehensible. I am the utterance of my name."

Was he saying that God is a woman? I pictured the deity I'd been taught to envision, white-bearded, enthroned. The woman next to me whispered to her husband.

"In the name of Jesus, son of Father of All and Mother Holy Spirit." Elijah crossed himself, folded his hands at his chest. Saul made the sign of the cross and surveyed the hall.

I thought of Mary Magdalene, St. Therese, and, then, of *Tlahzolteōtl* with her legs spread—all figures arresting, essential. I recalled my mother dismounting my grandfather's horse, tossing the reins at him. Women of power.

"If you bring forth what is within you, what you bring forth will save you," Elijah urged. "If you do not bring forth what is within you, what you do not bring forth will destroy you." Behind him sat Saul, framed by pines, stirring.

Beat your breath, something whispered.

"Move beyond what is in any book," Elijah said.

A man in front put his arm around his wife.

Be a cornstalk, I heard.

The Aztecs waited ten years for the maguey to mature, the sap welling from its pierced heart to yield the "honey" associated with semen. That nectar became *pulque*, the milk of She with Four Hundred Breasts. Man and woman—sacred, united, fecund.

That night, Saul asked if he could help wash my portion of the dinner dishes.

"Are you avoiding ecstasy?" I teased.

He plugged the sink, turned on the faucet, rolled his sleeves. "Asceticism devalues the spiritual significance of pleasure."

"If you're saying too much religion can spoil your love life, you're smarter than I figured."

Saul laughed. His hands seemed focused through a zoom lens. He used a cotton rag to stroke the inside of a water glass. First the lip, the soapy water dripping onto his bare arms. Then inside the glass, finally rinsing under the faucet, the steam floating about our necks and through our clothes, the water splashing.

He reached for another glass, the water sloshing against the porcelain sink. Then again, the rubbing.

"Do you have any family?"

He draped a cup towel over his shoulder, leaned on the counter. "When I converted, they disinherited me." He submerged the glass. "I'll follow anyone who sacrifices himself out of love for me."

Turning, he held out the towel in one hand, the glass, still dripping, in the other.

Stepping in between, I leaned my chest against his. He smelled earthy, ripe, human. Not a brother. Not a god.

CHAPTER 14
1966-1968

IT FOLLOWS THAT SINCE I prefer being alone, I haven't been inundated with requests to hop in the sack. Fifteen years ago, except for my classes, I began avoiding groups. *Relationship* became a technical term, used in much the same way as *patriarchy* or *materialist*. Finally, I stopped feeling available. My body could've been covered in bison skins.

Sex still interests me—the pleasure of arousal, the joy of coming—but the odds of getting lucky grow smaller each year. Once, I almost married an aging hippie who built movie sets, a carpenter, but certainly not Christ-like. He stayed with me between jobs, our fucking fooling us into believing we were well matched. I've considered trying the personals on the Internet, but I'm not brave enough for that.

My last offer happened two years ago. A persistent colleague (his Jack London specialization should've been warning enough) took me to dinner, then drove to a city park, of all places, and stopped under a tent-like pecan tree. He talked; I listened, noticing his bottom row of small teeth.

"Why is it," he said, staring out my window at the grounds, "that with our life expectancy at seventy-point-two years, we spend ninety percent of our time stuck in a chair?"

His cynicism almost won me over, but he spoke in numbers. Who could be charmed by that?

"Joke," he announced. "Two vultures boarded a plane, each carrying two dead raccoons. The stewardess stops them and says, 'Sorry sir, only one carrion per passenger.'"

I laughed, and then he closed in, rubbing a strand of my hair between two fingers, moving his open mouth toward mine. When I tasted him—sardines—I shoved his shoulder, turned to the window. "Just drive," I said.

Saul and the School of Jericho Prophets had become my official home. During the day, I answered phones while updating the ledger of school deposits and expenses. Evenings, I attended classes on interpreting the Beatitudes and transcendental meditation. Before going to sleep, I read books from a list Saul had assigned. I was halfway through *The Confessions of St. Augustine*; each time I finished one, he gave me a quiz. As often as I could, I walked with him to our private spot, a clearing next to a ditch used for the dump, a place not as bad as it sounds, brush covering most of the garbage. Mostly he talked: about political and geographical biblical history, about transubstantiation, about the morality of premarital sex and birth control. God was on our side, of course. We reassured each other by quoting scriptures. Proverbs was our favorite: "Trust in the Lord with all your heart and lean not on your own understanding." Because we prayed and followed our impulses, our lovemaking was a product of God's will. Saul loved me and he loved his faith. I basked in his life's clear definition, one enumerated by dictates I could memorize and quote, proven truths about community and obedience to a benevolent God spirit. I happily succumbed to my new mentor's influence.

That summer, my parents brought Hugh to our Heritage and Children's Craft Fair. My father and Elijah had developed a mutual respect, but my mother believed she had evidence that I'd been brainwashed. Instead of making fun of the women, she scowled, openly showing contempt. She jotted observations in a pocket notebook. Earlier, Hugh had said over the phone that she and Kurt had discussed hiring a mind-control expert to kidnap and de-program me, then restore me to the family. I was determined to convince her that Saul was a good catch—my converted Jew, fifteen years older, an assistant to a bed-sheeted man with an assumed name.

Soon after they arrived, Hugh, now a seventh grader, found a choral group in the parish hall. When Saul and I walked in half an hour later, he stood at the piano like Jerry Lee Lewis, playing a boogie-woogie version of "I Come to the Garden Alone." His fingers sped up and down the keys, pounding the chords like a jackhammer; once in a while, his elbow mashed a harmonizing cluster of discordant notes. His audience clapped, bobbing their heads. When he finished, they cheered; a few patted his shoulder. Mumbling thanks, he snapped his head back, flipping his oiled hair. Saul asked if he wanted to join us at the apple cider booth.

"You have talent," Saul said while we walked. "Where did you learn to play?"

My parents huddled over a handmade cabinet at the woodworking display. A baby cried at the soap-making demonstration; we drifted through a cloud of heat and lye.

"It's nothing. Easy. You seen him on TV?"

"This may sound strange, Hugh, but we don't have television here."

"Sam's seen him *in person*, in Waco." He either didn't know about Sam pawning our mother's bowl to buy the ticket, or he'd wisely chosen to omit that part. "You ought to see *his* impression."

"Sam plays the piano?" Saul asked, trying to reconcile that image with his perception.

"No, but he sounds *just like* Jerry." He raised his hands, grew serious. "Really, you can't tell them apart." He shook his head, incredulous. "Sam says I should make a record." He glanced sideways, checking my face. We knew our parents' plan for his future, and it didn't include music.

"That's a great idea," I said, and Hugh smiled, kicking the dirt. I slipped my hand into Saul's. "What do you think of my boyfriend?"

"Okay, I guess," he said, shrugging. When Saul awkwardly patted Hugh's slicked hair, he ducked.

My parents had already strolled to the cider booth. Dad handed Mother a glass. Peering over the rim of her sunglasses, she studied Saul.

Dad handed us four glasses of dark cider, cloudy with apple pulp. "Tasty," he said, nodding. His eyebrows had thickened, grown wayward.

"Saul knows the recipe," I said, nudging him. "Don't you?"

"A blend of bittersharp and bittersweet, with a small amount of crab apple."

"Gives it that kick, I bet." My father smacked his lips, the lower one faded, the top one folded under as though chewed.

"Has it been pasteurized?" my mother said, inspecting the cider through the side of her glass.

Appropriately swaddled, Elijah then ambled next to my parents. He invited my father to another of their theological discussions and smiled at my mother. She set her full glass on the booth's counter. *Leader as avatar or Messiah*, she wrote in her notebook.

Elijah said, "I hope you're happy with our new match." He beamed at each of my parents.

Mother quit writing.

"New tennis courts?" my father said absurdly, searching the grounds.

"Elijah—" Saul interrupted.

"I'm referring to our loving couple," he corrected, patting Saul's sleeve. "They haven't asked my counsel, but I'm hoping we won't have long to wait for a wedding." He pressed my arm, smiled again, and floated to the next group.

"I see," my father mumbled, each word dragging disappointment. "Mama, looks like you'll be getting your wish sooner than we thought." Kurt, who was engaged, had decided to postpone his marriage until his last year of medical school.

"No, no, no," I said, waving my hands. "Mom, don't blow a gasket. I don't know why Elijah said that."

"Your daughter and I—" Saul interrupted.

"I don't believe you've ever met Kurt," my mother said through gritted teeth. "He's Sarah's oldest brother." She flipped to a new page in her notebook. "And I'm going to call him right now."

"Wait," my father said, his mouth a slit. "Can we talk about this?"

Once my mother understood I wasn't getting married, she reluctantly accepted the alternative: a relationship she hoped would go nowhere.

Then, mid-summer, Sam and Terezie appeared in the cafeteria during lunch. He asked if I could sit with them in the sanctuary where no one would bother us. He had an announcement, he said. On the walk between buildings, he cupped Terezie's rear-end, and when she squealed, slapping his arm, he tickled until she giggled, telling him to stop.

Inside, we pulled chairs from the front row, forming a loose circle. Sam alternately held Terezie's hand and patted her leg. A shaft of light blazed through the windows, falling across the right side of Sam's face. He angled his shoulder, blocking the glare.

"What's your news?" I said, sounding more direct than I'd intended.

"Oh, nothing much," Sam said, reaching toward Terezie, "except this sexy lady..." he rubbed her belly, "is toasting a loaf."

When he looked at me, I frowned, thinking, *I don't get it.*

"A bambino...a Porky Pig." He flipped his eyebrows.

"She's pregnant?" I asked, thinking, *This mistake's too big. What'll we do this time?*

Terezie was acting too happy. "So, this is good news?" I asked.

"Hell yes! Can't wait to see my girl ripe as a tomato," he said, nuzzling her.

I shifted, looked at my hands. I didn't like them pawing each other in front of me and my friends.

"Hey," Terezie called, "Sarah doesn't like that." She pushed him back. "When's it due?"

"Not 'til February," Terezie said. "But our parents' friends can count, so the wedding's right away...July." When she picked an eyelash off Sam's cheek, he turned, his odor almond soap, barbecue.

"She's wearing one of those costumes, with the sleeve things," he pointed to my shoulder, "and an apron. I love those." Terezie closed her eyes, shaking her head. "At the Czech Moravian Brethren."

"What did Mama say?"

"What do you think?" he said.

"*My* parents—feature this," she said, "wanted to have the wedding at the capitol, on the front lawn."

Sam hugged her. "Let's have our honeymoon there instead." They laughed then he faced me, leaning on his thighs. "Sar, would you be our maid of honor?"

"Huh?" I said. "Really, I'm sure Terezie wants somebody else."

"Sweet," Sam said, "but it was her idea." He looked at Terezie, and she nodded, about to speak.

"Great. Thanks, Sar. Terezie's got it all figured out."

Terezie sighed. "You think I'm ready for this?"

The double doors opened, and Saul walked toward us. "Pardon me for interrupting," he said. "I won't stay. I just wanted to say welcome." He extended his open hand. "Good to see you again, Sam."

"Yeah, thanks," Sam said, slouching.

"Actually," I said, standing, "this is a private conversation."

"No," Sam said, "*actually*, it's as good a time as any to tell you what's going on."

"Yes, please do," Saul said, signaling me not to interrupt.

"Our family thinks Sarah should come home. We believe it's your fault that she's not."

"That's it," I said. "Sam, you don't know what you're talking about." I pulled Saul's arm until he walked alongside me toward the door.

"It's a mad tea party, Sarah," he yelled. Terezie put her face in her hands. "Time's standing still."

Two weeks later, I phoned Sam.

He said, "It's time for you to get on with your life. You've been stuck too long in his fantasy world."

I told him about the books I'd been reading and my plan to start classes somewhere. Still suspicious, he reluctantly promised not to ask again.

Sam and Terezie got married a week later in a miniature, gothic-revival cathedral. Its crude beams and freehand stenciling resembled decorations in a child's playhouse. Guests filled the forty pews, the aisle a cultural divide. One side held coiffed women who whispered and blinked, waving to one another. The tanned men vigorously shook each other's hands. On the other side, women sighed, heads bent, while being escorted to their section.

Mrs. Cervenka sat in a handmade shirtwaist, watching as though a written test would follow. My grandparents, striding like another wedding couple, joined my parents, who could've been Neiman Marcus models. They all looked at the gladioli, their laps, the crowd, anywhere but Sam, who grinned when I stepped to my place in front, opposite Kurt. Hugh rocked on his heels next to Cyril, a nature boy in a tuxedo.

Terezie wore a *kroj*, her pleated flax skirt embroidered with primroses and psychedelic doodles. Lace and eyelet trimmed her white cotton blouse; tissue paper packed its sleeves. When Mr. Cervenka bowed, leaving his daughter next to Sam, she swatted her arms, rattling the stuffing.

The preacher was a ham radio operator whose monotone invited intermittent responses. Whenever he paused, Sam jiggled his leg. As the preacher droned, Sam kept his head low, his hands folded. After he kissed Terezie, he held her, cradling her head, grinning at the church's dome, where a painted pelican pulled feathers from its breast.

On their way down the aisle, they stopped in front of my parents. Terezie handed my mother a lily, while Sam pressed his forehead to our father's shoulder, then hugged him. Mother whispered to Terezie, who smiled but watched the men at her side. Rising, my father patted Sam, saying, "Okay, boy."

Terezie surveyed the congregation then pulled Sam to her parents, who kissed both of her cheeks. He caressed their hands, talking through touch. Then my brother and his new wife strolled away.

The Cervenkas had rented the National Guard armory for the reception, the fraternal hall having been booked for a family reunion. The head table stretched along the wall where targets usually hung for rifle practice. Kurt's fiancée, a redhead popular for her culinary skills, pinned a sprig of rosemary, the fertility symbol, on each guest's shoulder; the baby was still a secret. Though Sam's trousers draped below his ankles, the guests noticed his sneakers. "Nice shoes," my parents' friends teased while moving through the receiving line. "*Dobrý přítel je nad zlato*—A good friend is better than gold," he said as he shook each person's hand. Whenever anyone complimented Terezie's dress, she grunted, "I stand by my man." Once in a while, she clasped her mother's arm.

Friends and relatives of the Cervenkas served a buffet of roast pork, fried sweet potatoes, tomato relish, squash bread, and *kolaches*. My family's guests waited in line as though lounging at a cocktail party. "NASA recently sent Holsteins into orbit," Blair Corcoran said to Kurt as Saul and I walked up. "It was the herd shot round the world," he cackled. Kurt winced then excused himself. Saul fidgeted. "Clever, yes," he said, forcing a chuckle along with Blair, while the Cervenkas' friends stared, such raucousness better than a picture show. Some of our group's children grew suspicious of the food. "What's that yellow stuff in the bread?" a little girl cried, yanking her mother's skirt. "Yuck," her brother moaned, his face contorting.

During dinner, the wedding couple sat between the sets of parents, who were flanked by the wedding party, including Saul who sat next to me, and Kurt with his fiancé, Randy, next to Saul. Our row of heads made a line-up for the shooting gallery, the lovebirds its bull's-eye.

"You and Saul have something in common," I said to Kurt, hoping to get them talking.

Kurt believed the scrawls in our mother's notebook confirmed his suspicions. He squinted. "Oh?"

"It's true. You both like history."

"Is that right?" Kurt said, adjusting his glasses. "So, Saul," he leaned, turning to stare, "what do you know about the Allies' Operation Shingle in Anzio in '44?" His fiancé tugged his tuxedo cuff.

Saul glanced at his plate then back at Kurt. "Didn't the Army hold off the Germans there?" He wiped his hands on his napkin. "I'm more interested in the Janowska concentration camp uprising in '43."

"Are you Jewish?" Kurt said, squinting again. "I'm confused. I thought…never mind."

"It's complicated, but—"

"I really don't want to know the details." Kurt moved his chair back. "Excuse me," he said and left, I guessed, for the bathroom.

"Well, that was rude," I mumbled to Saul.

When guests began shoving aside their empty dessert plates, my mother excused herself then walked to Mrs. Cervenka.

"Can you tell me the seasoning used on the pork?" she asked as though she'd caught the woman leaving milk at our back door. "I have to know."

Mr. Cervenka stood, scooted over. "Please," he said, indicating his chair. His formality couldn't hide his delight at her sudden attention.

"Thank you, no," my mother said, nodding a greeting at a nearby couple. "Is it sesame or caraway? It gives the meat an interesting flavor." She wasn't purposely being rude. She genuinely wanted to know this culinary secret and viewed her question as a compliment.

Mrs. Cervenka folded her napkin, scooted her chair back, and rose until her head was almost a foot above my mother's. "Is caraway, Mrs. Pelton." Her voice was an empty well, her face an iron skillet.

"I thought so," my mother said. "Thank you," she sang while she strode back to her seat, chatting with friends along the way. Meanwhile, Kurt had returned to the table. "Caraway," my mother announced to her future daughter-in-law, who'd recently spent a week at the New Orleans cooking school. That was the only time during the night that my parents and the Cervenkas spoke.

When the Snook Polka Boys started playing, Emil Kulhanek and Wade Nyank whooped and clapped, pumping their arms. "Wedding dance, wedding dance," Wade shouted, until an older woman swatted his hands. He flinched, pretending pain.

Hugh wandered to the portable bandstand, stopping in front of the lead accordionist. While the man's right hand jigged across buttons and keys, his left pumped the bellows. Hugh leaned precariously close, until our mother dragged him back to his chair. His sulking ended when the music whined to a halt. Sam took the microphone.

"This is the happiest day of my life," he said, smooth as a Rotary Club chairman, and people applauded. "Isn't she beautiful?" he said, pointing, and a whistle curled around the room.

Terezie's napkin became a curtain, hiding her face, revealing joy.

"We want to thank y'all for coming, but we especially want to thank our parents."

Tense, hopeful, the couples glanced at each other.

"But for the first dance," he said, "I'd like Albina to be my partner."

"Excuse, please?" Mrs. Cervenka said, blinking. She asked her husband to explain.

"And, Dad?" Sam continued. "Would you dance with my bride?"

Mother drooped. "Oh," she said, shading her eyes.

"Hold your fire," my father whispered. He patted her while he stood.

Terezie glanced from Sam to her parents. "Sam," she called, but he couldn't hear.

"And, Mother," Sam continued. He held out his hand, beckoning. "Would you come dance with Josef?"

Kurt grinned, covering his mouth. "Uh-oh," Hugh said.

"I know this isn't traditional, but please. Just once." While he walked to the head table, people turned their chairs to get a clear view. "Albina?"

Tradition, I thought. He'd once described it as a habit without a reason.

Mrs. Cervenka refused. "Sit," she hissed, turning away. Sam knelt, coaxing, as my father guided Terezie to the open floor. "Stop that," Mrs. Cervenka snapped at Sam. "If he does not," she said to her husband, "I will be leaving."

"Sam," Mr. Cervenka said, his voice heavy as a tree trunk, sharp as a saw, "your mother now you should look to, please."

"Albina," Sam pleaded, "why? You know you want to. It'll be fun."

"Get up," my mother said, stretching across the table, trying to catch his arm. Hugh slumped, disappearing. "Sam, what's wrong with you?" she said. "Everyone's watching."

Sam stared as though having to translate, then turned back to Mrs. Cervenka. "Just walk to the floor with me. We'll stand there, not even move." He pressed her back. "I'll have an excuse, finally, to give you a hug."

When Mrs. Cervenka walked away, her husband left with her.

My mother sighed, her shiny nail picking at the tablecloth.

Terezie ran, sleeves rustling, after her parents. Cyril followed her down the hall.

Then my father came toward Sam. "What's going on?" he asked, his back stiffening.

"I don't know," Sam said. "For some reason, Albina got mad."

"Did she say anything?"

Mother leaned on her elbows. "She didn't want to dance, but Sam, as usual couldn't leave it alone."

"What now, boy?" my father commanded. His body became a wall.

I thought of the times he'd whipped Sam, of their near fistfight in the study.

"What would be the *right* thing to do?" my father asked, glancing sideways, his voice a cracked chord.

Sam's jaw flexed; then he ducked and ran.

During the next half-hour, I visited each table with Kurt, his fiancé, and my parents. "What's that boy up to, Owen?" my grandfather said, tossing his napkin. "Doesn't *look* good." My grandmother's eyes narrowed, while Ruby, who'd come with them, raised her chin like a flag.

"Nothing to worry about, Dad," my father said.

My grandfather grumbled, "Expect you to take care of it."

"Sam's got everything under control."

We assured the guests that the couple was fine, that they and Terezie's family would soon return. Most people pretended to go along. Mrs. Cervenka's sister, though, tapped her plate with a fork, saying, "Craziest boy ever *I* seen." If Sam hadn't appeared, I'd have gone looking for him.

At first he sat, studying his guests. Mrs. Cervenka clutched her purse, wiping her mouth with a Kleenex. Terezie leaned, whispering, until he draped his arm around her, pressing her close.

At midnight, the band took a break, and a group of married women led the bride to a chair in the center of the tin building. Sam, ignoring Kurt's attempt to stop him, stood close by, his stance a military at-ease position. The women began slowly, somberly, singing a Czech song—"*Včera's měla z růží věnec/ A dneskaj už máš, a dneskaj už máš/ černý čepec*, Yesterday you had a crown of roses but today you have a black cap"— while they removed Terezie's white veil and hid her hair's crimped ends inside a *čepec*. When they finished, she slumped, patting her head. Amidst cheers, Sam broke through the circle, pulled his wife to her feet, then kissed her mouth's knobby scar.

Terezie was four months pregnant when she miscarried. For days, she and Sam cried, hugging each other and whoever else was nearby. They never mentioned their grief after that. He did, however, send a postcard with a cryptic message: "Don't trust anyone who wants to forgive you." In place of his last card's sketched legs was a doll figure, and underneath it, *Troll*. I worried that I'd somehow offended him. I asked about it, but he walked away, saying, "How do you know it came from me?"

One year to the day after Terezie lost the baby, I started commuting from Palestine to Waco for an anthropology course at Baylor. Conversations with Saul became heated while I read Dostoyevsky, Nietzsche, Heidegger, and a 1959 translation of the Gnostic *Gospel of Thomas*. I studied Coptic, and a professor's rare mimeographed transcriptions of other texts from the Nag Hammadi papyri sent me to Saul with more questions.

One day after lunch, Saul and I sneaked to our secret spot. He'd resisted because my questions of late had resulted in testy exchanges, sometimes exciting us until we flirted, aroused; other times we shouted, one of us leaving, silent, provoked. But this afternoon, before he could spread the blanket he'd brought as usual, I pulled him to the ground. The gray sky held us in a steamy cave; the pine brush cushioned our backs. For the first time, I became adventurous, guiding his mouth, hands. Afterward, Saul cupped my chin, pulling me to his downy chest.

"What have they been teaching at Baylor?" he said, sliding one hand behind his head. Trees cast turbulent shadows. "Can you register for a second course?"

I laughed. "Apparently, environment shapes sexual behavior." I waved toward the garbage hill.

"All right, all right." Saul stood, tucked his shirttail under his belt. "Another Garden of Eden. Like Adam and Eve, all that begetting."

He grabbed the blanket, pine needles scattering, and lurched up the slope.

"Some serious hanky-panky at that house," I shouted. "The Bible never explains that."

My parents hosted a Saturday dinner celebration of my twentieth birthday at their house. Everyone came, including Sam, Terezie, Kurt, his fiancé Randy, and Saul, whom I'd tried to convince to stay in Palestine. My mother served vegetables from a garden she'd planted; my father cooked steaks on the gas grill. We sat at the same dining table where my brothers and I had grown up, a parent at each end. Mother had been sitting there the first time she'd told us about Otis; years later I'd mashed gravy into her blouse. Tonight, our three new members would sit with us, and knowing how my older brothers felt about my boyfriend, I wondered whether there'd be more fireworks. I told myself to play the role my family expected (innocent female) and not to pop off when conversation got tense.

My father graciously invited Saul to say the blessing, and, surprisingly, no one seemed to mind. Dad sat stone-faced; his distraction was understandable, though. My grandfather lay dying in the hospital. I'd asked if I could visit, but he'd said, "Why? It wouldn't do any good."

I was the only one who could tell Saul was nervous, his mustache twitching while he studied our faces. He talked to Hugh about Bob Dylan. I complimented Terezie's hair. She ate two helpings, her farmer's hands slicing beef like a butcher. "This has a lot of marbling," she said, chewing. "It must be USDA Prime."

Sam was unexpectedly quiet. He seemed to hear what people said, but he wasn't listening. The effect was unnerving, like wondering if you have the flu. Since he majored in psychology, I asked, "So, Sam, have you sat in on any therapy sessions at school yet?"

"Huh," he muttered, "oh." He squeezed his eyes closed then blinked. "A few," he said.

"You'd be surprised what you might discover about yourself," Saul said, and the room became an echo chamber. He cleared his throat; his mustache quivered. "The unconscious is not just evil by nature. It's also the source of the highest good."

My parents glanced at each other, waited.

"Exactly," I said.

Kurt leaned across the table. "Your fanaticism doesn't belong here."

Saul raised his hands. "Forgive me, I—" he said.

"Kurt, really," I snapped.

"Saul was quoting Carl Jung," Sam said, expressionless. "So who, then, would you say's the fanatic?"

CHAPTER 15

By Cornelia's fourth visit, we've established the idiosyncratic habits of friends. "Hi, Doc," she says, leaning on the doorjamb, holding a giant cup of juice. "How's our desperate non-housewife?" I know she's alluding to a TV show, although I've never seen it. "Discover any new species lately?" Sipping from a straw, she sinks into a chair.

"Have you considered that I might be busy? Maybe I'm on my way to class."

"You've got exactly," she checks her cell phone, "two hours and twenty minutes. Great!" She coughs, rising again, "Lunch." She pulls an apple from her fanny pack, takes a bite. "Will you still love me without *kolaches*?"

We walk toward our bench outside the building. When we reach the exit door, she puts on rhinestone-framed sunglasses but also shades her eyes with her hand. Wearing shorts and a Joan Jett tee, she looks like the throngs walking past or lounging on the grass, except each slow, sandaled step favors the heel. "You move our bench, Doc?" she says. "That must've been a bitch."

When we finally sit, she coughs. "Aargh," she says, imitating a malevolent pirate, slapping her chest, then taking a slug of juice.

"Mmmm," I say, stretching, covering her need to rest, "this is just what I like." The tower clock chimes like a pipe organ: 2:30. A group of students walk past, bantering

"I have a theory," Cornelia says, crossing her legs, her sandal dangling like a stripper's glove. "You study other cultures so you can understand yourself." She sets her cup on the bench. "Actually, it's Mom's theory." She presses her side, closes her eyes.

"You're probably right."

She looks at me again. "And to understand anybody you're close to, right?"

"Culture influences our sensibilities, dreams, styles, perceptions of power. Yes, I'd say one studies a culture in order to ascertain origins of societal codes of behavior."

"You're a trip, Doc." She shades her eyes again, her bubble-gum nails poised like a geisha's. "Ask a question, get Anthropology 101."

"I distinctly heard you say—"

"No, you. I meant *you*, Doc, not any geek off the street. You're trying to understand yourself, right?"

"Absolutely not. My work is purely professional."

"Nothing personal about proving that the rest of us are robots."

"That's a gross oversimplification."

"Second theory: To you, behavior is like a math problem, so you can convince yourself that X makes Y."

"I wonder if there's an X that could explain your rudeness."

"No fair. You're as messed up as the rest of us."

"Excuse me?"

"Why did your brother kill himself?"

"Be careful. I don't want to talk about that."

"But I do. I need to. He was married to my mother, and I hardly know anything about him."

"Ask her then." I check my watch. "I appreciate you coming, but I have to get back to my office." I take a step. "You should see my stack of papers."

"Okay," she says, grabbing my arm, "just one question." She squeezes. "Please."

A man dressed in a suit, carrying a basketball, trots by, pockets jingling.

"Depends on the question."

"You're not going to like it, but it's important, and you're absolutely the only possible person I can ask."

"I'm not promising anything."

"I can imagine *why* he killed himself," Cornelia says. "What I want to know is *how*."

Her face expands, the shadowed eyes now holes, sucking. "This subject," I say, "is off limits, you understand? Besides its morbidity, your question is out of my realm."

"You don't understand," she says. "I can't ask anybody else."

"Of course, this will be difficult for Terezie, but as your mother, she…" Then I realize why she's asking. I take several steps then bend over, queasy. I hit my thigh, raise back up, squeeze breaths. Finally, I walk over and lean into her face. "Think about your parents, for God's sake. How dare you suggest something so hideous?"

"But I *am* thinking about them," she says calmly. "They're the reason. But please, you can't ever say that."

"How could your death possibly be something your parents would want?"

"Dad sold his bookstore, Mom's giving up her job, and they're moving to Minnesota of all places, he's losing his kidney, they're bankrupt and the house is being foreclosed, your brothers have filed a lawsuit, Uncle Cyril's gone crazy, and Mama doesn't know how she's going to pay him back. Besides, after the transplant there'll still be tons of bills, but the doctors won't promise anything. What would you do?"

Youth's essence is intensity. In spite of her failing kidneys, Cornelia invites watching, touching, her body carrying its subliminal desire to procreate. Each cell and follicle pulses, moist and animate. Sam, I realize, was only a few years older. "Thank you, Cornelia," I say, "for telling me." I cup her cheek. "Now you have to listen very carefully. I understand why you feel helpless. You're right that the situation is serious. Harming yourself will only aggravate the problem. The fact that you want to protect your parents is admirable, but your death at your own hands will only ensure their suffering."

"But if I was gone, they'd be able—"

"Thirty-three years ago my brother died, Cornelia. Thirty-three years, and I'm not the same person. At fifty-four, I'm still grieving.

Please don't do this to your parents."

"But I can't just do nothing," she says, bending over until her head rests in her lap.

"Sit up," I say. "Come on. Here, dry your face." I pull a handkerchief from my sleeve. "I have an idea," I say, "but I have to work out a few details. If I promise to tell you everything in no more than one month, will you trust me? Will you wait?"

The tower clock chimes. When she hugs me, the rhythm of her breath echoes inside my head, my chest.

When I close the door to my office, something in my stomach feels like ice, my mouth goes dry then fills with saliva. Darkness everywhere, except one tiny bit of yellow light. I'm sitting by a fire on an angled floor, inside a rock shelter carved out of rattlesnake-infested cliffs. The Lower Pecos winds below; pictographs cover the back limestone wall. The headless white shaman is leaving his shadowed mortal body. He's got cat feet and paws; feathers cover his arms. When his twelve-by-twenty-four-foot image steps off the wall, I'm not afraid. He flies above me, his body spread like an airplane. I expect chants or animal calls, but instead Cornelia says, "If I was gone…" A master switch snaps, and I'm sitting in my office chair, orchids on the windowsill, university email messages waiting on my computer screen. Rescued by Cornelia.

CHAPTER 16
1968

SAM GRADUATED from the university in May and worked at Family Health Services arranging foster care for abused children, counseling unwed mothers, and helping people find jobs. To supplement his caseworker salary, he drove a cab three nights a week. Stubble shaded his muscular cheeks and chin. "My tribute to the Rolling Stones," he said, wisps of sun-streaked hair barely reaching a knotted rubber band at his neck.

Sometimes I stayed overnight in his and Terezie's Austin apartment, a stop only a half-hour outside my usual route. Terezie, who would complete her degree in music education that fall, never talked about the miscarriage, and I didn't ask about it or about other children.

Labor Day weekend, Sam convinced me to stay until Sunday. Friday, Terezie and I watched him play intramural football on the University practice field. When we got home, Terezie got a phone call from an elementary school principal saying she'd been hired for the spring. Sam was so excited he hopped in the car and brought back a bottle of champagne. "Teaching is the greatest act of optimism," he said. "Here's to you, babe," and he clinked our glasses. After we'd drunk most of the bottle, he pulled her to the piano, and she played "The Tennessee Waltz" while we sang, her thick fingers mechanized, her foot tapping the pedal. We got hamburgers and chocolate malts at Dirty's and watched *Night of the Living Dead* and *Rosemary's Baby* at the Chief Drive-In.

I slept on a daybed in the front room. Cyril woke me when he arrived Saturday at 6:00 a.m. Sam grabbed two graphite rods with spinning reels from behind the curtains next to me and his metal tackle box from the bedroom closet. I pictured him standing in our farm creek, catching that bass with his hands. He'd said I was the curled mouse we'd found inside the gullet, my babies the tiny clams.

They hung coffee cans of limburger bait on strings around their necks. Giddy as boys playing hooky, they banged their way to the door.

When Terezie got up an hour later, I asked if she had a project for me. She tried to change the subject, but I insisted, saying I couldn't keep coming unless I pitched in. We decided to paint the kitchen, a space small enough for us to finish in a few hours. While she bought the paint at a store on the drag a few blocks away, I cleared out small appliances and dishes from the counter and shelves and took everything off the walls. I was taping around the window when she came back.

"Look," she said while setting a sack and gallon of paint on the front room floor. "Since the shelves don't have doors, I bought this paper"—a blue Delft design—"to go with this yellow, my favorite. Is it too bright?"

I started scrubbing dirt and grease. "I hope Sam likes it," I said.

"Your mom won't. That's for sure." She stood back, gazing around the room. "I can't put it all together the way she does." She shrugged. "Looks great, right?"

"Sure does," I said, not knowing how I really felt, except disappointed for not being more honest. Terezie didn't know how to be anything else.

"Are you going to marry Saul?" she said facing the wall, her paintbrush busy.

"Probably not," I said, surprising myself. I'd finished cleaning shelves and reached for a brush.

"Why do you live at the compound then?"

I took a breath, determined not to censor myself. "I thought it would give me a place to slow down and think."

"Do you believe in evolution?" She dipped her brush in the paint, dragged it across the rim.

"I'm not the kind—"

"Do you interpret the Bible literally?"

"No. As a matter of fact, I've been studying Eastern religions."

"And Coptic. Why?" She stood on her tiptoes, reaching for a corner. "Are you planning to be a preacher?"

"No, that's not why—"

"A diplomat?" She turned around. "Maybe a politician?"

I laughed. "That's a lot of questions."

"Yes, it is," she said.

"Well, truthfully, I guess I don't know. I just want to study for awhile."

She looked at the floor then began painting again. "What makes you want to stay with us so much?"

I stopped moving. Terezie was the truth scavenger. And me? I was wearing a mask.

One October evening when I arrived as planned, Sam's voice came through the door telling me to come in. When I did, I found him in an apron juggling four tomatoes. "Follow me," he whispered, his voice wavering with each arm stretch. "We've been,"—he paused to reach for a wobbled toss—"banished to the kitchen." Bobbing, grunting, he finished in slow motion, miraculously clutching two in each hand. "George is studying," he said, motioning toward the next room where Terezie, surrounded by books, sat on their bed. Mozart played softly from a radio on a table. Leaning into a circle of lamplight, Terezie scribbled on a legal pad in her lap.

"You're in charge of the salad," Sam said, nudging me forward, dropping tomatoes into my arms.

As I made the garlic, oil, and olive juice dressing, Sam slid a pan into the oven. "What are we having?" I asked, stirring, ready to rinse lettuce.

"Christ's messenger, the bird of peace." He used a mixer to whip cream he'd poured into a bowl. "I shot them Saturday with a friend." He stuck his finger into the white peaks, then poked it, cream-covered, into his mouth. The bowl went into the refrigerator next to sliced strawberries. "Just call me Killer." He knew I disapproved of hunting, but raising the issue was pointless. He thought it was fine as long as he ate everything he shot.

He asked about my class. While he basted the doves, I asked his opinion of Confucianism. I carried a pocketsize copy of the *Tao Tĕ Ching* in my purse.

"Tao's the way to go," he said. He closed the oven door, wiped his hands on his apron, then took plates and glasses off the cupboard shelves. "I'm not a fan of kow-towing to your elders. You might've noticed; I'm not good at it. What do *you* think?"

I told him my professor had said that great ideas were like buried seeds waiting to sprout in a better climate and that Confucius and Lao Tzu would outlast Mao Tse-tung. "Lao Tzu's teachings on gentleness and humility are as important as the Sermon on the Mount."

Sam leaned against the counter, folded his arms. "Does your boyfriend agree with that?"

"No," I said, taking place mats out of a drawer.

"You think gentleness and humility can be political?"

"I don't know. Our system certainly needs them."

"Nietzsche thought those with power ignored morality. If that's the case, how long can any religion last?"

Nietzsche was my private signal to change the subject. "Think the doves are ready? You burn it, you still eat it, mister."

While we set the table and served the plates, Sam sang, "Busted flat in Baton Rouge, waitin' for a train." He and Terezie had heard Janis at a pub. "Freedom's just another word for nothing left to lose." Barefoot, he danced me around the narrow dining area, bumping chairs, walls. I felt like Anna in *The King and I.*

"Sam!" Terezie shouted from the bedroom. "Could you keep it down, please?"

I'd forgotten she was in the apartment. At least, for awhile, I'd had a happy Sam to myself.

"Nice moves," he whispered, grinning. After he twirled me, I patted his cheek then clapped. "Dinner is served," he called toward

Terezie. Halfway to the bedroom, he threw his palms on the floor, his feet in the air. He walked on his hands to his wife.

On each of my three November visits, I found Terezie alone, her purple eyes red-rimmed, her t-shirt and shorts wrinkled, food-spotted. "That son of a bitch," she fumed the first time, "he hasn't been home in two days." When she cried, I awkwardly hugged her, then cried too, made coffee. We tried to watch old movies on TV, or she tinkled concertos on their mottled upright. Sometimes, she'd sit quietly in an old rocker, a row of Czech puppets watching from a shelf. I'd try to say something funny about Sam, and she'd almost laugh.

Each time, he appeared the next morning before we were up, the scratch of his key bringing exhausted relief. He brushed aside Terezie's accusations, his expression all animated flattery, his hands bearing a gift: the first time, a wheel-shaped bottle of perfume; the second, a snake's rattle, milky, tough as a toenail; the third, a book about saints.

While Terezie glanced at the book's sketches, he rubbed her feet and told stories about his late-night passengers: an unemployed court reporter looking for a buyer for his screenplay; a guy camping at Barton Creek who'd never been in a cab. "It pays to be friendly," Sam said. Terezie fried eggs; I made more coffee. After he'd eaten and while I washed dishes, he carried his wife into their bedroom, kissing her chest. "Hello," I yelled at the closed door, ready to rap it with my fist. "Excuse me, you've got company." I imagined his taut flanks, her sensual mouth. Then I packed my things and propped their front door open as I marched away.

Some days, Sam skipped work, dozing or staring at the TV. One mid-November night, the three of us sat in lawn chairs on their apartment's backyard deck, talking late. Sam, barefoot, in blue jean shorts, finished a six-pack. As his speech slowed, he became more physical: catching a fly in his fist, tugging his ponytail. His body smelled rank, addictive, while he massaged Terezie's neck. He told stories about his job at Family

Health Services ("A little boy cuts himself tattoos; one's a smiley face, I kid you not"), and recited a line from Gogol's "Overcoat" ("This Person of Consequence had only lately become a person of consequence, and until recently had been a person of no consequence").

"I don't know if I can go back," he said.

"Is it really that bad?" I said, trying to imagine what he faced. Droves of desperate people must have expected help. They probably blamed him for their messy lives, calling him a bureaucrat. How ironic was that?

He stood, slapped his stomach, grabbed another beer. "Here's to man, and the son of man, which is a worm." He clinked my bottle, drank. "Hey, you still with the preacher?"

"Saul," I corrected.

"What?"

"His name is Saul."

"Like I said, you still with the preacher?" He noticed a beer stain on his black t-shirt. "Excuse me," he chuckled. "I must be full." He waited, but we didn't laugh. "What I'm trying to say is, I know some guys. Why don't you let me fix you up?"

"You trying to get rid of me?"

"Sam," Terezie said, "you're drunk." She tugged his arm until he sat. "And you're boring."

Sam whistled, the ringing carrying down the block. "Damn, George. Did I insult your artistic sensibility? My wife," Sam lifted his bottle again, "the great virtuoso."

I didn't know until my next stopover that Ruby had died. My parents hadn't thought to mention it, even though my brothers and I felt as close to her as we did to our grandparents. A framed photograph of a woman appeared with others Sam and Terezie kept on a bookshelf. Dressed in knee-high boots, tie, belted coat, and trousers, she leaned against a roadster parked next to a biplane. "That's Bessie Coleman," Sam said, "Ruby's sister. The first black woman pilot, what they call a barnstormer. Ruby's Missy Mama." I leaned in, my nose almost touching glass. *This is like one of Otis' Master Sam stories*, I thought. "Their dad was a Cherokee sharecropper, but he couldn't take it. Left them in Waxahachie, went back to 'Indian country,' he called it. Ruby said he didn't give them anything except his wide head. Ha!" he snorted. "Anyway, I guess she wanted me to have it." Now I regretted not having a memento of Otis. The stories would have to be enough.

That night, Sam treated us to dinner at his favorite Tex-Mex restaurant. Dishes clanked while waitresses shouted their orders at the kitchen window. Sam ordered glasses of Big Red.

"We're celebrating," he said, dipping a chip into guacamole.

"What for?" I said, dipping mine.

"I don't know," he said. "Any suggestions?"

"Jalepeño peppers," Terezie said, munching.

"To the jalepeño," he said, holding a chip in the air.

"The jalepeño," Terezie and I sang. We each took a bite.

Terezie described a third-grade boy at the school where she was student teaching. She told a story about him accidentally sitting on his peanut butter sandwich. To the delight of his classmates, he'd turned the stain into a scatological routine.

"I know a kid, too," Sam said, leaning back. He'd finished the basket of chips and raked the guacamole bowl with his finger. "He's the one I told you about, the one with tattoos." I nodded. "He's not doing so good, but we think we can help him." He lifted his arms as the waitress set down his enchiladas. He rolled a tortilla.

"Great kid. Five going on ten." He took a sip of his drink. "His foster parents adopted him, and everything looked cool. But, without going into details, things aren't so great now. Right?" He looked at Terezie.

"He's a good kid," she said.

"I need to ask a favor," he said shoveling a forkful of rice and beans.

I was flattered. Finally, I could do something for them. "What?"

"His new mom does this thing with women's hair where she straightens it and weaves in wigs and stuff. Anyway, she makes pretty good money, but she plays hard and isn't around much. Dad just up and split. I'd like to get Clarence out of there, but there's not enough evidence yet. Meantime, I don't like him being by himself."

"How terrible. Poor kid."

"He stayed one night with us, and it was great. Right?"

"I said he was a good kid," Terezie answered." Her tone was not subtle.

"As you can see, she's not a hundred percent with me on this, but she's getting there."

His buildup made me nervous. "Just tell me what you want."

"I want the boy to live with us."

I glanced at Terezie, who looked away. "Really? Can you do that?"

Sam stared at his plate. "Not exactly, but this is a special case." He brightened, leaning on his elbows. "His so-called mom and her new boyfriend are going to Vegas next weekend. So I thought he could stay with you. I need a little more time to figure out how to make this work." He chewed a bite of tortilla and licked his fingers.

"That's so exciting!" Sam smiled; Terezie didn't. "But why can't he stay with you again?"

"If he does and somebody finds out, it could spoil our chances."

"But *I* can't get in trouble, right? I mean, everybody'd be cool about him staying with me?"

"Absolutely. We'll get approval first."

I'd get to help my brother adopt the child he wants. What could be better than that? Bringing the boy to the compound would be easy. He'd probably think it was camp. Still, something didn't seem right. "Terezie, what's he not telling me?"

"When his supervisor finds out," she said, watching him, "he could get fired. He could lose any chance of ever getting his license."

"That's *not* going to happen," he said, shrugging. He shoved away from the table, leaned back, crossing his ankles, his arms. "And even if it does, having Clarence would be worth it."

"I don't understand," I said to Terezie.

"This is crossing the professional line—it's an absolute no-no— but he's being the usual jughead. To be honest, I'm not even sure it's okay for you to keep Clarence for the weekend."

Sam threw his napkin at his plate, splattering picante. "You said yourself that you like him," Sam said. "You said you'd think about it. What happened?"

"You're right; I did say I'd consider it, and I will," Terezie said. "Because I see how much it means to you, and I think he's great. But only if Sarah agrees to help."

"Excellent," Sam said, turning, rolling up his sleeves. He scooted his plate, hiding the puddle of sauce. "I can't wait for you to meet him. He's one tough dude."

"I don't know, Sam," I said, thinking, *convince me.*

He poked my ribs, tickling. "You'll see. It'll be great, *Aunt Sarah.*"

"Stop that," I said. "Adoptions are a big deal, Sam. He's a kid, not a puppy."

Sam cocked his head. "You don't know what you're talking about. Don't do this."

"Don't do what? Get you fired?"

"I can make this work." He squeezed my shoulder. "I need your help." His request was the confession I'd longed for. "Have I ever asked you for anything else?"

"Isn't there a way to adopt Clarence without getting you in trouble?"

"I can figure it out. I just need more time. He's only five. He'll be all by himself if you don't take him." His words pressed; his eyes were a torch. "I'm close to having the evidence. I'm working on my supervisor; it won't take much longer. Now, are you going to help or not?"

Terezie slumped.

Would I help Sam adopt a son, or take the blame for something Terezie couldn't bring herself to do? The answer leaked from my mouth. "I can't. It's not right, Sam, and you know it."

"What?" he growled. "You've got to be kidding. You *have* to do it. Terezie won't agree unless you do."

I shook my head. "Please, Sam." My heart collapsed, a burning house.

"Thanks! Thank you very much," he said, standing, knocking his chair. He tossed money on the table, and while everyone watched, he walked out the door.

The next weekend, I went home to Nugent. I considered telling my parents about Sam's moodiness, but, instead, Kurt distracted them. Apparently, he was failing anatomy at Galveston, and his pre-arranged fellowship with Denton Cooley at Baylor was already in jeopardy. He'd come home, too, but I didn't get to spend much time with him. He and my father talked in the study.

Sitting in the living room, pretending to read the paper, I watched. They sat on either side of my father's desk, books and the kettle of bones between. "Bones are composed of two types of tissues," my father said, and Kurt pushed his glasses up, agape. "Compact or dense bone, a little like Sam's head," he laughed, "and spongy or canallous bone, like, well, I guess your head. But we're going to change that, right?"

"Yes, sir," Kurt said, scooting forward. He was twenty-three, built like a halfback, engaged to be married, and he could've been Hugh that morning so long ago.

"Two-point-six million red blood cells are produced each second by the marrow." What he meant was, "Let men laugh when you sacrifice desire to duty." They stayed two and half days in that room, their meals brought on trays, huddling again the following two weekends.

I had my last stopover at Sam's during the first week in December. I hadn't seen them for three weeks, time enough for noticeable changes. I didn't call beforehand and arrived mid-afternoon, earlier than usual, so I wasn't surprised when Cyril answered the door. "Thank God," Cyril said, nervously touching my shoulder. "Good," he said, nodding, "come in. Look, Sarah's here." He pulled me to his sister, who sat next to a chair propped upside down on the daybed. For some reason, all the furniture, including the piano, table, and chairs, had been shoved into the center of the room.

"What's up?" I asked, assuming that Terezie had called Cyril to help with a redecoration. I hoped I could help.

"Your brother decided to try something new," Terezie said. "Not exactly my taste. What do *you* think?" When she hugged her knees, Cyril paced the room. "Sam…" he said, shaking his head. This was the first time I'd seen Cyril criticize Sam.

"I detect his style," I said, "contemporary chaos." The braided rug draped their rocking chair. A brass lamp lay decapitated, its linen shade resting on a stack of books. "Where is he?" Obviously, something was wrong.

"In his temple," Terezie said, chewing her lip.

"His what?"

"The bedroom," Cyril whispered, pointing but not looking at the door.

I found mattress, bed frame, table, and aquarium piled in the middle of the bedroom. In the corner, swirled curtains formed a bloated cocoon. Sunlight glowed inside the room's white walls. Sam sat near a window, naked, his legs folded into the lotus position, his head shaved, eyes closed. I couldn't believe he'd lost so much weight. This was anything but his true self.

"Hey," I said trying not to sound alarmed. I closed the door, but Sam didn't move. "Sam?" I said, touching his shoulder. I squatted, checking his face.

He blinked, focused his gaze. He smiled.

"What are you doing?"

"Purifying," he whispered.

"Bullshit," I said. "I want to know what's going on. Did you know Cyril's here?"

He closed his eyes. I wondered if he was stoned.

I shoved him, stood. "I think he might be taking Terezie home to her parents. Sam, this is just plain weird."

"The only way to cure suffering is to tame the flesh." Slowly, he lifted his leg, lodging it behind his neck, straining even though he was double-jointed. He tipped to the side. "Be faithful," he panted, his face blanching, "to that which exists nowhere but in yourself."

He's snapped, I thought. "You're scaring me."

"You're only bothered by the unfamiliar." Sweat dripped from his scalp to his cheek. "I've taken control."

"Have you eaten? Where are your clothes?"

"Purity can only be attained by abstention from pleasure."

I walked to the chest of drawers, found his jean shorts. "At least put some pants on, Mr. Indispensable."

His smile hinted at mischief, giving me hope. When the phone rang, we jumped. "Did you and Terezie have a fight?" Could something have happened to that little boy?

Someone knocked. Cyril peeked in, his tenderness a jolt. "Sam?" He waited, but Sam looked straight ahead. "He says he's a client."

Sam eased his leg down. He stepped, feet smacking, into the corner next to the swirled curtains, picked up the receiver. "Hello," he said, nude, wan, staring at me. His face sagged, then hardened. "What happened?" Flicking sweat from his forehead, his fingers rubbed an imprint—two streaks, pink, then gone. "Jake, I met your supervisor. He wouldn't do that." Sam bent over then froze, listening. "You know," he said, raising himself, "you're full of shit. You need that job."

Terezie tiptoed in, walked passed Cyril and me, then stood in front of Sam. He glanced while she shadowed him, shifting from side to side, her hand a plea on his naked arm. "I can't talk to you now. I told you never to call me at home." He climbed onto a window seat, Terezie his acolyte. "Jake, Jake," he yelled. "*You're* the problem." He held the receiver away, shook his face, vibrating his cheeks, then brought the receiver back. "Yeah, is that right?" he said. "It's pointless," he shouted. "Don't you understand?" He stared at the ceiling. "Uh-huh, sure, why not? Come see for yourself tomorrow." When he stretched one pointed foot behind his back then lifted it, he reached over his bald head, arching his body like a bow, and he pulled the foot even with his shoulder, his other arm spread, balancing.

Terezie turned, eyes pooling. As soon as I could, I left, sadly relieved to go.

Terezie phoned one Sunday just before Christmas. I slipped out of Elijah's morning service to take her call in the main office. "Sam's been in an accident," she said, her voice flat.

Fistfight? I wondered. "What now?" I asked, annoyed, thinking Sam had to change jobs, do something to get out of this cycle of bad luck.

"About four this morning," Terezie said, "he dropped a fare at the airport then drove off the second story ramp."

"Are you saying he was in an accident?"

"His spine's fractured." Heavy breathing became a cough.

"Who was driving?"

Terezie cleared her throat. "The doctor says he won't ever walk again."

"What?" I moved the phone closer, set it in my lap. "Sam's passenger's in the hospital?"

While Terezie patiently made me understand, I stayed calm. "Can you come?" she asked, whimpering. "Please?"

Saul insisted on driving, and during the next six hours, I tried to imagine what I'd find in intensive care: Terezie, of course; my parents; maybe Kurt and Hugh; and Sam. I wondered what he knew about his condition, and how much pain he felt. I pictured him on a gurney, his speckled eyes incredulous, his pouty lips strained.

When Terezie saw me, she blinked twice then wept on Cyril's chest. His arms hung, clubs. Saul stepped forward, and she shifted her embrace to him. Mumbled consolations began as I shoved my way toward Kurt, who stood, reading stapled sheets of paper.

"Any update?" He'd have heard the doctors explain Sam's condition to our father, and now he could translate that for me.

"It's a T4-6 spinal cord injury. The prognosis is incontrovertible."

"How did it happen?"

"That's what nobody can figure out." He handed me the paper. "His accident report says at 3:53 a.m., he crashed through the rail and sailed off the ramp like it was an exit." He turned a page, pointing. "Dry pavement. No faulty lighting. He either fell asleep or somebody screwed up the lane markings. Apparently, a number of accidents have happened in that exact spot." He took the report back, checking. "I think we should sue."

"Did Sam say anything?"

"Yeah, it's in the report." He squinted, shuffled the pages. "Here," he said, sighing, shaking his head. In the section marked, "Investigator's Narrative Opinion of What Happened," someone had written: "Driver says he dropped off a fare. He then moved to the ramp's outer lane, but as he proceeded, the moon, being smarter than he was, told him to make a sharp left."

"That's ridiculous," I said.

"Exactly."

"Why would he say that?"

"You know Sam," he said, folding the paper, pretending to straighten his glasses as he wiped his eyes. Our father walked around the corner. Kurt joined him.

Terezie's parents arrived, ushering her to the family waiting room. When I moved toward Sam's bed, Saul approached, while my father sprinted after two doctors down the hall. He'd only taken a few steps before he stumbled, then fell, landing prostrate in the passageway. Before I could move, one of the men trotted over just as Kurt bent down. Dad began talking, rising to his knees, so Saul and I instead slipped past the curtained doorway into Sam's room.

My mother sat in a chair next to the bed, holding Sam's hand. She stood when we walked in. "He's sleeping," she whispered.

"Are you all right?"

"No." Her eyes watered. "He's my child. It's tough." She faced the window, blew her nose. "I'm glad you're here, though," she said. "You're better at this."

"But Mama, I'm not." I'd never seen her cry.

She turned around, straightened. "You and Sam have always been close."

I walked to the bed. A metal device fit over his head with posts drilled into his temples. Tubes hooked to his wrists. His eyes were closed; one hand lay palm-open. A starched sheet and blanket covered his body, but his feet made a bulge. He can't feel them, I thought. Sam's trapped inside his body like that mouse inside the bass. I leaned, needing to hear breathing, and smelled antiseptic, sweat, something like glue.

"I'm going to check on your father. He's not as strong as you think," my mother said, patting my back.

"Daddy fell." She blanched. "Don't worry. He's okay."

"We'll be right outside," she said.

Sam's eyes opened; he blinked. I tried to smile. "Hey," he said.

Does he need a nurse? I thought. Pain killer? Does he know it's me? I remembered Mary Jo sprawled across the train tracks; again, I hated myself for not knowing what to do. "Can I get you anything?"

"Terezie," he said, "she's tired. She needs something to eat."

"Don't worry. Her parents are here."

"Hey," he said to Saul, who stood in the corner, my sweater over his arm.

"Sam," Saul said, stepping to the bed, "what exactly have you heard?"

Saul's take-charge manner, his lean, mobile body suddenly made me furious. "We don't need you right now," I said.

"Excuse me?" he said.

"Leave." I pushed him. "Out."

"All right, all right," he said, nodding, passing me the sweater then stumbling through the door. I lay the sweater and my purse on my mother's chair.

Sam said, "Sar, touch them."

I moved to the foot of the bed, reaching toward the cover.

"No, underneath," he said, his hooded eyes darting. He lifted his arm, rattling the tubes. The icy air smelled of alcohol, adhesive tape. The blinds lay flat, a plastic plank.

"Let me get a nurse." I turned toward the doorway.

"Don't be scared, not of me."

"No, I just—"

"I want you to do it, just us." He motioned with his hand.

Slowly, I folded back the quilt, then the sheet. Wrapped in a hospital gown, his body lay limp, his feet turned out. I recognized his shape, his muscled calves, but his joints and limbs seemed tacked on, slabs of clay, cadaver-like.

"Pinch something," he said. His breath was spoiled fruit, warm, turning.

I remembered him smoothing the cadaver's mouth, his relaxed talk about the genitals. "You know what?" I said, unfolding the cover, pulling it into place. "This isn't a good idea."

His eyebrows lowered beneath the metal band at his forehead.

"You're not supposed to feel anything the first few days." I patted his hand. "Sleep is what you need." I leaned in close, scowling. "And you better not give me any trouble."

While Saul drove us back to Palestine, I told him I needed to be alone.

"That's to be expected," he said. Cows lounged at a manmade lake under an elm grove. "You have a great deal on your mind."

"You're right. But that's not what I mean." That morning, Sam had been moved to his own hospital room. Surrounded by our mother, Terezie, a nurse, and vases of flowers, he'd watched glumly as I walked out the door.

"What do you mean?"

"I'm moving to Baylor. I can't see you anymore."

At first, I wondered if he'd heard me. Then he squeezed the steering wheel, his fists a clinched nerve. "I understand," he finally said.

"No you don't. Don't say that," I snapped.

He gazed, his thin, mustached face no longer familiar. "This is a particularly difficult time—"

"Stop. You've got to listen." I turned, leaning against the door. "Our relationship is over. I'm moving out tomorrow, and I want you to leave me alone."

"Now is not the correct time—"

"I don't think I can be any clearer." Was I shouting? "Sam needs me. I don't have room for anybody else."

After he pulled the car over, he reached toward me.

"Saul," I said, jerking away. "Please. I don't love you anymore."

He leaned on the wheel, burying his face in his arms.

CHAPTER 17
1969

THE REHAB HOSPITAL: cellblock rooms off endless shiny hallways, averted eyes, limp bodies in wheelchairs, on gurneys; moaning, repeated shouting of a name (*Betsy, Betsy, Betsy...goddammit, Betsy*), an odor of Pine-Sol, lime Jell-O, piss. These impressions are clear now, but their implications didn't register then. I believed Sam dutifully inhabited this inferno, but only temporarily, that he would endure rigors of rehab then somehow be transported home where his life would be altered, of course, but because he was Sam, it would resume normal definitions, that his mangled body, like Antonín Cervenka's, would be transformed. Sam would become the exemplary paraplegic.

I sat next to his bed, which was one of twelve in the room, a scene straight off a World War II movie set. "Goddamn nurse won't come turn me," he said, his face already thinner, his lips chapped, crust at the corners. "Sores will cover my ass. They don't give a fuck."

I scampered toward the doorway, frightened by his language, his mood, the place. "Should I go get her?" Now I was sure that his accident had been my fault. His appeal for help that day in the restaurant had carried larger implications, suggestions I'd been too self-absorbed to notice.

"No. Won't do any good." He flinched, shifted his beefy shoulders. "Smell anything? I think I've gone and crapped again. You smell it?"

I shook my head, not knowing then about the rubber pants he probably was wearing, his urethral catheter, his loss of bowel control, fear of infection.

"Can't use a toilet, and they won't fucking tell me if I ever will again." His eyes reddened; he exhaled, slowly. "A goddamn eunuch."

I didn't allow myself to think about his bowel/sex connection. Anthropology was my reference point. "I'm sure they know what they're doing. They'll teach you. It'll be like learning a new language."

His hand slid under the covers. "Smell anything?"

"What you need is a road trip. Can you leave to get something to eat?"

He stared, his arm making a tunnel in the sheets. "It's funny, going off the ramp—can't remember. But I had some french fries—salty, greasy so a little came off on your fingers, and cut skinny, you know, so they crunched. If I had some now, I'd lick the goddamn sack."

"Want to? I'll take you."

He laughed. The sheet quivered, bulging below his waist. "How about that—a fucking boner. Hey, Betsy," he shouted, "supper's ready." He laughed. "Come and get it."

"Sam, don't," I said.

His arms slapped the top of the covers. He turned his back, reached for a glass of water, sipped. "There's only one thing scares me," he said, staring ahead again. "That's falling. I'm lying here, flopped like a goddamn channel cat, and all I think about is rolling off this fucking bed." He shoved the glass back onto the table. "Pitiful. Nothing but a shit-faced organism. Protoplasm on a plate."

"No wonder," I said, panicked, "it's this place. You'll be all right once you get home."

"I'm not leaving," he said, frowning. "And I'll slug anybody who tries to make me."

My mother told me to answer the phone. Sam now lived with Terezie in an apartment one block from my parents, and every couple of weekends I drove the half-hour from Baylor so I could visit him. Sometimes we'd go out to eat, and once at a pub just across the county line, he'd insisted that we dance. "'Scuse me, sugar. Make way for the gimp," he shouted, and people stumbled, clearing a space. A lousy band was playing—a horn, two guitars, drums, a singer who thought he was Bobby Darin. He wasn't. Sam requested "Do You Wanna Dance?" and at first, the guy thought it was a bad joke. It was, but the group honked the tune anyway. Sam jimmied his wheels back and forth to the rhythm while I swayed. We even did the hand jive. Yanking on the pushrim, he'd twirled his chair, and a woman at a nearby table had clapped.

I expected the call to be from Terezie. She'd already talked earlier to my mother, wanting to know if Sam was at the house. Apparently, he'd been gone overnight again, and she couldn't find him anywhere. This morning while she railed, my mother had made excuses for him, then gradually grew peeved, her chin the familiar rubber patch. Now two hours later, she shrugged, handing me the phone.

"Hello," I said.

"Is this Sarah?" a woman said, husky as a blues singer.

"Yes."

"Just a minute."

Then Sam said, "Sar, I need a favor."

Since my mother was watching, I pretended it was somebody else. "Sure. What's up?"

"I'm with someone. Can you drive your car down the block and meet us? I need you to take me home."

"No problem. See you there," I said, hanging up. Here we go again, I thought, nervous, relieved. Sam was bouncing back.

"Who was that?" my mother said, her glare a scalpel.

"Someone from high school. You never knew her. We're going to meet for a Coke." I grabbed my purse, pulled out my keys. "I won't be long, about an hour, I guess."

A block away, Sam sat in a red Triumph convertible with a girl it turned out I did remember. Petite, with black, unratted hair, she'd had a comic's wit, Elizabeth Taylor eyebrows, and an unforced smile. Not seductive, more like Natalie Wood. When a group of us stood together, she looked like the grown-up. Weeks before graduation, someone convinced her to play Mrs. Waters in *Tom Jones*. In one scene, she and Tom stood behind a screen while we heard smacking, moaning, groans.

When they appeared, we saw lipstick dotting Tom's face, and we cheered. Unfazed, Mrs. Waters shaded her eyes from the stage lights and gazed into the audience, studying us.

"Hey, Sarah," she cooed, gorgeous now, coltish, oestrual.

"Hi," I said. "What's going on?"

"Just two friends getting reacquainted." She rubbed Sam's back, her hand dainty, her fingers probing. "I always had a crush on your brother." She leaned into his neck, whispering, "Call me when you're in Dallas, okay? I'll fit you in." He put his arm around her. "A freebee." She kissed him. "For old times."

Sam opened his door, pushed his wheelchair out of the back seat, unfolded it, and positioned it next to him in the street. He shifted himself onto the green leather seat, clanked the footrests into place, positioned his legs, then rolled himself to my car and repeated the same steps in reverse. While I crammed the folded chair behind him, the girl sped down our street, her radio's decibel-level cranking.

"How's it going?" Sam said, grinning, his eyes unfocused, floaty.

"What was *that*?"

"What?" He blinked, putty-faced. That wasn't sage I smelled.

"Terezie called Mom." Why did I enjoy saying that? Me, the tattletale. Pathetic.

He smiled, slowly nodding. "Then I guess you'd better get me home."

When I turned into his driveway, our mother stood with Terezie at the apartment door. They crossed their arms, a phalanx.

"Sar, what did you tell Mom?" he said.

"That a friend wanted to meet me for a Coke." How stupid, I now thought. Of course, she knew. What a mess.

The women glared. Terezie crushed wads of her bathrobe in both fists.

Sam opened his car door and reached for his chair. He propped the contraption open on the pavement next to his seat. "It's okay, Sar," he said. "I'd better take it from here."

CHAPTER 18
1970

THERE WAS A TIME when I researched paraplegia. The primary cause: accidents. The largest group: young, virile males. One minute, invincible; the next, numb in a hospital bed. An alien force transforms your body and leaves you inside, trapped. An irritable nurse wipes your ass. You're told what you can and, especially, what you cannot do. But no one talks about sex.

Along with your leg and genital spasms, you get erections, usually when you'd rather not. They can, however, be convenient for lovemaking. A little rubbing of the inner thigh, the penis, the scrotum, and presto. The only thing missing is any sexual urge or sensation. For that reason, you're inventive with your fingers, your tongue. During coitus, you probably watch in order to have a sense of participation. Your orgasm, if you're lucky enough to have one, is a combination of leg and genital spasms, sweat, a sensation of warmth, an ill-defined mental relief. One man claimed he passed out for ten seconds.

One Friday in late August, nine months after the accident, Sam told Terezie he didn't want to go to water therapy, and he asked me to go with him instead. I'd come to Nugent the night before, according to my mother's instructions, to help prepare a family Sunday feast. Sam phoned after Terezie had left. My mother irritably agreed to shop for groceries alone. "He'd better switch his appointment to Saturdays. He's lucky I made you come two days early."

Susie, the physical therapist, was as thick-waisted as she was thick-skinned, a no-nonsense matron leading her troops through each inveterate drill. With the help of two male attendants, Sam and three other men were strapped into canvas floater belts and lowered into the ninety-five degree womb. As I stood next to Sam, his face almost level with mine, his muscled arms treading water, I blocked my conscious memory of his paralysis. We were there because of his disability, but somehow I had my brother back, pre-accident, all to myself.

Susie instructed me to massage his bobbing seaweed feet. "Press here," she said pointing to his instep, "and bend the toes." She squeezed and rolled them, each wrist crank an expert latch twist. The yanks sprayed drops, while flowing tracks dribbled down her arms. "He won't break." She dropped his foot, *plunk*. In spite of the chest-high gelatinous water, his skin felt dry, tear-able. Using the heel of my hand, I rubbed the bottom of his foot, a slow, rhythmic kneading, and even though he couldn't feel it, Sam leaned back, eyes closed. Next, I curled the toes, pressing each one with my thumb, along the curved top, across the flat nail. Then the stretched spaces between, the loops of connecting skin soft as a wrist's underside. "You asleep?" I asked.

"Mmmm," he said, turquoise encircling his face. Waves slapped the steps, trickling into a nearby side drain.

"Now stand at his feet," Susie instructed, "and grab his calves. Lean right up next to him." His toes, then, rested against my chest. "Massage those calves. I mean give them a real work-out." While I pressed and squeezed, his feet rubbed my breasts. I felt his legs for muscle, sliding all my weight against the little I found.

"Terezie must have the strongest fingers in town," I said, working my arms, trying not to notice his feet brushing. Sam's eyes opened, his glare an impulse he couldn't resist. *"What...?"* I said.

From the sidewalk above us, Susie stood, water dripping from her suit and body, creeping across concrete, seeping into pavement. She gave her next order to the whole group. "Stretch the legs open and wrap them around you. Concentrate on the inner thigh muscles."

"She's kidding, right?" But each of the other couples was already clutched, their poses straight from a sex manual. "You don't really want to…" I motioned toward Susie, shaking my head.

Sam smiled.

"Pelton," Susie barked, "is there a problem?"

"No, I guess not," I said, tugging at Sam's ankles, pulling them in slow motion through the buoyant water, wrapping them behind my waist. He lay back, treading, his swiveling palms triggering ripples. I bent and straightened his left knee, never looking at his face. Then the right knee, concentrating on my applied pressure, the necessary positions for my hands, my toes as they gripped the gritty floor. Sunlight shone through condensation on tall windows, rays speckling the surface, white patches bobbing, a symphony of flash. As his leg drifted forward then back again, air pockets bubbling under his trunks, I remembered his fingers straightening the cadaver's puckered mouth.

"Thanks," Sam said, resting his palm on my arm.

"Huh?" I said, jumping. "Oh." I shook my head, bent his left knee.

"Pull my leg around again," he said.

"Okay," I said, positioning his feet at my back, trying to be casual.

"I love the water." He sloshed an oozy handful at my breast. "I wish we could live here."

"King and queen frog," I said stupidly.

"Like floating in space. Black." He grasped my shoulders, closed his eyes. Then, I felt him—the man, not my brother—swelling against my belly. I held onto his arms, and for one intoxicating moment, we stayed clasped like that, together.

"Hey, Sergeant Susie's watching." Panicking, I pulled his hands down, reached for his right ankle. I guiltily hoped he'd felt himself becoming aroused, that he'd liked pressing against me.

His eyes popped open. He squeezed my shoulder again. "Listen. Stop." He grabbed my hands, leaving his fugitive legs undirected, drifting. As he floated backward, his expression crumpled. I caught him then, wrapped his legs around me. His hands rose, and while he rested them on my shoulders, he pulled out of the water. He slid his arms to my back, and he hugged me, rubbing my neck, stroking my hair. "It's okay," he said. "It's only me." He felt strong, solid, and he was wet, smelling of chlorine, sodden canvas.

"Sam?" I said, burying my face at his ear. I wanted to ask why he'd been so moody during the months before the accident, to remind him of the fish he'd gutted, his natural enthusiasm for its mysteries, his insistence that I live unafraid, eager to see even the most difficult truth. If I had to do that, why didn't he? But my questions would hurt him. I didn't know how to convince *him* of something *he* needed—a naïve hope, of course. How could I know what he was thinking?

"Shhh," he said. "Just hold me."

He didn't say anything else until the drive home. "You need to see the ruins of Malinalco near Mexico City," he told me. "Promise?"

CHAPTER 19
1970

WHEN THE FAMILY GATHERED for lunch, we thanked Sam for requesting our unseasonable menu—beef tender, an early Thanksgiving feast.

Terezie parked their Impala at the end of the front walk, since Sam's wheelchair couldn't fit through the back door. Kurt met them as Sam balanced on the armrests then swung himself onto the seat. "Here, I'll do that," Kurt said, taking the handles. Terezie positioned Sam's feet on the footrests. While Kurt bumped him backward up the curb, she locked the car. The chair's wheels rumbled on the pavement, vibrating Sam's cheeks. Kurt pulled him up the porch steps, front casters swiveling, Sam's head pressed against his brother's chest.

"Where to?" Kurt asked once they'd squeezed through the entrance.

Mesmerized, Hugh stood unmoving in their path.

"Hugh, buddy?" Sam said, reaching out.

Hugh flinched, then shuffled, almost tripping, to the side. Blushing, he covered his mouth.

"Thanks, man," Sam said, then used the pushrim to help Kurt get him across the carpet to the dining room. His chair fit easily under the round table, where the men joined him, relieved to be eye-to-eye.

"After lunch, we'll adjust that seat," my father said, sitting at the next place. He checked the space beside Sam's thigh. "It's too narrow. There should be a half-inch between you and the chair." He sat back, watching the women through the doorway. "Otherwise, it could interfere with your circulation. You don't want a pressure ulcer."

Sam inspected his fork then set it down. "Even the smell of Mom's cooking is fattening," he mumbled. Nudging my father, he winked and nodded at the kitchen. "You think," he shouted toward the stove, "they'll bring us something before we starve to death?"

"You boys," my mother said as she set a plate of tenderloin before him, "you're a bottomless pit."

"You don't know how much I've been looking forward to this," Sam said.

In spite of the heat, we ate like jackals, sopping the last drops of gravy with sourdough rolls. Woozy, we secretly longed to stagger to our cars, drive home for a nap. But before we could rise, Sam asked for a second helping.

"There's plenty," my mother said, jumping to refill his plate. We slumped in our seats, politely watching our cheerful invalid gorge himself. Clearly, he was better adjusted, I thought.

After lunch, our father floated upstairs, Hugh left to meet friends at a movie, and we women cleaned up the dishes. Once we'd finished, we walked into the living room, where Sam and Kurt debated the hunting abilities of beagles. They waived their arms, taunting each other. "Face it," Kurt said, standing to go to the bathroom, "you know I'm right."

"How long you think you'll have to wait," Sam said, "before *that* happens." We laughed, back in familiar territory, assuaged. He wanted to talk about movies, so we sat, impatient but graciously quiet, we believed, in order to appease him. Terezie dozed and my mind drifted, but he didn't notice. He described one we hadn't seen, its plot convoluted, exhausting. Perspiration misted his lip as he shared the final scene about a prisoner waiting to be put to death. "So the guy turns to the priest, says, 'Hey, it's okay. I've done more than most. There's nothing I feel like I missed.'"

After that, he described a dream. "I'm walking, more like floating, but I feel my thighs catch whenever I take a step. The way your leg tightens, the flexing."

Twice before, I'd seen his legs spasm, knocking a foot off the wheelchair pedal. I didn't learn until later that he suffered spinal pain, had stones in his kidneys and bladder.

"I'm moving down these steps, and it's a cobblestone street, like in some European country, Italy or Hungary, maybe."

I pictured him striding through coral light at dusk, two steps at a time down a crowded walkway, Duomo bells ringing, people turning, drawn to his energy, his body, his seductive expression.

We waited, expecting him to tell what came next.

My mother came to Baylor, unable to tell me over the phone. I knew the news was bad when I received a note that said to meet her at my dorm. We sat on my bunk; she held my shoulders and described what Sam had done.

"I was afraid to tell you," my mother confessed, shuddering. Her puffy eyes remained surprisingly dry. "From the time you were born, he stayed close. He always took care of you."

My tears were more for her than for Sam. Those would come later. For now, my mind was a sewer clogged with images: Sam saying, "I need your help," then later sitting naked on his apartment floor; his description of the movie, when the inmate said, "There's nothing I feel like I missed"; and worst, his final moments. Had he said anything to himself, to anyone? Had he prayed?

"He left instructions," she said, "not much though, really."

"What? He left a letter?"

"Terezie found it in his motel room. He wanted her to have his things; that's all."

"You mean he left a will? He took time to write something?"

"Oh, he'd written it before then."

"How do you know?"

"Because that prostitute had signed it as a witness, that's why. Poor Terezie."

"You mean the high school girlfriend who came to see him?"

"The very one."

"*She* signed his will?" I pictured her kissing him, whispering, "For old times."

"Your father refuses to talk about him," my mother said. "Not a word. The only thing he's said is that with four children, the odds were we'd lose one."

Sam, already a statistic. Had our father been waiting to see which one of us would go? Or had he suspected early that the odds-on favorite would be Sam?

My mother described a visit she'd had from Sam two days before. "He asked if he could have lunch, so, of course, I dropped everything." She inspected the veins on the backs of her hands, traced one, straightened her ring. "I'm so glad I did. Now I think that, without knowing it, I suspected something." She brushed her skirt. "When he called, he said getting dressed took so much out of him, he didn't think he could go anywhere. So I made us Ruebens, and we ate right there in the car." She pressed her lip. "He loved Ruebens."

I nodded, picturing him the Sunday before, gorging.

"After he called, I went straight to the meat market." Her fingers sliced air. "Without a doubt, I found the best corned beef I've *ever* tasted. Sam even said so. Lettuce straight out of my garden. I used my homemade mayonnaise, too. Sam noticed. He ate a garlic pickle from the batch I'd put up." She gazed, picturing him. "He called me an artist." She chuckled, shrugging. "It really was a good sandwich."

"He ate two helpings last Sunday."

"Wasn't that something?"

"I didn't know anybody could hold that much."

"That was one of his favorites, no question." We sat, the silence filled with all we couldn't say. "We stayed a whole hour in his car. He's never done anything like that before."

"Sounds like you had a good talk."

"We did. Yes," she nodded, "we said a lot. He knew more than I thought."

"Like what?"

"Oh, that he was born while Daddy was away."

"But we all knew that."

"Well, you didn't know how hard it was. And it was—hard, I mean. Sam understood."

"Good, I'm glad." But did he encourage her feistiness? Did she tell him she'd read *The Feminine Mystique*? Probably not, but that's what I imagined.

"Sam and I were just alike," she said, not for the first time. "He knew what he was in for." She stood, picking up her purse. "Frankly, I would've done the same thing."

That evening, Hugh shared details about the suicide. Sam had driven to the Oasis Motel on IH 35 in the secondhand Studebaker that my mother had rigged with hand controls. He phoned Hugh that afternoon and said to come over. He explained that Terezie was still at the private school where she'd begun teaching.

"Did he tell you why he was there?" I asked. We sat in our parents' backyard, at the same wrought iron table where Otis had described his master's spirit, lifting.

"He said the air conditioner was broken in their apartment." Hugh cried, as though I'd accused him. "So they were spending the night while it was being fixed."

I nodded. "Sam could make us believe anything."

"I didn't know," Hugh sobbed, cupping his face, dropping to the table.

"Of course you didn't." I hugged him, his shoulders taut, knobby. "No one blames you. We all feel guilty."

"You do?" He peeked, rubbing his eyes.

"I need to know what he was like when you saw him. You understand?"

Hugh sat back, exhausted. A breeze bounced the pecan tree's limbs. A grackle cawed. "I smoked a cigar," he muttered, trance-like. "He had a box on the table, and when I got there, he gave me one." He wiped his cheeks with his sleeve. "It was terrible." He turned, laughing, then hiccupped.

"Really?" and I joined him, teetering toward hysteria. "Leave it to Sam," I said.

"We got pretty drunk, too."

"When you left, he was drunk?"

"Yeah." He frowned, his chin tightening.

"What did you talk about?"

"Music, mostly. He helped me write a song." He cocked his head, remembering. "Can you believe that?"

"He thought you had talent."

"You know what it's called?" I shook my head. "Come in the Back Door, 'Cause No Bleedin's Allowed on the Living Room Floor."

Our laughter was tender relief. When he sang, he transported us to childhood. Sam, who'd been playing softball with Hugh in the side yard, dove to catch a wild pitch. Sliding, he hit a rock that shaved his elbow. The line had come from our mother as he burst through the front door.

"After you wrote the song, what happened?"

Hugh wandered to the other side of the patio. He picked up a twig, snapped it. "We phoned Josef and Albina."

"Why'd you do that?"

"I don't know. For something to do, I guess." He shrugged. "Sam'd been calling a lot of people. He just asked me to think of somebody else."

"What did they say?"

"Nothing."

"What did Sam say?"

"Nothing, really." He threw the twigs into a hedge.

"He had to say something, Hugh."

"Just that sometimes he drank their farm cream out of a glass." He sat again. "He told them about me selling some to my friends." He shook his head. "The jerk."

"Did you call anybody else?"

"No. We went outside after that." He scratched his ear, leaned back. "We drank a bottle of wine by the pool."

The last word floated between us, shimmery, ominous. "Didn't y'all talk?"

"A little."

I didn't move, my waiting a reluctant gift.

"He said girls'd always been his best friends." He tapped his propped foot, bouncing his leg. "We talked about me becoming a doctor." Of course, Sam would get around to that. "I told him I didn't think I was smart enough."

"Oh, Hugh."

"I'm not!" he snapped, thumping his foot on the patio stones.

"What did Sam say to that?"

"He said sometimes courage is as simple as thinking I could be somebody else."

I had to walk, swallowing hard, hiding my face. I wouldn't be the one to explain that Sam had been talking about himself. Unlike the mouse lying limp inside the creek bass, Sam had escaped his trap. "Is that all?"

"Yeah, pretty much."

I didn't have to ask where Sam was when Hugh drove off. He would've waved, still sitting by the water. Maybe he watched a cat squeeze through a nearby fence; there's always a fence at a motel pool. Perhaps a dog barked; cars would flit like wasps down the freeway. Clouds, twists of bakery dough. When he rolled to the edge, chlorinated moisture rose. As he hit the break release, he closed his eyes, remembering a line not from Sartre, not from Homer, but from Mae West: "Between two evils, I always pick the one I never tried before."

Three hours later, Terezie phoned, asking frantically if Hugh knew where Sam was. During a room search, she and the motel manager discovered his scrawled instructions taped to the TV. When they found him, his belt wrapped his body to the chair, on the bottom, next to the drain, in the deep end.

Terezie was inconsolable. But mostly, she was angry, screaming *selfish*, as though Sam would repent and appear. "You bastard," she railed. Sitting on the boxy sofa in her parents' house, she explained why she thought his death had been her fault.

Sam, Terezie swore, had been happy during the therapy session the week before our family's lunch. "For a crip," he'd teased a guy trying to keep from flipping facedown, "you're not too bad." I remembered him saying it paid to be friendly.

But during the exercises, Sam's mood had changed. Terezie performed the bending and unbending, the curling and straightening as usual. Sam, though, had something else in mind. "This turns me on," he'd said, serious, reaching for her breast. "Let's do it in the water." Terezie had simply told him to behave, whirled him around, caught his waist from behind. The next week, he'd refused to go.

When Terezie finished her story, I think I said the right things—consolations, reassurances, whatever—I can't remember. I didn't mention that I had taken Sam to therapy instead. I picture her blotched face, makeshift shelves of books above, a pillow and folded bed sheet beside her on the sofa, her long fingers scratching air.

I didn't drive home immediately. I parked at the picnic table beside the creek. I sat on the bench and watched mayfly duns skip the water's surface, heard the buzz of cicadas, the grumble of spring croakers, the cranky barks of blue jays. Twice, a black bass leaped, so I walked to the bank.

Flathead minnows swam in the shallows, pools slapping puny waves against limestone rocks. When I reached a hand toward the surface, the colony of fish jerked sideways, underwater pilots in synchronized maneuvers: flip, jag, hover. I waved again, my arm a flag, and they darted back.

They disappeared as I waded in, the silt just as I remembered: silk and feathers. My skirt floated, a snarl of paisley air pockets. The sun reflected off banks onto creek patches, migraines of white. Honeysuckle choked Georgia cane and hackberry limbs, while watercress and onions stood thick in the mud.

As I stepped off the creek bottom—air warm as sleep, animal clatter a nuisance, light flashes a litany—a nibbling started at my ankles. Bream? Hawksbill turtle? Water snake? My dress, now saturated, tugged at my waist, shoulders. My kicks slowed, the water a second skin, my boundary of self shifting: present merging with primordial. Underneath, hydrophytes and pond moss flapped their tentacles. Crawdads crawled along the bottom; bluegills and pumpkinseed sunfish fed on hellgrammites, freshwater clams, cadis fly larvae. Was I hominid? Plankton? Finally, my true self?

A nutria's nest perched at the creek's bend, its gnawed limbs trashy. Somewhere below, the rodent ploughed ahead, webbed feet paddling. A kingfisher, its spiked crest a headdress, coasted downstream, searching for river suckers. A green heron hunched on a cane stalk in the shallows. When its head darted forward, the neck uncoiled, stretching the beak toward a target. A croaker was flipped headfirst, and swallowed. Devoured, like the mouse inside Sam's fish. Possessed, like Sam's toes in my palm. Like his swollen part I'd purposely cushioned against my belly. *Unthinkable.* But I'd pushed him away. *Unforgivable.* I'd pushed even when he asked for help.

The water wrestled, pinning my arms, and I let it. As the surface crept up to my chin, I leaned back. Clouds muscled across blue. Then, again, came the nibbling, back of my knee, my thigh, my neck. A universe, like the one inside a fish, teemed below—deep, where I now longed to go. I wanted a place without color. Without clatter, or weight. No smell of soap or baking bread. No sermons. Only food for rain.

Until the locomotive came rumbling, its soldered face an omen. *Over here*, it chattered. *Beat your breath.*

I don't remember running toward the tracks. Train cars clicked by as I scrambled up the trestle, pebbles sliding, useless. Hinges whined. Currents of hot air pressed then sucked as each compartment whipped past. I raised my arms, swaying with the gusts, knowing one or two steps meant silence. Letters and colors lurched into vision, then converged, streaks blurring. My dress clung as vibrations rattled up my back, through my chest, my jaw. When suction from the last car pulled me onto the tracks, the metal hummed in my feet. I straddled a rail, and the music throbbed inside my legs. As the train's snaky tail looped at a bend, twisting into clouds, my body stiffened. I could breathe but was safely numb.

I made two pledges during my drive home. Like Josef Cervenka had for his father, I gave Sam a promise: "I'll live for both of us." Then I emulated my mother, tossing the family's reins. Five months later I was gone.

CHAPTER 20
1972

MOST OF MY DAYS at the Ciudad Universitaria were spent at the Central Library. Walking across its volcanic rock pathway, past its iconic walls of O'Gorman murals, I was happy. When the librarian set out the accordion-folded pages of the Codex Fejérváry Mayer, I knew I'd become what Sam intended: a truth scavenger. The farm midden and Nugent's 1915 lynching had been my introductions, but my life's work would be the study of cultures that first appeared in 20,000 BC in the Valley of Mexico.

As a professional collecting and analyzing data, I accepted my role as an outsider. The pitfalls were obvious, especially since this scientist was a middle-class, Anglo-American female. I attempted to move beyond my high school fetishism toward a psychological connection to these ancients in two ways. First, I learned Nahuatl, then I interpreted documents like the *Mexihca* codices, their illustrated scenes alongside pictographic systems of glyphs. Although the people did not recognize an interior life, and their rituals were grisly and well documented, the ceremonies were ideologically complex. Costumes and movements joined opposites—warriors with fertility, female and male, sky and earth—disrupting the familiar; attempts to impose order were futile. The sacred energy that managed these shifts united with its statue or human vessel, rebalancing and regenerating the universe.

Six months before I arrived, a heavy rain had unearthed a major discovery thirty-three miles northeast of Mexico City, in *Teotíhuacan*.

At its peak in AD 500, this metropolis had covered eight square miles with a population of 200,000, making it larger than its contemporary, imperial Rome. Sometime between the birth of Christ and AD 150, the Pyramid of the Sun and the Pyramid of the Moon had been built, and the city's main axis, the Avenue of the Dead, had been extended to three miles. The 1971 discovery occurred at the base of the Pyramid of the Sun, a structure 738 feet square and twenty stories high.

My anthropology professor, who'd been part of the original team, later invited me along with two other students to crawl through the man-made entrance they'd uncovered. Standing at the foot of that truncated monument, I remembered the hobo's pyramid of stones at my family's farm and the one I left the same day by the tracks, all three, ours and the *Teotihuacanos'*, expressions of gratitude meant to honor.

Just inside, the cramped enclosure required light from our spelunking helmets. We crawled down an ancient stairway as though rappelling a mountain, the steep stone steps cut into the walls of a shaft twenty-three feet deep. Although each ledge held, my foot barely had space to balance; every dusty surface felt on the verge of disintegration. Our professor, his helmet's light probing, his voice soaking into rock and mud, led us to a tunnel at the bottom that turned out to be 112 yards long.

I stayed as close to him as possible while we crawled through the damp darkness, my knees throbbing, picturing Long-tailed shrews, albino salamanders. The air thinned—we could've been, instead, on a mountaintop—and I grew dizzy, gulping, my lungs filling but not getting enough oxygen. I curled against the tunnel wall, refusing to move. Patiently, the professor, his ray of light aimed at my feet, guided me through a regulation of my breathing. We crawled for another fifteen minutes, his light beam roving crags ahead. When he finally stood, his head disappearing as he rose, my heart lurched; then we joined him.

The cavern, he said, his voice echoing, had been formed by an enormous bubble of gas in lava that streamed from deep within the earth. Dark as a blank and humid, it was huge, our lights illuminating its regions. Attached to the floor were ceramic pieces surrounding a flagstone, situated directly beneath the pyramid's center. When light from the monument's narrow entrance had flickered across the stone, shamans, perhaps the city's founding fathers, had held elaborate rituals. I wondered how their ceremonies compared to the ones at the White Shaman site in the Lower Pecos. An amorphous shape had appeared there, and now I hoped it would reappear here. Our voices ricocheted; our lights streaked across walls slick as obsidian and a ceiling covered in what looked like fossilized toucan tongues.

The cave ended in a four-petal flower shape, the chambers like those mentioned in *Tōlēteca-Chīchīmeca* history. Inside, skull carvings and jaguar sculptures, symbols of death, had waited centuries to be found. A greenstone figurine with inlaid pyrite eyes had also lain undisturbed, alongside basalt blades and a conch shell.

The *Teotihuacah* believed that the cave was the womb from which the sun and moon first arose. When the pyramid was built over this holy place, the structure became an *āltepētl* or "water-hill," around which the community then settled. In other words, the pyramid was the center of the universe. Now, we stood in the footprints of its shamans, Christ's contemporaries.

As we squatted inside a chamber, the professor described an archeologist's first attempts in the early 1900s to excavate the pyramid. "At its highest level," he said, "skulls of children, none older than eight, were found at each corner." The victims' tears had been shed for *Tlāloc*, the god of water.

I gathered a fistful of groundcover and sniffed: dust, alkali, metal. So, I thought, this is time, its dark elements, and I'm like Jonah inside the whale's belly, like the mouse inside the bass's sac, like Sam inside his paralyzed body. Was this cave anything like the one at the Caley Creek battlefield, where 240 Caddoes, Kickapoo, and Comanche had been *routed*? Was my father's kettle of bones so different from the shrines atop the pyramid? I pictured the man in his overalls, hanging, then Otis lying stiffly, and the cadavers in my father's lab. Like Houston, they'd all lifted, become stars.

Sam told Hugh that courage was being able to see yourself as something else, and now I did. The amorphous shape would not appear in the cave, I realized, because it was inside me.

CHAPTER 21

AT THE ROCKPORT HOUSE, Terezie makes me go inside to alert my brothers that I've brought her and Cornelia. I've convinced them to come by saying they've been invited, which is, at best, an exaggeration. In fact, the last time I spoke to Kurt, he said, "For God's sake, keep them the hell away from us." My family doesn't expect *me* today, much less their ex-sister-in-law and her daughter, but this is one Thanksgiving when, like it or not, we are going to sit down together. Somehow, we have to start talking again. Only then, can we figure out what to do for Cornelia.

After that, maybe we can finally share what we've heard about Sam's secret. How long has Kurt known, I wonder, and why didn't he tell us? Did Sam, upset over news of Ruby's death, confide in him? Kurt must've told Hugh before they took Cyril to court; Terezie knows too, of course, and even Cornelia. What about Kurt's wife, Randy? Did Hugh tell Debbie? Am I really the last? I'm an anthropologist. How did this happen?

"Do I know you?" Noreen says, standing at the door. Her ponytail hangs in perfect ringlets.

"I'm your Aunt Sarah. Now be a good girl and go get your father."

"Man!" someone whoops from down the hall. "Did you see that?" Laughter.

"Daddy," Noreen calls, shuffling toward the voice, her curls bouncing.

I turn toward the car and wave, give a thumbs-up.

"What happened?" Hugh says, suddenly materializing, frowning, barefooted. "What's the matter?"

"Happy Thanksgiving to you, too, Hugh. May I come in?" I brush past him toward the room where our family always gathered. Our grandfather's billiard table underneath a Tiffany island lamp; his portable bowling alley along one wall. The casement windows angle open, but logs crackle in the stream stone fireplace. As two White-faced ibis sail over the bay just past the dock, I remember our grandfather saying patients gave him Chinese pheasants, peacocks, and a pair of Japanese deer. Our father's pear and plum trees still shade one side of the house.

"What the..." Kurt says, his feet lurching from the coffee table to the travertine floor.

I throw my hands up, slap my thighs. "Okay," I say, "so I crashed your party. But this is my house, too, and we *are* family. Would it be terrible if I asked you to let me stay?"

Emma rises from her chair by the bank of windows, flapping her hands, her long face and prominent chin sloped as a crescent moon. She says nothing, frantically panting. Kurt approaches her, his arms resting at his sides. "You remember Aunt Sarah," he says, his voice a bassoon. "We're very glad she's here. She's going to have lunch with us." Behind them, a White Pelican swoops toward the water then rises as though leaping from their heads, its pumping wings whispering *comfort, comfort*.

"I *thought* I heard a strange voice," Randy says, the slotted spoon in her hand reminding me of Ruby in Gran's kitchen telling my mother to leave. "Is something wrong?" She's wearing designer slacks and matching knit top, complete with a coral necklace and paisley scarf.

"Only that I've crashed your celebration. Do you mind? I'm happy to help."

"Aunt Sarah, way cool," says Kurt Jr. walking past his mother. He puts something yellow in his mouth then licks his fingers.

"Kurt Jr. and I would be glad to set the table, right?" How am I going to tell them about Terezie and Cornelia? Surely, the doorbell will ring any second.

"Who's that?" Noreen says, pointing outside the side windows toward the fruit trees.

Debbie walks next to her daughter then leans to look, her leather skirt hiking. "She's right. It's two women, and they're doing something." She bends closer, shading her eyes. "Are they digging? It looks like they're digging. Hugh?"

I don't need to join the others as they conjecture about Terezie and Cornelia. Hugh recognizes them first. "What are *they* doing here?" After a few seconds, the adults turn, synchronized as a Motown group.

"Look, it's Thanksgiving," I say, my arms stretched. Okay, yes, I'm hoping for a miracle. "All they want to do is have lunch with you. Nobody has to say anything about the lawsuit. What do you say; can I bring them inside?"

"But what are they *doing*?" Debbie repeats.

"Sure," Randy intercedes. "I say bring them on. There's plenty of food. Why not?"

"Because it's my holiday; that's why," Kurt says. He flops back in front of the TV. "I'm not going to spend my day off with people who're trying to rob us."

"You expect me to tell them to go? For God sakes, Kurt, they're not ax murderers. She was Sam's wife; doesn't that count for something?"

"You mean that lady out there's Uncle Sam's wife?" Kurt Jr. asks, his mouth hanging open. "She's real? I mean, a actual person?"

"This is between the grown-ups," Randy says, shaking her head, walking toward the kitchen.

"I don't get it," Kurt Jr., says. "Why do y'all hate her?"

"Thanks," Kurt grumbles.

Then Emma begins laughing, a giggling interspersed with hiccups. She bites her hand.

"Time out," Kurt says, standing, floating toward his daughter. "Want to play puzzle?" he croons. "Let's go to your room."

Fingering her blouse button, she follows her father. "Room," she says. "Room. Room."

"Oh, my God," Debbie squeals at the scene out the window. Noreen is standing next to Terezie and Cornelia, who both squat next to my father's pear tree, its leaves crimson. Debbie runs out the door first, me right after.

"Honey, what are you doing?" Debbie asks while placing her arm around Noreen's shoulder.

"They have to clean that up," Noreen says, pointing to a hole near the tree's trunk. "It's a mess."

"Now, don't you worry, honey," Terezie says. This tree's going to be fine. As a matter of fact, loosening up the dirt will give it a little air so it can breathe." She scoops soil into the hole and pats. "What's your name? Mine's Terezie."

"I don't think we've ever met," says Debbie, "but I'm Debbie, Hugh's wife, and this is our daughter, Norine."

"Norine, honey, I knew your grandmother, and you don't just have her name. Why, you lucky thing; you got her gorgeous green eyes, too."

"Were you a friend of my grandmother's?"

"Well, once upon a time, I was married to your daddy's brother, Sam."

"But he died. I know."

"Yes, he did. And now I have a daughter of my own." She rises and helps Cornelia struggle to stand. "Debbie, Norine, this is Cornelia."

Norine frowns while holding and flipping her ponytail like a switch. "Why'd your mom have to pick you up like that? Something wrong with your leg? What's that thing on your nose, there?" She points.

"Why you're a regular Curious George," Cornelia says, wheezy. "It's a nose ring, and I'll show it to you if I can have some water. What do you say, doll face?"

"Sure, come on. It's okay; lean on me," Norine says, grinning. Helpless to stop them, Debbie follows.

Terezie starts after them, but I pull her back. Somehow, I have to explain what happened in the house. "What were you doing?"

She opens her hand, and my Marcos point lays across her palm. I'd have recognized it anywhere, the beveling along its lateral edges, the scalloped grooves chiseling its rim. Sam said Tonkawa left it after camping at the farm.

"How did it get *here*?" I've always wondered what my father did with it.

"A few days after you found it at the farm," Terezie says, "your dad drove to Austin and told Sam to put it back."

"You're kidding." How could I not know that?

"Sam was furious. I thought it would kill him. That's when he got thrown in jail in Laredo, remember?"

Is that possible? Did he go to Mexico right after that day at the farm?

"He kept the Marcos in his wallet until your grandfather died. Then we buried it here." We look up, the tree's tint surrounding us, its radiance the miracle I asked for.

"Here," Terezie says, placing the flint in my palm then closing her hands around mine. "He would've wanted you to have it."

I thumb its side and edges, planed as cut-glass crystal, and think, *silica, ashes*. This is an artifact of my family as well as the Tonkawa, present *and* past. While we walk toward the house, I say, "Don't expect much of a welcome." I hope Terezie will be more forgiving than I am.

"I don't care what they think of *me*," she says, her clear skies darkening. I picture her standing in her chinos and Christmas sweater next to Randy, the runway queen. "But I expect them to be kind to Cornelia."

"Of course," I say. "I'll do everything I can to ensure that."

"Maybe once they get to know her," she says, chipper again, "see for themselves what a good girl she is, they'll…"

Kurt walks with Emma through the kitchen to the game room. He flinches when he spots Terezie, then nods stiffly, muttering, "Hello." While he and Hugh resume watching their football game, Kurt Jr. and Norine take turns pitching balls down miniature bowling lanes. Cornelia watches from an arm chair. Kurt Jr. trots, stretches, and tosses like a double-jointed athlete, each move gauged by Cornelia's reaction. "Shame on you, Norine," she teases when he throws his hands on the floor, kicks his feet up, then arches his back and inches haltingly forward. "Why'd you flip that boy upside down? You put him back, right this minute."

Norine giggles, covering her face, her curls bunched to one side.

Terezie, Cornelia, and I try to be last filing into the dining room, but Hugh stops, bowing, motioning us forward. I politely simper but think: Why do I feel obligated to follow his direction? Why can't I say that we want to wait so we'll know where to sit after everyone's settled?

He smiles. "After you, ladies," he says, smug, oblivious.

When I see our parents' round table, I act unfazed, but I picture us sitting there during Sam's last dinner. Today, our parents and Sam are replaced by the Pelton children—same table, shifting faces—a subversion of *possession*, of *always*.

Randy serves our plates from the kitchen before I can remind her that I'm a vegetarian. I take a bite of cranberry sauce, queasy from the scent of roasted meat. Pumpkin pies and dessert plates wait on the double-hutch buffet along the back wall.

Cornelia seems to be enjoying herself with Kurt Jr. flirting on one side and Noreen watching adoringly from the other. If she's pretending not to notice the tension between Terezie and my brothers, she's doing a great job. She asks Kurt Jr. how Barbie and some pop star are alike. When he shrugs, she says, deadpan, "They're both blonde, brainless, and made of plastic." Even Kurt laughs, spewing sweet onion relish, making everyone howl again. "It wasn't *that* funny," Cornelia wheezes.

"Can't help it," he says, grinning, wiping his mouth. "I'm a sucker for dumb blonde jokes."

I say, "You missed the point, A.K."

"What's A.K.?" Randy asks. Her voice hovers between pissed and party-mode.

Emma taps her fork against her knife.

"That's what Sam called him, right Hugh?"

"Yeah," Hugh says, stifling a smile, dropping his glance. He now thinks Sam exemplifies what happens to someone who rejects Christ.

Kurt hands Emma a roll, sets her fork next to her plate. "I'd forgotten about that," he says. He speaks directly to Randy: "It stands for ass kisser."

"Rad!" Kurt Jr. yells, hugging himself.

Kurt squints, scratches his head. "He said I'd wear a dress if Dad told me to." He turns to me. "But I couldn't. Sarah's were too tight."

Kurt Jr. peeks at Cornelia, giggles.

"I don't get it," Noreen says. "Mama? Boys don't wear dresses. That's stupid."

"Anybody for more gravy?" Debbie says, standing. "What about you, honey?" she says to Noreen. "Want another roll?"

I stir my food, take a bite of relish. "This reminds me of Mother's cooking," I say.

"We have her oyster dressing every year," Randy says. "I'll give you the recipe, if you don't have it."

"Actually," Debbie says, "Randy's made your mom famous. She's shared a lot of her recipes." Randy straightens her napkin. "And she always puts your mom's name in the title."

Randy stands, picks up her plate, then grabs mine. She disappears into the kitchen. Terezie and Debbie gather more dishes and follow.

I smile at Cornelia, my ally. Like me, she's hardly eaten anything.

My sisters-in-law begin serving pie, pouring coffee, bringing refills of milk for the children. As much as I resent the men sitting like Ayatollah, I grudgingly help. I do, however, insist that Cornelia stay put. Before we eat, everyone pauses for a tradition that began after I moved to Mexico. I'm starving. I take a bite of pie, then notice they have their hands in their laps.

"You can't do that," Noreen said. "You have to wait."

"Oh," I say, stupidly. "Sorry. I didn't know." What next? I think. This is, after all, the Bible belt. I foolishly thought that Hugh's blessing, which was heartfelt and apropos, was a sufficient nod toward God and country. So okay, I'll agree to say the Pledge of Allegiance—I'm as patriotic as anyone—or join hands and recite the Lord's Prayer, but that's where I draw the line. I'm not going to spout some homily or give testimony. They might as well ask me to speak in tongues. I can listen; yes, I'm actually good at that. In fact, watching this tribe will be interesting. Hugh takes the lead.

"I hope you ladies will bear with me," he says, "'cause about now, everybody expects me to sing."

"Yeah," Noreen says, staring at me, "and you can't eat."

"She knows, honey," Debbie says, squeezing her daughter's hand.

"But I saw her. She took a bite."

"Okay, thank you," Debbie says. "Now let's listen."

Frowning, Cornelia picks up her fork, but when I shake my head, reassuring her, she puts it back.

Hugh continues, nonplussed. "I always thought it was a plot to keep me from preaching."

Debbie pats Noreen. Kurt says, "Amen."

"Amen!" Hugh repeats, chuckling. "Actually," he clears his throat, "Debbie helped me pick this one. I wanted something everybody knew. It's 'Faith of Our Fathers.'"

"But *I* never heard of that," Noreen says.

"Shh," Debbie says, placing her arm around Noreen's shoulders.

The sound that comes out of Hugh's mouth doesn't belong to him. I've heard the hymn; I know it by heart. This time, though, I expect a Jerry Lee Lewis version—energetic, jazzy—instead, a bassoon croons soft as silt. "Faith of our fathers, living still," Hugh sings, his voice the Duomo bells surrounding Sam while he walks down an Italian street. The notes take shape, change colors, scattering like chips of jade, like nuggets of turquoise.

After lunch, I follow Hugh, Noreen, and Kurt Jr. to the dock to feed thawed, freezer-burned flounder to the pelicans. "Let me," Noreen says, reaching into the bucket. Two Browns, a species recently removed from the endangered list, swim toward us. Swans with Donald Duck eyes and suitcase mouths, they are caricatures of prehistoric majesty.

"Try this, slackers," Kurt Jr. calls, tossing the birds a pickle. They watch it arc then plunk into the water.

"No! You can't do that," Noreen shouts. "Daddy told us!" She pulls out a flounder, shaking it. "Only *fish*! He says! Like this." When she pitches her offering a few feet away, the nearer bird swims up, cranes its serpentine neck over the dock's edge, opens its mandibles like giant tweezers, then pins and flips the fish into its distensible pouch.

"Now you!" says Noreen, cavorting like a Shetland pony. "Here," and she hands Kurt Jr. the bucket, while Hugh and I sit in rattan chairs under the awning.

When Kurt Jr. sails his flounder at the water, the second bird swims over, dives under, and scoops the target into its netlike pouch, the seawater draining from its mouth. Three white pelicans fly toward the children, so Kurt Jr. throws another flounder into the air, and one of the birds hovers, nabbing its catch, its colossal wings pedaling.

I remember seeing a pelican painted in the dome of the gothic church at Sam's wedding, an image that sent me to the library to discover a second century Egyptian legend. A mother pelican, it said, plucked her breast to feed her young with her blood so they wouldn't starve. I think of Ruby, her sacrifice. Even Dante and Shakespeare used the bird as a religious symbol. "Christ, the pelican," I say to Hugh, wondering if he recognizes the reference.

"Like what tender tales tell of the pelican," he says, stroking the skin above his almost invisible lip, "bathe me, Jesus Lord, in what Thy bosom ran."

"Dante?" I ask, dubious.

"St. Thomas Aquinas. But you're the scholar. I thought you'd know that."

"I should have," I say, annoyed. "I guess you've become the expert."

"Maybe," he says, looking away then turning back. "But I would like to know the real reason you brought those women."

"My turn," Noreen yells when Kurt Jr. tosses a fish in the air.

"Cornelia's a wonderful girl, don't you think?" I say.

"Yeah, great. And she'll get her transplant, if that's what you're worried about."

"Really? That's not what Kurt says."

"Look, Terezie just has to sign that agreement. It's as simple as that."

"It's only money, Hugh. Why are you willing to let it endanger this girl's life?"

"There's an important principle at stake."

"What, that Terezie's no longer a member of the family? That Cornelia's not related?"

"Yeah, that's right. Those people aren't my responsibility. My job is to be a good steward of God's gifts. 'A man can receive nothing, unless it has been given him from heaven.' Through God's grace, we were given our inheritance, Sarah, and now we're obligated to be good managers of that."

I'm not going to argue that Sam and his heirs deserve a share, and that God intended them to have it. Instead, I decide to try a different tack. "Wouldn't Christ share what he had if it could save a life?"

"My obligation is to provide for my wife and daughter. God'll take care of Terezie and Cornelia."

"Maybe sharing our inheritance is part of God's plan."

"No," he says, standing. "I see this as a test of my responsibility as a steward, and I won't do anything that'll hurt my family. I just won't." Turning, wiping his face again, he marches toward the children.

I hear their voices, the water's slap against the dock, but the only image I can muster is Hugh's face as a boy, confessing that he's been with Sam right before he committed suicide. Hugh, I now think, *had* to know what Sam was thinking. Why in hell didn't he stop what happened next?

"You're all murderers," Terezie yells, backing out the door. She holds Cornelia, who slumps, sobbing.

How, I wonder, does Terezie know what I'm thinking? All these years, I believed she blamed herself for Sam's death.

"You're the only one stopping that transplant," Kurt says, watching Terezie motion me over.

That's when I realize that I left them alone in the house.

"If you and your shyster brother weren't so greedy," Kurt says, leaning against the doorframe, "you could do the responsible thing and get your daughter into surgery."

Cornelia wheezes and stumbles with Terezie toward the side of the house.

"What's wrong with you?" I shout at Kurt. "I don't know you people."

CHAPTER 22

As I PULL UP TO THE FARM GATE, I notice it has the same chain, now casually wrapped around an adjacent pole. Once inside, I allow the car to creep down the dirt road. Buffle, goat weed, and blue stem grow alongside, overtaking the fields like a forest. From the plank bridge, the creek bed is stony, trashed, vanished as childhood.

A slight young woman has appeared on the road, obviously the buyer, who has seen me from the house. I step from the car, the door ajar, ignition dinging.

"Hello," I say, extending my hand. She rakes me with her eyes: my cropped gray hair, jeans, stretched henley. I wonder how she feels about the sale's postponement. Does she know about Terezie? Cornelia? What are her plans for the place? "I'm Sarah. My parents own a small farm up the road," I lie, hoping she'll speak freely. I point toward the highway.

"Oh." She shades her eyes. "Hello." Asian-American, probably Taiwanese.

"You'll be neighbors," I say. Her small fingers soften my formal handshake. "I heard the Peltons were selling the place." In the distance, a broken fence droops against sagebrush, and behind, a ledge must be railroad track. I picture my grandfather's peach trees. "I remember," I say, "when another family lived here."

"Would you like to see the house?" she asks. Broad-faced, dark-haired, she has ethnic features but no accent. Unlike me, she probably says *y'all.*

"Yes, thank you. I would." I close the car door, and we step between wavelike ruts dried hard as limestone. "When will you begin work on the place?"

"We started Thursday, but we've been out here a lot, hoping, you know." She turns, her elbows locked, her arms swinging. "My name's Lilu, by the way."

I nod but am confused. "So the sale is going through?" Maybe, I think, our Thanksgiving fiasco convinced Terezie to give up and sign the settlement agreement, forfeiting her claim to the coastal house. Or, worse, maybe Cornelia's health has deteriorated. A lot can happen in a week.

"There's a question about a will, but their lawyer says not to worry. It shouldn't take more than a few months, so Hugh told us we could move in. You know the Peltons?"

I'm not sure what to say, so I straddle a rut, then keep walking, thinking I'm going to have to move fast to get this farm sold. Cornelia won't wait another month.

Four puppies, shorthaired, compact as cinnamon rolls, come yapping. A carport skeleton, its wood sap-smelling and blonde, stands next to the house, which has rotten boards at the windows; half of the roof is gone.

In the doorway, a bare-chested man stands with a little boy, who giggles and arches backward in his father's thin arms. The man darts into the house. The boy runs to Lilu, and when she picks him up, he stares, thumb in his mouth. The man reappears, a starched cotton shirt tucked into his Bermuda shorts. He's combed his hair, which is shaved around his ears and across the nape of his neck.

"This is Sarah," Lilu says, enunciating carefully, motioning. An overbite makes her *S*s whistle. "Her parents have a farm down the road."

They whisper in Mandarin. She waves an arm; he glances, looks away.

"Small," I say. "Over there." I point north.

"Fong," the man says, tapping his delicate chest. "How do you do." He dips his head.

"Are you going to live here?"

"Oh, yes," Fong says, bowing. He sweeps his arm toward the house, caved barn. "Not much, but we can fix." He finds a bottle cap, puts it in his pocket.

"Will you work the fields?" I ask. When a puppy tugs at my pant leg, I thump its nose. Lilu claps her hands, hisses. She sets down the boy, who squeals after the dogs.

"No, we have restaurant, El Taco Taipei. Enchiladas, egg rolls too, we got." Fong pats his arm.

When they invite me in, I know I should leave, but climb the creaky stoop instead. The boy clambers up, his sticky hands a nuisance, the top of his head a purple thistle.

Wallpaper has been partially stripped from the first room, which contains two low, thickly varnished tables, a straw mat, four cushions, a wire-screened cabinet holding jars, ceramic jugs. A curtain of beads painted with a mountain hangs in the doorway to the next room. When Lilu passes through, the beads shimmer then reconfigure, a glass pool reflecting an imagined landscape. She returns with a bowl of scraps; the boy scurries outside, calling "hssst, hssst" to the puppies. I think of our farm's clattering turkeys, played with, fed, then eaten.

"You remember?" Fong asks, pointing to the walls.

I picture Mr. Cervenka on the boxy sofa, his mottled hands folded in his lap. "A god, he was, next to them bees," Sam told me he said. Now both men are dead. Otis spent time here too, his work shoes dusty, pruning shears tucked in his overalls pocket as he stood at the door.

I admire the room's sparseness, the owners' easy welcome, their possession of the farm already natural. They could be Confucian, judging by the shrine in one corner. Draped in red silk, the table holds a teapot, a bowl of Texas sage, another of sliced bananas, a clock with Chinese numbers, a small stack of dollar bills, sticks of incense burning in their holders.

In the center leans a smudged photograph of a woman walking barefoot, carrying yams and coconuts in baskets hung from a long pole balanced across her shoulders. Instantly, I admire her: her splayed toes and makeshift rag hat, her open-mouthed concentration. But her eyes are dark holes, familiar, tugging. "If I was gone," she seems to say, "they'd be able to…" her voice trailing.

It's been seven months since Terezie first came to see me. Kurt now speaks through his attorney, while Hugh pretends he never offered to pay Cornelia's hospital bill. They fired their first attorney when he made it clear that Sam's adoption wouldn't bolster their argument. All the while, I return to the same thought: Sam wasn't the brother I knew. And what does that say about me? Digging out the truth has become the hardest thing. My father loved Ruby enough to risk losing his family, countering his most closely held beliefs. And why was my mother willing to adopt Sam? Why did Ruby give him up?

Now, Cornelia's spending more time on dialysis; she might at any moment carry out her threat. I shouldn't have any trouble persuading my brothers to sell me their farm shares at a slightly reduced rate. Then the Taiwanese couple can have their new home, and Terezie can get what's been hers from the start. I can't worry about whether she'll give up the rest of the estate. Right now, minutes count. I'll have time to stop by Hugh's house today if I hurry.

"Would you like some iced tea?" Lilu says. "We've got a thermos." She steps toward the curtain again, dragging her son, who's hugging her leg.

"Not right now," I say and start to add that I must go, but the impatient, dignified woman in the photo fills me with longing. Cornelia's going to leave, I now realize, once Terezie has her money. Never again will she sashay into my office saying "Hey, Doc," then sit on our bench, breathing into my chest. Who else will ever do that?

I pick up the photograph, wondering if the woman is Lilu's mother or grandmother.

Didn't Debbie say Cornelia has *longer* than six months? Terezie is bound to prevail in court. After all, *Genius is nothing but a greater aptitude for patience.* I finger the snapshot like a charm, rubbing its slick surface. Pocketing the photo would be easy, but, no, a violation, impossible. I must put it back.

"Ours," the boy mutters, snatching the picture, hugging it to his chest, glaring, his hunched shoulder an accusation.

Stooping, I say, "Thank you for letting me hold it. Is she your grandmother?"

"Don't," he says. "Noooo," he shrieks, jumping into his mother's arms.

"Don't speak to Dr. Pelton like that," Lilu whispers. When she pulls his fist from his eyes, he kicks her stomach. "She's a professor. Show respect."

Fong replaces the photograph on the altar. Incense coils toward the open roof.

"Well, I'll be," I say, plopping onto a cushion. "How did you know?"

Lilu sits, folding the boy into her lap. "Pictures from the newspaper, at the library."

"So what else are you not telling me?" Next, she'll say she's a fashion designer or a dental assistant.

"I don't give a flip about your family's problems," she says, her gaze a threat, "but you've got to work things out with that sister-in-law. I mean it. Y'all better sign those papers."

"Lilu, what happened to your manners?" I ask, intrigued.

"Look. Whether you like it or not, this is going to be our home," Lilu says, her *S*s whistling.

Fong clears his throat.

"So tell me: What exactly do we have to do to get it?"

The roof hole angles sunrays like a heat lamp. A ginger aroma mixes with paint, motor oil. "Just ask," I say, shrugging, surprisingly reconciled, while their altar clock chimes twice.

The barefoot woman in the photograph shifts and stares, her blue irises transparent. Her body mutates, now naked, made of granite speckled with seed-shaped red garnets. She lifts the pole from her shoulders and sets the baskets on a sunken patio surrounded on four sides by adobe rooms with a reed roof. She squats, defecating on the packed earth. *I don't live in your* Cihuacalli. *I'm not looking for protection,* I tell *Tlahzolteōtl. I need a different kind of help.* Her hands move behind, grasping ground while she balances on her haunches. Her collarbone extends, encircling her chest and shoulders. I kneel, and those eyes follow, each a miniature cosmos. She licks her lips, grimaces. *I loved my brother too much*, I say. *I couldn't help it.* The letters take shape, are coated in mud then float toward the goddess. Her hands snatch; her mouth gobbles. *I hurt him, I saw it in his face. And then he died.* Something scrapes my heart. *Please, please forgive me.* Mud rings *Tlahzolteōtl*'s mouth and drips from her chin, her hands. She smacks, licks her fingers, my confession swallowed, my guilt gone.

A hummingbird appears in the roof's hole, moving backward, hanging like a star, then lifting. I point, thinking *Sam*, knowing the bird's appearance is coincidental but enjoying the idea just the same. I laugh, my stomach muscles hugging. I move toward the couple's beaded curtain, conscious of my breath—lungs filling, releasing, filling—glad to be standing inside this broken house with people who are giving it new life. I don't need to know why. Suffering can't be explained or accepted, so I'll live with questions. Sam taught me to recognize my obsession with the spiritual, to move outside my head. The *Mexihca* believed balance was the way to "gain a face" during this struggle-filled life. Will I always believe this? Maybe not. Transformation is inevitable, destruction necessary in order to create. I've destroyed the myth I created about Sam and can love this truer brother. In this way, I will keep him alive.

As I send the beaded mountain swinging, the thistle-headed boy comes running, his sticky hands outstretched. I dodge, laughing again. "No!" I say, shaking my finger. He grabs, and together, we clap.

BOOK GROUP
DISCUSSION GUIDE

Sarah's university colleagues close their office doors when she walks past, her brothers haven't spoken to her in years, and she lives by herself in a sparsely furnished house. She has no friends, and she hasn't been involved in a romantic relationship for years. Do these facts make Sarah an unsympathetic character?

At end of the first chapter, Sarah raises her hand to block out everyone in her family except Sam. Why does she do that, and why does she feel close to this brother?

When Sam guts the fish, his actions seem grotesque, even cruel. He says that sometimes you have to do ugly things. What does he mean, and what does this imply about him?

Sarah's mother, Norine, seems strong willed and independent in chapter one when she throws the horse's reins at the grandfather. But when she tells the story about Otis dying, she seems racist and wants Sarah to submit to gender expectations. How do you explain this change?

When Sarah recalls Otis telling his Master Sam stories, she says she hopes he didn't skew them according to what she wanted to hear. Later, when she sits in the USO with her girlfriends and the two soldiers, she admits she's confused about how to act with Tyrone, who is black. Is Sarah racist?

References to a steam engine and a fish act as motifs throughout the novel. What do these images symbolize?

Why is Sarah having hallucinations? What triggers them, and why do they always include a *Mexicha* god? How do they operate as a structuring device in the novel?

Sarah's research focuses on rituals that include an *iziptla*. What is an *iziptla*, and how does it relate to Sarah and Sam?

What does Sarah's life-long interest in the Mesoamerican culture, various theologies, and metaphysics reveal about her? Is it an admirable pursuit or an obsession?

Sarah's father is a moralist, biblical scholar, traditionalist, and dedicated physician. How could someone with his convictions become romantically involved with Ruby? How would you describe his feelings about Sam? Some of the scenes between Sarah and Cornelia incorporate humor. Can you find any other passages that are humorous?

What is the source of Sam's ambiguity, rebelliousness, and unpredictability? Is his behavior an emotional reaction to his parentage, could he be suffering from a mood disorder, or do you detect something else?

When Sam's taxi drives off the ramp, is that an accident or does he do it on purpose?

Why does Sarah press against Sam in the pool during water therapy? Is she sexually aroused, or are her actions a manifestation of her longing for an emotional connection? Would you describe her actions as immoral?

Do you agree with Kurt and Hugh that since Terezie has started a new family and the Peltons haven't seen her in thirty years, she does not have a claim on the grandparents' coastal house?

Do you agree with Kurt that he has a moral obligation to be a steward of his inheritance, even if his commitment jeopardizes Cornelia's health?

What does Sarah's story suggest about family relationships, a balanced mind/body connection, and the effects of suicide?

Acknowledgments

Thank you, Victoria Barrett, for including *Body and Bread* in your stellar lineup at Engine Books. Thank you, too, for being the rare editor with talent and initiative to become a true partner. You have made certain that my little book is the best that it can be. And how do you thank an agent who has believed in you for eight years? It's impossible, but here goes. Thank you, Esmond Harmsworth, for your wisdom, tenacity, and sense of humor. I've wanted, for a long time, to feel I earned your faith in me. I hope this book makes you proud.

Surely, my teachers already know how grateful I am, but thanking them publicly is an act of vanity I can't resist. Remarkable mentors all: Robert Boswell, Chuck Wachtel, Richard Russo, Douglas Unger, and Mary Elsie Robertson. I hear your voices still.

When you've worked on a book for twenty years, there are too many people to name. Generous friends have read and commented on stories that became the manuscript and later the novel in its various permutations. I thank them all. Here are a few: members of my first writer's group, Daedelus, and fellow students in the MFA Program at Warren Wilson College. Close readers include Alison Moore, Grace Dane Mazur, Dale Neal, Helen Fremont, Faith Holsaert, Elizabeth Brownrigg, Susan Sterling, and Margaret Kaufman. For their inspiration and support, I also thank Martha Rhodes, Debra Monroe, Naomi Shihab Nye, Barbara Ras, Joan King, and Robert Ayres.

I am grateful to Dr. Veronika Tuckerova for her assistance with the Czech translations. *An Analytical Dictionary of Nahuatl* by Frances Karttunen was an indispensible guide. Thank you, Dr. Karttunen, and I apologize for any mistakes. The Nahuatl inclusions were meant to honor the people, their language, and their history.

I am not an immigrant, member of the medical profession, historian, religious scholar, or anthropologist, so I relied on research to furnish credibility. For information about Czechs who settled in Texas, I used *We're Czechs* by Robert L. Skrabanek; *Czech Voices, Stories from Texas in the Amerikán Národní Kalendář*, translated and edited by Clinton Machann and James W. Mendl, Jr.; and *The Czech Texans* by The University of Texas Institute of Texan Cultures at San Antonio.

For information about the medical profession, I read *The Doctors Mayo* by Helen Clapesattle; *With Scalpel and Scope, A History of Scott and White* by Dayton Kelley; and *For the Good of Humanity, A Century of Surgery at Scott and White 1892-1992* by Patricia K. Benoit. Nugent, Texas, is modeled after my hometown, Temple, so I used *Temple, Backtracking 100 Years* by Martha Bowmer. I also used *My Master, The Inside Story of Sam Houston and His Times* by Jeff Hamilton, as told to Lenoir Hunt; *Sexual Adjustment: A Guide for the Spinal Cord Injured* by Martha Ferguson Gregory; and "Hers: Waterborne" by Suzanne E. Berger, from *The New York Times Magazine*.

Research on religions included *The Existence of God* by John Hick; *Reason and Religion, An Introduction to the Philosophy of Religion* by Rem B. Edwards; *The Gnostic Gospels* by Elaine Pagels; *A History of God, The 4,000-Year Quest of Judaism, Christianity and Islam* by Karen Armstrong; *The World's Great Religions, Volume 1: Religions of the East* by the editors of *LIFE*; and *INANNA Lady of Largest Heart, Poems of the Sumerian High Priestess ENHEDUANNA* by Betty De Shong Meador.

Research on indigenous people included *The Indians of Texas, From Prehistoric to Modern Times* by W.W. Newcomb, Jr.; Texas A&M University's website, *Center for the Study of the First Americans; Aztecs* by Inga Clendennin; *A Scattering of Jades, Stories, Poems, and Prayers of the Aztecs*, edited by Dr. J.J. Knab and translated by Thelma D. Sullivan;

Aztecs: Reign of Blood & Splendor by the editors of Time-Life Books; "Weaving the Aztec Cosmos: The Metaphysics of the 5th Era" at the Web site *Mexicolore*; and "Aztec Philosophy" at the Web site *The Internet Encyclopedia of Philosophy*.

Thirty-five years ago, my husband, Don, said, "You ought to write a book," and I laughed, but his words became a mantra. I thank him for that and for the evenings he listened to me reading excerpt after excerpt, forever encouraging. I thank my son, Don Jr., for being proud of his mother. I hug my daughter, Julia Nan, for reading every draft and offering her remarkably astute advice. I'm grateful to my parents, Julia Martha Barton Brindley and Hanes Brindley, for teaching me to ask questions and appreciate the nuance of words. I thank my surviving brothers, Hanes Jr., Glen and George Brindley, for being keepers of our family stories and for allowing me as a child to tag along. We, each in our own way, thank our lightening-rod brother, Paul, for jolting us into awareness.

Thank you to the editors of the following journals, where excerpts originally appeared: *Columbia: A Magazine of Poetry & Prose, Quarterly West, Voices de la Luna,* and *VíAztlan: A Journal of Arts and Letters*. Excerpts appearing in *Art at Our Doorstep: San Antonio Writers and Artists, New Growth 2, Poets of The Lake,* and *Writers at The Lake* are published with the permission of Trinity University Press, Corona Publishing, and Our Lady of the Lake University.

ABOUT THE AUTHOR

 **NAN CUBA** is founder and executive director emeritus of Gemini Ink, a nonprofit literary center. She received a Fundación Valparaiso Residency Grant in Mojácar, Spain and is currently an associate professor of English at Our Lady of the Lake University. As an investigative journalist, she reported on the causes of extraordinary violence in publications such as *LIFE, Third Coast,* and *D Magazine.* Her creative work has appeared in *Quarterly West, Columbia: A Magazine of Poetry & Prose, Harvard Review, storySouth,* and *Connotation Press,* among others. She is coeditor of *Art at Our Doorstep: San Antonio Writers & Artists* (Trinity University Press).